AFTER THE
SLEEPOVER

BOOKS BY KERRY WILKINSON

A Cry in the Night

THE ANDREW HUNTER SERIES

Something Wicked

Something Hidden

Something Buried

STANDALONE NOVELS

Ten Birthdays

Two Sisters

The Girl Who Came Back

Last Night

The Death and Life of Eleanor Parker

The Wife's Secret

A Face in the Crowd

Close to You

After the Accident

The Child Across the Street

What My Husband Did

The Blame

The Child in the Photo

The Perfect Daughter

The Party at Number 12

The Boyfriend

Truly, Madly, Amy

SILVER BLACKTHORN

Reckoning

AFTER THE
SLEEPOVER

KERRY WILKINSON

bookouture

Published by Bookouture in 2023

An imprint of Storyfire Ltd.
Carmelite House
50 Victoria Embankment
London EC4Y 0DZ

www.bookouture.com

ISBN: 978-1-83525-026-6
eBook ISBN: 978-1-83525-025-9

PROLOGUE

Leah's foot crunched on the gravel as she took a step towards the overhanging trees, which swayed ominously overhead.

'Can you believe it's happened again?' the waiting police officer said, as Leah approached. She sounded surprised that she'd spoken, unable to keep her thoughts to herself. 'Is that why you're here?'

'I don't know why I'm here,' Leah replied.

'It's boys this time – but there are three of them again. They were sleeping in their tents and then... gone. Just like you with your friends.'

Leah nodded, unsure how to reply. It had been twenty-five years since her trio of friends had disappeared. Twenty-five years since the night of the sleepover.

'It's unbelievable, isn't it?' the officer added. 'Same town, same ages, same thing.'

The two women stared at each other for a moment, before the officer seemed to realise she'd overstepped.

'Sorry,' she mumbled, before pointing along the path. 'It's that way. They're waiting for you.'

PART ONE

ONE

ONE DAY EARLIER

FRIDAY

The thing with film premieres is that they don't usually involve a child feeding a freeze pop to a dog.

Leah Pearce watched as the little girl sat on the edge of the play area's unmoving roundabout. The girl was taking one lick of the fluorescent pink popsicle for herself, then allowing her little French Bulldog to have a slurp. A skittling of wind had the swings rocking gently, though the park was otherwise unoccupied and unused.

A couple of hundred voices were talking over one another in the community centre behind and Leah needed a few seconds of silence.

If everyone could just stop talking, her evening would be a lot easier.

'Shush,' she whispered, to nobody in particular.

On the roundabout, as the freeze pop dwindled, the dog crept onto the girl's lap, desperate not to lose out on the final few tastes. The girl laughed and told the pup he was tickling her, before shooing him away. He sat staring, giving it the big eyes.

'You OK?'

Leah turned to where the other woman had approached. Esther Merrivale was a person Leah had barely known a year before. She was the older sister of Leah's missing friend. *One* of Leah's missing friends. There had been three of them, after all. It was now a quarter of a century since Leah, Victoria, Jasmine and Harriet went to sleep in Vicky's living room. When Leah awoke the next morning, she was the only one there.

But Esther and Leah were now friends of a sort. Secrets did that to people.

'It's so busy, isn't it?' Leah replied.

The two women watched for a moment as the girl fed the final crystals of the freezy to the grateful dog. 'There you go, Mr Popodopolous,' the girl said.

Esther snorted softly. 'Do you think that's the dog's name?' she asked, quietly enough that only Leah could hear. The answer seemed self-evident.

Oblivious to the noise and the drama of the film premiere, real and on screen, the girl hopped up. She brushed down her hands and started to run across the play area, with Mr Popodopolous barely a pace behind. They disappeared through the gate and started across the field.

Leah was tempted to follow.

The place in which she grew up had never hosted a film premiere before, if that's what this could be called. A Leicester Square movie launch had its stars, with their dazzling good looks and impossibly white teeth – but it didn't have a portly, middle-aged, town crier in bright blue garb ringing a giant bell.

'Owen's asking for you,' Esther said gently. She tapped Leah on the elbow; it was time to go. Leah was the star, after all.

The two women followed the path to the front of the community centre and through the doors. The cacophony of voices boomed around the high ceiling, bouncing and increasing in volume. Leah winced as she followed Esther around the rows of seats towards the stage.

For a film premiere, it was decidedly low-key, with most of the guests being locals who'd applied for free tickets. That was apart from the front row, which consisted of some councillors, the mayor – who was wearing the full ceremonial jewellery – plus the town crier, who had tucked his bell under his seat.

The film's director, Owen, was on stage by himself. When he spotted Leah, he touched his chest; one step away from doing that heart thing with his hands. Leah had come to know him a little over the past year. His relentless efficiency and enthusiasm had become hard to stomach. Where was his chronic sense of self-doubt and imposter syndrome, like a normal person?

Esther guided Leah to one of the seats in the front row. She was dead centre, which wouldn't have been her choice.

Although, if she'd truly had a choice, Leah wouldn't be here at all.

Esther was at her side, then there was the local newspaper journalist, whose name Leah had either forgotten, or never known.

Owen tapped the mic and immediately launched into introducing himself. He'd done something similar almost a year before, though he'd stammered a little more then. The past year or so had changed him.

'Thank you for coming,' Owen said, as the mass of voices dimmed. 'My name is Owen and it's been twenty-five years since my older sister, Jasmine, disappeared, along with her friends Victoria and Harriet. The documentary you're about to watch has been a lifelong project for me. We're taking this movie to Tribeca and the BFI next month, then Toronto and New York in September, hoping to find a distributor. There was only one place that felt right for its premiere, though. The place where it all happened, the place where I grew up.'

He paused and took a breath, before adding a solemn: 'Home.'

Leah wondered whether he'd been practising, because the pause was perfection. Like a politician delivering a rehearsed line that actually landed and wasn't a load of old guff. She also figured there weren't a whole host of places lining up to launch the film instead.

'Before we start, my crew and I would like to thank the community for your support over the last year and a bit. People who've opened your doors, or made yourself available for interview. For all the emails and tips, even those who simply made us cups of tea. We can't thank you enough – however, there are two people I would like to single out.'

Another pause. He'd definitely been practising.

He had told Leah a couple of weeks back that the 'premiere' was a bit of a stunt. He'd be showing his most recent cut of the film, in the hope of drumming up a little more publicity, before touring it around the festivals. It still wasn't certain he'd get a buyer.

For now, it was more smoke and mirrors. Fake it until you make it.

Owen looked down to the front row. 'I'd like to welcome them on stage, if that's all right. Please give a warm welcome to Leah Pearce and Esther Merrivale.'

Esther was on her feet first, which didn't give Leah a lot of choice. None of this had been in the email, though it explained Owen's insistence on Leah being front and centre.

Suddenly, Leah was on the stage, arms by her side, trying not to appear too uncomfortable as people clapped. It was hard not to wonder why they were applauding. Leah's friends had disappeared, she had spent twenty-five years somewhat answering questions about that, and then a movie had been made. She hadn't achieved anything because of it. Not really. It was her son, Zac, who'd pointed out that she now had an IMDB page and was listed as the 'star' of Owen's documentary. It was all a bit strange.

Leah and Esther returned to their seats, waiting for someone at the back to get the projector up and running. There were no giant Cokes, or popcorns in the community centre. Nothing more than people rustling the crisps they'd brought from home.

As the lights went down, Leah finally had her silence, though it was more a collective intake of breath. She felt it, too. An anticipation for something that really had been twenty-five years in the making.

The premiere was to be the first time Leah had seen the movie, though Owen had emailed a summary of its contents. She didn't know what would happen at the end, though she knew it definitely wouldn't be the truth.

Nobody knew that.

Not all of it.

The darkness became light as the town sign faded into view, and then zoomed away as a drone headed up to take in the town. It felt so small on screen, surrounded by green. This little pocket of home. Leah scanned the image, finding the community centre and then trying to work towards her own home. She didn't get the chance before things faded, to be replaced by the front door of Vicky's house.

That was the next ninety-five minutes or so. The familiar but the not. It was kind of, sort of, Leah's story. She went to a sleepover at her friend's house, woke up the next morning, and the other three had gone. The film laid out the various theories – some more wild than others. There were psychics and alien enthusiasts who had their say. There were police officers and neighbours who had theirs. There was almost nothing that Leah either hadn't already known, or hadn't found out during the filming process.

As the movie neared its conclusion, Leah realised it wasn't

really a film about her at all. Nor her friends. It was about the town and how generations of people had coped with an unsolved mystery hanging over them. The end was inconclusive, as it was always going to be. Owen hadn't discovered the truth, and he never would. There was a hopeful finish, not that the mystery had been solved, but that a community had overcome. That neighbourhoods and people were important.

In a way, Owen had failed. He'd returned home to find out what had happened to his sister, but he still didn't know. In another, he'd created a love letter to small communities and home towns. That was likely why he got the standing ovation he deserved. Leah clapped, too – not because it would have been strange if she didn't, but because she appreciated what he'd done.

Then there were canapés and cheek kisses. Thank yous and good nights. Leah spoke to the other people she knew, including Harriet's parents. Owen's own mother and father had returned from France for the evening and seemed happy enough, even though their son hadn't answered the question of what had happened to their daughter.

The after-party wasn't a wild EDM thrash in a field, it was the mayor telling Owen that she loved his movie, while sipping fizzy wine from a slightly scuffed flute.

For the most part, Leah watched. She mingled a bit, perfecting the hello-but-not-now wave, which she combined with the thin-lipped, nodded don't-come-near-me smile. This wasn't her scene. She might be bafflingly listed as the star of the movie but the person who wrote that was wrong. The town was the star.

This was no longer the place from which children went missing. It had been for twenty-five years and, now, maybe – *finally* – everyone was ready to move on.

TWO

Leah was sitting in her kitchen, drinking tea, and reading the write-ups from the night before. The local news website had rushed a 'world exclusive' review, which Leah struggled to read because of the sheer number of pop-ups. The gist seemed to be that the film was good.

There were the Facebook comments on the town's page, which ranged from people being annoyed they hadn't got tickets, to general praise and excitement that the town was going to be on big, or little, screens around the world. Nobody really mentioned that a quarter of a century had passed and that three girls were still missing. Or that the movie was a small-town, small-budget, documentary that had just had its premiere in the back hall of a community centre, and was unlikely to find a big audience.

As Leah scrolled on her phone, a message arrived from Ben. His son was friends with Leah's. The pair had bonded a year or so before and things had become, well, complicated.

We still on for 8?

Leah replied with a quick: 'Of course'. And re-read some of the messages she'd had about the film. Harriet's mum, Deborah, said she thought Owen had done as good a job as possible – although Leah suspected, deep down, the other woman had wanted more. She had waited so many years for answers about her daughter she still didn't have.

There was movement from the stairs, so Leah put down her phone and waited for her son to enter the room. Zac was fifteen and built like a grown man. The sort of kid that people called a 'gentle giant', even if – really – that meant he was clumsy and frequently tripped over his own feet.

He was clutching his phone as he entered the kitchen, which wasn't uncommon, though the concern on his face was.

'People are saying Dylan, Alf and Mo are missing,' he said.

Leah's 'What do you mean?' got a bemused yawn and a stretch. He straightened himself and she knew her son well enough to realise he was trying not to appear as confused as he was.

He held his phone up higher. 'Dunno. Suresh said his dad was out walking the dog and saw a load of police cars. He asked what was going on and they told him Dylan, Alfie and Mo disappeared overnight.'

Leah started to reply and then stopped herself as she realised she was repeating the same question. It was all a variation on 'What?', though ever more disbelieving.

As Zac picked out some slices from the bread bin, Leah's phone buzzed, with another message from Ben.

Have you heard there are 3 boys missing? Josh says they're in his year

Leah felt a prickling at the back of her neck. It would be

nothing. Perhaps three boys off for a midnight adventure, who were yet to return. No big deal.

Except there was a time in which adults had insisted three girls had done the same thing. That was twenty-five years before. And the girls had never returned.

'Do you know them?' Leah asked.

Zac had slipped four slices of bread into the toaster. He'd developed that teenage ability to eat anything and everything, while growing only upwards.

'I messaged Alf but there's no answer,' Zac replied, while tapping into his phone.

Leah tried to remember whether she'd heard the names before. If they were friends with Zac, she didn't think he'd mentioned them.

'What about the others?' Leah asked.

'They're in my year,' Zac said, still on his phone. His puzzled expression deepened.

She was about to ask whether he was *actually* friends with any of them when the door sounded. Leah glanced into the hall, where a large shape had appeared on the other side of the rippled glass of the front door. The shape was adult-sized, except Leah didn't know anyone who'd be looking for her so early on a Saturday.

Leah caught her son's eye, who gave an *it's-not-for-me* glance, before returning to his phone.

He was right that it wasn't for him. The shape at the door was in fact two people: both police officers in uniform. The taller man stood to the side, letting his colleague do the talking.

'Are you Leah Pearce?' she asked, although it seemed obvious she knew the answer.

'Is everything all right?' Leah asked.

The officers exchanged the briefest of looks, as if doing a mental paper-scissors-stone to decide who was going to ask the important bit.

'There's nothing specifically for you to be worried about,' the woman said. 'I'm Constable Evans. We're sorry to ask this but there's been an incident at a farm just outside of town. There are three boys missing.'

Leah stared back at her. 'OK...?'

Another silent glance between the officers.

'The thing is, one of the mothers is asking for you. She says she knows you...'

THREE

'What's she called?' Leah asked, trying to remember the names of the boys. Alfie, someone and someone else. She was so bad with that sort of thing.

The officer checked her pad. 'Jennifer Bailey, though she says you might know her as Jennifer Hook.'

The name sounded vaguely familiar, like being reminded of a chocolate bar that was discontinued years before.

Evans picked up on the confusion, adding: 'You were at school together...?'

There it was. Jennifer Hook. The Cadbury's Spira of people Leah knew.

'We were in the same class,' Leah said. 'We don't *really* know each other.'

Leah tried to picture Jennifer, but there was only the vague notion that she had dark hair. They might have nodded to one another while filling up with petrol a month or so back. Leah doubted they'd ever said more than a hundred words to each other – and all of those would have been at school.

Evans checked her pad again, presumably making sure she had the correct people. 'She specifically asked for you. She asked if you'd go to see her on the farm...?' The pad snapped closed. 'You don't have to. We only came to ask and give you a lift if you need one.'

The male officer took a step backwards before Leah interrupted him with a 'No, no, it's fine.' She told them she needed a minute to put on some proper clothes and then disappeared back into the house.

Leah got dressed and told Zac the police had asked if she could visit the farm. He was bemused about why, although she didn't know any more than he did. She told him she'd message if anything happened – and then she was off, driving across town after the police.

They led her out the far side, onto the narrowing country roads. Beyond the tall hedges, the green fields stretched far, towards the line of trees in the distance. The sun was up, the sky a greying blue. There was a chill, though it felt as if the day would be warm later.

The police car indicated and turned onto what turned out to be a rocky track. Leah had driven past the path hundreds of times, yet barely noticed it among the swaying bushes and overgrown borders. The only indicator of anything beyond the hedgerow was a rickety, faded, 'Barnacre Farm' sign, that was riddled with moss. The sort of banner that usually accompanied the abandoned building of a business that had long since gone under.

Leah didn't fancy the track in her car, so parked on the verge and headed after the police on foot.

Another officer was waiting at the top of the trail, leaning on a gatepost. Wisps of blonde hair peeped from underneath her black and white police hat – as she folded her arms across her front, trying to protect herself in the bristling wind.

The officer's eyes widened with recognition as Leah neared. 'Oh, it's you,' she said.

Leah blinked back, wondering if they might've been at

school together as well, before realising the other woman had a good ten years on her. It was just that general recognition people had for her in the local area.

'Is it that way?' Leah asked, pointing along the track, knowing it was.

'Yes,' the officer replied. Her arms were unfolded now, voice chirpy but curious.

Leah's foot crunched on the gravel as she took a step towards the overhanging trees, which swayed ominously overhead.

'Can you believe it's happened again?' the waiting police officer said, as Leah approached. She sounded surprised that she'd spoken, unable to keep her thoughts to herself. 'Is that why you're here?'

'I don't know why I'm here,' Leah replied.

'It's boys this time – but there are three of them again. They were sleeping in their tents and then... gone. Just like you with your friends.'

Leah nodded, unsure how to reply. It had been twenty-five years since her trio of friends disappeared. Twenty-five years since the night of the sleepover.

'It's unbelievable, isn't it?' the officer added. 'Same town, same ages, same thing.'

The two women stared at each other for a moment, before the officer seemed to realise she'd overstepped.

'Sorry,' she mumbled, before pointing along the path. 'It's that way. They're waiting for you.'

The lane was riddled with ankle-deep potholes and shingle that slipped and skidded as Leah trod across it. A wire fence lined the path, with fields of browny-green stretching towards trees on one side and a distant building on the other.

Four police vehicles were parked at the bottom of the track, close to a large house. Paint flaked from the sills and there was a fist-sized patch on the upper floor that had been covered with black gaffer tape. The roof was speckled with more moss, as water dripped from a hole in the drain, where the downpipe was supposed to be.

Constable Evans was waiting at the side of her car. With a slim, humourless, smile, she led Leah through the unlocked front door of the farmhouse, into a gloomy hall. Crusty wellington boots were piled with shoes in a cluttered heap that smelled of dirt. Thick beams lined the ceiling, inches from Leah's head. If Zac had been there, he'd have had to duck.

Into the kitchen and a woman was sitting at the table with an untouched cup of tea in front of her. When she looked up, there was the merest speckle of recognition between her and Leah. Jennifer Bailey, Jennifer Hook, wasn't the person Leah remembered from the petrol station the other week. When Leah had pictured nodding to someone, it had been someone else. This person was a stranger.

This Jennifer's hair was purply-blue, which matched her zigzag nails.

'You came,' Jennifer said. She looped her fingers through the handle of the mug, though didn't lift it.

Leah wasn't sure what to say and offered a weak, 'Of course...'

There were now two officers in the kitchen, plus Jennifer. Leah didn't know anyone, nor had she ever been in the farmhouse. It was all new.

'Nobody else knows what it's like,' Jennifer said.

Leah found herself sitting across the table from the other woman. The chair creaked and so did the floor. The entire house felt as if it was sighing.

'What happened?' Leah asked.

Jennifer glanced to Constable Evans, who was standing in the doorway, opposite a different officer in another frame. The kitchen felt crowded.

'Dylan was camping out back with his friends,' Jennifer

said, angling towards the field past the window. 'They did it a few times last summer, when we had that nice patch of weather. They usually come in when it's morning. Teenagers, you know? Always hungry.'

She waited a beat and Leah wondered if the other woman knew they had sons in the same year.

'I came down for a cup of tea,' Jennifer added. 'There was nobody inside, so I went out and...' A pause. 'Three empty tents. They're just... gone.'

FOUR

Leah had been on the other end of the questions and it was always the same. People didn't know what to say, so they asked the stupidest things imaginable.

Except, now things were the other way around, Leah found herself doing the same.

'What do you mean "gone"?' she asked. The words were barely out of her mouth before she realised how thick it sounded. How she'd have resented anyone asking something similar all those years before. 'Gone' could only mean one thing.

Jennifer didn't particularly acknowledge the question. She was biting her fingers and at least two of the fake nails were missing entirely. 'I tried calling Dylan but he's not answering,' she added. 'There's no sign of any of them.'

'Who else was over?' Leah asked.

'Alfie. His mum and dad are away all weekend, so he was staying over 'til tomorrow night. Then Mo. Do you know him? They're all in the same class.' Jennifer didn't wait for a reply, before turning to look at the officer to whom Leah hadn't been introduced. 'Did you—?'

'They're on their way back down,' he replied.

That got a nod. 'They have family up north,' Jennifer added. 'I think it was her mum, something like that. They were visiting, so Mo was staying here as well.'

Leah didn't know either of the two boys. Actually, she didn't recognise Dylan either. Three boys from her son's year at school. The parents might be in the giant parent WhatsApp group that Leah rarely checked. There were splinter ones for smaller clubs at the school, or just the parents of Zac's actual friends. Leah sometimes wondered if there were others to which she hadn't been invited. A 'No Leah' group. She told herself not to be so egotistical, then wondered if everyone else thought the same.

Jennifer was staring at the mug. She'd let it go a while back, though still hadn't touched the tea. At some point, Constable Evans had disappeared. There were now only three of them in the kitchen.

A wave of discomfort suddenly passed through Leah. Her legs felt itchy, her temples bristling. There couldn't be three missing boys in this town: there just couldn't.

She stood, not sure why, and crossed to the sink. There were unwashed plates and glasses as Leah plucked a teacup from the mug tree next to the kettle. She filled it with water and passed it to Jennifer. It felt like something to do. Perhaps something other people might do in a crisis. A person could make drinks and maybe knock up a sandwich, because what else was there?

Jennifer took the mug and drank, then put it down next to her tea.

As Leah turned back to the sink, she noticed movement through the window. Dark dots of police officers were grouped towards the far side of the field, near the trees. Someone was pointing, then a different guy indicated the opposite way.

Leah remembered watching a different search from her own bedroom twenty-five years ago and she shivered.

The remaining officer in the kitchen must have followed Leah's line of sight because he was suddenly talking.

'We've got more officers on the way,' he said to Leah. 'We've started searching beyond the property, mainly around the river.'

Jennifer spun in her seat and stood, crossing to stand by Leah as they watched the distant search party.

'Dylan goes fishing,' she said quietly. 'I found his rod out there this morning when I was looking for him. I thought they might've gone down that way because he sometimes goes night fishing. I ask him not to, but he's a teenage boy...' She looked for support and Leah nodded along, even though that wasn't particularly her experience with Zac. He wasn't the outdoors sort.

Leah had been wondering why Jennifer had asked for her. They weren't friends and, as far as Leah knew, hadn't spoken since school. Even that was a guess, because Leah didn't remember any specific conversations back then. It didn't feel like a question she could ask, and it certainly wasn't the time. Except the last couple of weeks of local news, and the Facebook pages, had all been about the documentary, with Leah front and centre, whether or not she wanted to be. Plus, Jennifer had been in her year at school. Leah might have been the girl who was left answering questions about her missing friends – but they had all lived through it.

'We got no answer at your neighbour's place,' the officer said.

'He was in last night,' Jennifer replied. 'I saw his lights.'

'We'll keep trying.'

Leah continued standing, with Jennifer at her side. She wondered if she should hug the other woman? When everything had been reversed, Leah had largely wanted to be left alone. But Jennifer had asked for her.

Jennifer had her phone in her hand and was tilting it for Leah to see a list of calls. 'He phoned from his tent last night,' she said.

The most recent name on the call list was 'Dylan', as were most of them.

'He'd been messaging, asking me to take down crisps, so he didn't have to put on his shoes. Because I wasn't replying, he called. Cheeky sod.'

Jennifer glanced towards the counter and the open multi-pack of crisps, then pressed the screen to call Dylan again. She moved the device to her ear, then lowered it.

'It's not even ringing,' she said.

'Do you have Find My Friends?'

'His last known place is here – but I can't find his phone. It must be with him but either off, or he has no service, or...'

She didn't finish the thought.

'Have you tried his dad, or...?' Leah hesitated part-way through the sentence, knowing it could be a touchy subject. Could there be a second mum? Leah herself was divorced from Zac's father – and others had far more complicated situations.

Jennifer's jaw tightened. 'He's not at his dad's.'

Leah exchanged a glance with the officer, who turned away. They'd be looking into all that sort of stuff.

She and Jennifer stood for a few seconds more until the back door clunked and opened. Constable Evans was back.

'Can you come this way?' she asked, talking to Jennifer.

Jennifer moved slowly, a pace, then two. She stopped next to the fridge and turned towards Leah. 'Are you coming?' she asked, though it sounded more like a request than a question.

Leah followed the other two women out the back door and onto a crunchy square of gravel that gave way to a dusty yard. A wire fence separated the hard ground from the acres of soil. Clumps of wild grass were dotted among patches of brown and green. Leah knew little about farming but, even to her, it felt as if the land hadn't been worked in a long time.

The trio walked across the yard towards three small tents on the edge of the soil. A pile of rocks were nearby, with blackened scorch marks inside.

They stopped a few metres short of the tents and the officer pointed towards the trees. 'We're trying to figure out the property boundaries,' she said, speaking to Jennifer.

'I've never really known,' Jennifer replied. 'I've always assumed it's the trees. I've got the plans but they're somewhere in the attic. It was Dad's house.'

Evans was nodding. 'We're going to get a helicopter up soon. We might have had issues over low flying if it was private property...' She tailed off, then added: 'Just letting you know we're doing all we can.'

There was a buzz from some sort of radio and Evans said she'd be back. She hurried towards the house, leaving Leah and Jennifer alone. The empty tents sat in front of them, pulling and demanding Leah's attention to the point that she had to turn away. There had once been an empty living room, now there were empty tents.

'What's it like?' Jennifer asked. Her haunted words hung on the breeze.

'What do you mean?' Leah replied.

'I guess...' Jennifer stopped and took a breath. Tried again. 'What if they don't come back?'

FIVE

Leah started a sentence that began with 'I think' but then abandoned it. This question was why Jennifer wanted her. She was the go-to person for missing teenagers, whether or not she wanted to be. Who else was there to ask what to feel, and how to act? Leah had lived it for twenty-five years.

Except Leah knew something Jennifer didn't, something *nobody* else did. She knew what had happened to her friends years ago and where they were.

Leah was spared from answering by the *chuka-chuka* of a behemoth that materialised from nowhere. A helicopter swooped low over the house, circled across the field, and dived towards the trees in the distance. The speed at which it appeared and then disappeared was almost unworldly, leaving only a ticking from somewhere beyond.

In the time it had taken for the helicopter to fly over, they had barely moved, except to stop their hair windmilling.

'I think your son's in Dylan's class,' Jennifer said.

Zac had told Leah they were in the same year but they could still be in the same class for individual subjects.

'They're still so young,' Leah said, knowing it wasn't really a reply.

But they *were* young. Five one day, fifteen the next. A skinny boy and then a filled-out young man. Leah still remembered the moment on the landing, in the gloom, when she'd realised she had to look up to take in her son.

'I really thought they'd gone fishing,' Jennifer said. 'There's a stream on the other side of next-door's farm. Technically, it's a river – but you can walk through it, depending on the time of year.' She waited and, when Leah didn't reply, added: 'I sometimes go over and sit on the bank. It's so quiet. You can just... *think.*'

She looked to Leah and there was a moment of understanding. Leah craved that sometimes. Not only the quiet of an empty house but an empty everything, with no passing traffic, or noisy neighbours.

'Does Dylan catch much?' Leah asked, being polite.

'I think he's only caught two or three fish in the last year. If you follow the water upstream, there's as many shopping trolleys as anything living.' Jennifer stopped again and Leah felt the weight of the other woman looking to her.

Somehow, Leah had again ended up staring at the tents. There were three of the pop-up, festival sort. They'd start life barely bigger than a shoebox and then explode into a sweltering sweat lodge that could just about fit a person. They would then either break, blow away, or never again fit into their original container. The type that would be abandoned in a muddy field.

'Is your son into fishing?' Jennifer asked.

'No,' Leah replied, and then: 'I don't think so. He plays games with his friends, or they go to Laser Quest. He tried skating for the first time the other week, but I don't think he liked it.'

It didn't feel like the response Jennifer wanted. The other

woman bit her lip and continued as if Leah hadn't spoken. She wanted to talk.

'Dylan's always watching those YouTube or TikTok things. Kids who make loads of money opening boxes. That sort of thing. He shows me and then tells me how much they make. It's unbelievable. He's really into his fishing and does these videos about it. I think he's hoping he can make something of it.' A pause. 'He probably needs a better river.'

There was a resigned sigh as Jennifer followed Leah's stare towards the tents. Camping had never been Leah's thing. She had a perfectly good bed at home.

'I found Dylan's rod on the bank this morning,' Jennifer added. 'He's really protective over it because he saved up and bought it with his own money. He'd never just leave it there. I was trying to tell the police that but I don't think they were listening. The police have it now but I dunno what they're going to do with it.'

Leah thought on that for a moment. Jennifer might have asked for her because she was seemingly an expert on local missing teenagers – but that didn't mean she had the answers. 'They'll be checking fingerprints, something like that,' Leah replied. 'I'm sure you'll get it back.'

It was another of those things that felt the right thing to say. Leah wasn't sure if police still looked for fingerprints. It felt like a relic, where putting on gloves was some sort of magic get-out-of-jail-free card for a crook.

Jennifer nodded across towards the other farmhouse. It was over to the side and, from a distance, looked broadly the same as Jennifer's place. 'Charles goes berserk because Dylan sometimes takes a shortcut across the back of his field. It's the quickest way to the river.'

'Charles is your neighbour?'

A nod. 'His wife died a few years ago and he's gone mental ever since. They didn't have any kids, so it's just him by himself.

He went through a stage of putting up signs in the lane, saying how everything's a hoax. The council made him take them down, so he dumped everything on the steps of the town hall.' She waited for Leah to meet her eyes, then added: 'He's a real nutter.'

'What does he do when he sees the boys on his field?'

'Shouts at them, or comes knocking on my door and shouts at me. Dylan said he came out with a shotgun last year. I called the police but he told them it was a walking stick. They couldn't find any evidence of a gun but I don't know how hard they looked.'

Leah followed Jennifer's stare towards the neighbouring property. Aside from the top of the farmhouse, it was hard to see much of anything beyond the hedge.

'He's got a scrapyard over there,' Jennifer added. 'Loads of old cars and trailers. Rusting old rubbish. I don't know what he does but you'll hear him welding or grinding for hours at a time. We're in a bit of a dispute because I'm trying to sell.'

'Why's that a dispute?'

'They want to put up wind turbines but need both farms. It's both or nothing. He says he'll never leave. I've considered selling to someone else for the land but I'll get much less than if we work together.'

There had been stories for years about a potential wind farm outside the town. Each new update would have the town's Facebook page exploding with insults as those against decided those in favour were scum of the earth. And vice versa. It was always a ticking clock until someone got compared to Hitler.

In the distance, the helicopter surged over the trees and hovered momentarily, before dipping towards another area. Leah wasn't sure she'd ever seen a helicopter around town before. She wondered if this was procedure, or if the police were particularly worried. Had there been other missing children over the years, after her friends? Had they turned up quickly enough that nobody had heard about it?

'How long have you lived here?' Leah nodded to the house. She was trying to think of something to take Jennifer's mind off the immediate.

'Always. Mum and Dad used to run the place as a dairy farm back in the day.' Jennifer pointed across to a barn that had holes in the side and no doors. 'It went out of business when I was about nine or ten. Dad always refused to buy anything at the big supermarkets because he said it was their fault for buying milk in bulk. Something like that.'

'Where did you shop?'

Anything to keep the conversation going.

'We got stuff off his farming friends for a while but, in the end, we didn't have much choice. One day, there were Asda carrier bags in the cupboard under the sink and that was it. Dad ended up getting a job at the meat plant.'

The two exchanged a glance and didn't need to say anything more. The plant used to be on the edge of town and, if the wind was blowing the wrong way, the foul stench of flesh would hang. People called it a 'meat plant' because it was better than saying abattoir. Complaints about the smell had continued up until a few years before, when it had gone out of business.

Moving from raising cows to being involved in slaughtering them felt like a very abrupt change, though Leah didn't say that.

'What happened to your mum?' All the talk had been of Jennifer's dad.

'She said was going out and never came back.'

Leah had visions of another missing person: 'What do you mean?'

'I didn't know for ages. Dad just said she was gone. After I kept asking, he said she was having an affair and left us for some guy. I literally never saw her again.'

'Not even letters? Phone calls? Texts?'

'Nothing. Things had been hard after the farm closed. This was the only job she'd really had. Then Dad would take all the overtime at the plant and was hardly home. I guess I wasn't around much either. I sort of get it...'

Jennifer stared towards the house and it felt as if there was at least some understanding between them. Except, maybe, she was talking about herself as well. It was a big house for one person.

'Dad got cancer about eighteen months after that. He was gone not long after.'

That was spoken with a lot more finality, and with little obvious regret.

With everything that had happened overnight, into the morning, it felt as if Jennifer wanted someone to talk to. Someone to take her mind from the worry.

'How old were you?' Leah asked.

'Twenty? Bit older. Something like that. I was never home because I was seeing this lad. He ended up moving in. We got married and had Dylan, but not in that order. You probably know Steven Bailey.'

Leah pictured a skinny lad with a shaved head and a wispy moustache. 'Isn't he the one who lost the class rabbit over the Christmas holidays?'

That got a roll of the eyes. 'The first time we ever went out, I asked him about that. He reckoned his dad killed it but said he couldn't tell the teacher that.' Jennifer considered things briefly, perhaps considered Leah herself, weighing up what to say, before adding: 'I think *he* probably killed the rabbit.'

'Why?'

'That's just what he's like. He deliberately ran over a cat once. I was in the car and he swerved towards it. There was a bump as it went under the wheels. When we got home, I asked why he'd driven at the cat and he said he didn't know what I was talking about.' She stopped for a sigh that Leah knew well enough. She had an ex as well. He didn't kill cats but...

'Where is he now?' Leah asked.

'On the coast somewhere, with that girl from his work. Her dad's some city banker-wanker type. Bonuses and all that. She's got some waterfront flat. I found it on Google Maps: this horrible glass thing, near an old post office. I think—' Jennifer cut herself off, probably realising she'd dipped into full stalker mode. She waited a moment, probably considering how much to reveal. 'Steven doesn't really want to see Dylan. Dylan goes there every six weeks or so but sometimes not even that.'

Leah worked in community support and was amazed at how many times she heard similar things. She occasionally wondered if it was her. Did she attract these broken souls? It sometimes felt like it – but, on this occasion, it felt as if Jennifer didn't have a lot of other people in her life to talk to. It felt like the other woman was lonely. Leah knew that feeling.

'Should I help look?' Jennifer asked. She was looking over the tents, towards the trees. 'They said to wait here in case Dylan calls, or comes back, but I know the woods quite well.'

The police officers who'd been on the edge of the field had disappeared past the tree line.

'I think they probably know best,' Leah replied, although she wasn't sure it was true.

They stood together quietly for a while, listening to the distant ticking of the helicopter blades.

'Did you ever go on any of the searches?' Jennifer asked.

Leah shivered as she stared across the wide open land. 'I was too young.'

'My dad did. They searched the woods at least twice and even checked our barn. It wasn't falling apart then.'

Leah turned to take in the barn again. It was the sort of place that would get searched by the police. In a crime drama, it's where the bodies would be.

She knew her friends had never been in that barn, nor the woods.

'I don't know what to do,' Jennifer said. She'd moved a step or two closer, without Leah realising. 'I keep thinking this is all a bit overblown. I know I called the police but it's a bit much, isn't it? The helicopter and everything. Dylan will be off at someone's house and I'll have to say sorry to everyone.'

Leah had no idea what to say. Should she tell Jennifer that Dylan *would* be back? Was that false hope? Or real hope? Did people want the truth in situations like this? It was another explanation of why Leah was there: people assumed she knew.

'I'm sure the police know what they're doing,' Leah said – and it sounded weak, even to her. Some poor soul by themselves in a restaurant insisting that, no, they hadn't been stood up and that, yes, he would be along any minute now.

Jennifer took out her phone, tapped the screen, then put it away again. 'He's still not answering,' she said, before trying a second time. 'He's going to be in so much trouble when he gets back. He'll be grounded the whole summer.'

Leah let that sit. What were the stages of grief? Anger was in there somewhere and so was denial – but were they already at grief itself?

It had been a few hours and there had to still be a chance that Dylan and his friends had gone off somewhere without saying something. Perhaps it would all be a big misunderstanding?

As they stood, Leah caught movement in the corner of her eye. When she turned towards the neighbouring farmhouse, a figure was striding across the field towards them. For a flickering moment, Leah thought it could be Dylan. He was back, and it *was* a misunderstanding. It took her a couple of seconds to realise it was an older man. He had long grey hair at the sides, with either a centre parting that had got wildly out of hand, or a massive bald spot.

Jennifer had spotted him, too. 'Charles,' she said, ominously.

The two women moved around to the side of the house as Charles stopped mid-field and waved them across, like a teacher beckoning a naughty child.

'This is what he's like,' Jennifer said, as she started walking towards him.

Leah kept pace until they'd reached him.

'Have you seen Dylan?' Jennifer asked, though the question was batted away with a backhanded wave.

'What's all the noise about?' the man demanded. He was on tiptoes, arching forward and pointing. 'I've had people banging on my door. Is this you?'

'Dylan's missing,' Jennifer said, with a forced politeness. 'And his friends. They were camping in our field but there's no sign of them. Did you see anything overnight?'

That got a shrug and a rapid shake of the head. 'Why would I have seen anything?'

'I'm not sure. I just—'

'They'll be by the river, where they always are. Did you look there?'

'Of course but—'

'I told you I saw him trying to set a fox trap down there. Maybe he caught himself up in that. You should've stopped it when I told you.'

Leah watched as Jennifer sighed and then caught herself. There was a time and place for arguing with neighbours, and it probably wasn't while a child was missing.

'Dylan said it wasn't a trap but, regardless, he's not out there.'

'I know a trap when I see one. Anyway, I'm not surprised he's run off.'

Until Charles said that, Jennifer had maintained a fierce

expression of tolerance. Something about the way she narrowed her eyes made Leah take a step forward.

'What do you mean by that?' Jennifer growled, as Leah moved between the neighbours.

Charles eyed Leah and then Jennifer. It felt as if he was sizing them up, before making his choice. 'Just keep it down,' he snapped.

He didn't wait for a reply before turning and stomping back towards his property.

It took a few seconds for Jennifer to sink as Leah realised the other woman had been on tiptoes.

'That's one of our happier interactions,' she said, humourlessly.

Leah didn't doubt it. He seemed like something of a nightmare neighbour.

They turned back to the house together, as the back door was opening. Constable Evans had returned.

SIX

Mo's parents were waiting in a crowded kitchen. Ali and Aisha had hurried down the motorway after finding out their son was missing. They, understandably, had the panicked look of confused parents, desperate to know what was happening with their child.

Leah was a spare part, unsure if she should return home, or if there was something she was meant to be doing. But she couldn't simply leave.

That left her watching and trying not to be in the way as Aisha headed to the back of the house to make a call. Ali followed, before making a call of his own. There were conversations with Constable Evans, then a new police car appeared and there were more talks with them. Jennifer and Aisha had a moment as mothers together, then Ali wanted to see the tents. Worried, panicked, people wondering what they could do, while being told the only thing was to wait. The frustration was evident. The natural instinct was to stomp into the woods and look for the boys – but what if they trampled across important evidence? Nobody wanted to have to sit and wait, let alone parents whose children were missing.

It was almost ten minutes later, as she wandered around the front of the house, that Leah realised there were small children in the back of Ali and Aisha's car. A pair of anxious faces stared through the glass and Leah found herself giving a small wave, because she had no idea what else to do.

Minutes later and Aisha was at the car, still on her phone. Ali arrived not long after, talking to one of the officers – and then they were both back in their vehicle, presumably to head home. Leah watched Ali do a three-point turn and then bump the car back to the road. Mo's parents had been at the house for less than fifteen minutes.

The last thing Leah saw was the troubled face of a young girl peering through the back window. She couldn't have been older than seven or eight.

Leah was trying to think of a way to tell Jennifer that she should go. She wanted to check on Zac and possibly ask if he knew Dylan or the others that well. There didn't feel as if there was much she could do at Jennifer's house.

Before Leah could turn to look for the other woman, there was a chuntering howl as the helicopter whipped over the top of the house, heading away from the woods and towards town.

Constable Evans was at the front of her house, holding onto her hat as the air blasted from above. When the chopper disappeared out of sight, Leah crossed to the officer.

'Does this mean they found something?' Leah asked.

That got a shake of the head. 'Not yet. They need to refuel but I'm not sure if they're coming back anyway. It's a lot denser than we realised.' She paused a moment and then indicated the house. 'You're not really friends, are you?'

'I don't think we've spoken since school.'

'I'm sorry for bothering you in that case. There wasn't time to check everything. She said you were friends and asked if we could pick you up. I just do what I'm told.'

Leah told her it was fine. It felt as if the officer was going to say something more, though her radio buzzed and she stepped away before speaking into it. Instead, Leah headed back into the house, where Jennifer was again sitting at her kitchen table. She was alone, typing on her phone, though looked up as Leah entered.

'I'm so glad you came,' she said. 'I know we're not great friends or anything. They asked if there was someone I could call. Steven's nowhere around and it's just me and Dylan. I didn't know who to say but you've been everywhere all week. All year, really. I suppose I just…'

She didn't finish the line, instead picking up the stone-cold cup of tea, sipping, and then realising. Jennifer got up and dumped the liquid into the sink, over the top of the dirty dishes.

'You don't mind, do you?' she asked.

'Of course not,' Leah replied.

Hours later, as Leah got through her front door, she heard footsteps on the stairs. Zac usually stayed in his room, only appearing when he was hungry, or if the Wi-Fi had gone off. It felt like it had been a long time since he had awaited her arrival home with such eagerness.

He bounded off the bottom of the steps, tripping on the bottom one, and only stopping himself from falling by grabbing the stair rail.

'Did they find them?' he asked.

Leah gave a little frown, though didn't remind him – again – about not running on the stairs.

'No,' she replied. It had been almost six hours since she'd headed off to Jennifer's house.

'Do they, um— What's going on?'

Zac was usually laid-back and unflappable, though he couldn't get out his words quickly enough.

'Are you all right?' Leah asked.

'Yeah. Of course. Yeah.' Zac was still speaking too fast. 'I sit on the same table as Alfie in physics. I only saw him yesterday.'

Leah put down her bag and ushered her son into the kitchen. The fridge was cluttered with plastic tubs of food and she nudged them to one side to find the can of Coke she knew was at the back. It was for emergencies, when only a sugar rush would do.

'Did he tell you he was going camping with Dylan?' Leah asked.

'No but we don't really talk about stuff like that.'

'How well do you know Alfie?'

'We play FIFA sometimes, plus he was Mufasa when we did *The Lion King* at school.'

Ah, yes. The musical was what could've been expected of twelve- and thirteen-year-olds. The biggest surprise was that nobody got cancelled after the very white cast's attempts at singing the opening Zulu lyrics. Leah vaguely remembered the blonde boy under the bad wig playing Mufasa. Zac had been Timon or Pumba. Leah could never remember which was which.

'Do you have any idea where Alfie might've gone?' Leah asked.

By the time she had left Jennifer's house, Alfie's parents hadn't arrived back from their weekend away.

That got a shake of the head, though Zac held up his phone. 'That's what everyone's talking about. He likes fishing and football but nobody knows more than that. Someone went out and looked around the pitches in case they were playing but there's nobody around.'

Leah sat at the table and drank from the can. One thing to say about the current generation is that they rarely waited to be told what to do. If there was a classmate to find, they cracked on.

'What about Mo?' Leah asked.

Zac tilted his phone again, presumably indicating the chats he was having. 'I don't really know him, but he's top set for everything. He won some sort of county science cup last year.'

Leah remembered something about that from the parents' WhatsApp group. There had been large-scale disinterest from the other parents.

'Do you know Dylan?' Leah asked.

Something crossed Zac's face.

'What?' Leah pressed.

'He got suspended at the start of the year for touching a girl's, um...'

Zac glanced away. He might be built like a man but still had that squirming awkwardness when it came to girls. He mimed touching his own chest and then caught himself.

'Her... boobs?'

'Yeah.' Zac lowered his hands and found a spot on the wall at which to stare. 'Alfie once said that Dylan's dad isn't his real dad,' he added quietly

Leah thought on that for a moment. Jennifer hadn't mentioned another man, though she'd been insistent that her ex, Steven, wasn't the person for her.

'What do you think he meant by that?' Leah asked.

'Dunno.'

As Leah had another drink from the can, her phone buzzed. If it had been any name other than Ben's on the screen, she'd have ignored it. At some point, they were going to have to tell their respective sons they were seeing each other. That day felt as if it was creeping nearer.

Because of that, they were careful in what they sent to one another. This message felt different, because Ben didn't really do insistence.

Can you come over? Urgent

SEVEN

The kettle was starting to bubble as Leah let herself into Ben's house. He had a key for her place, too. Those spares were something else about which Zac and Josh didn't know. It had only been a couple of weeks since Leah had approached Ben's door, ready to drop off Zac, when she'd started to reach into her bag for the key. She'd caught herself just in time, and rang the bell instead.

As Leah entered the kitchen now, Ben was pouring boiling water into a mug.

'A cup of tea doesn't seem very urgent,' Leah told him.

He put down the kettle and grinned, reaching around her waist. Leah allowed him to pull her closer as he pecked her forehead.

'That doesn't seem very urgent either,' Leah added.

He smiled as he poked the teabag with a spoon. 'Josh is at his Mum's 'til tomorrow. I've got the place to myself.'

'That's still not how I'd define urgent.'

Ben scooped out the teabag and dunked it into the small compost bin that was under the sink. He splashed in some milk and gave it a stir, before washing up the spoon, drying it, and returning it to the drawer.

They say that opposites attract and, when it came to tidiness, this very much applied. If Leah had been making the tea, the teabag and spoon would've been in the sink.

Ben picked up his grim-looking dark green protein shake from the counter and supped the top. He would've been on a run that morning, though had long since learned that Leah neither needed, nor wanted, to hear about it.

'Josh told me that Dylan once brought a gun to school,' he said.

It was such an abrupt change in tone that Leah fumbled a 'What?', making him repeat himself.

'I don't know if I should be telling the police,' Ben added. 'I went through the class WhatsApp group but nobody's mentioned it in there. I'm not sure who else knows.'

Leah needed a moment to think. Guns might be a common sight in some places but not where they lived. Leah didn't think she had ever seen a real-life gun in the UK.

'What do you mean?' she asked. 'A real gun? An air rifle?'

'Josh said it was some sort of pistol. Dylan showed it to him one lunchtime at school.'

Even though she had teased Ben about the meaning of 'urgent', Leah had known Josh was away. She had expected her and Ben to have the house to themselves; that they would be heading upstairs, with little in the way of chat. This was *actually* important.

'Why did he have a gun?' Leah asked. 'Where'd he get it?'

Josh didn't know. 'I asked the same things. I asked if it looked real but how would he know? He said it looked like the ones on *Modern Warfare*.'

Leah knew that was a game but had no idea what the guns looked like within it. Presumably they were realistic.

'Did he say whether Dylan showed the gun to anyone else?'

'I don't know. I asked Josh why Dylan had chosen to show him the gun and he said it was because they were talking about a game. Dylan said something like he only plays with real guns.'

Leah sipped her tea, thinking. The picture Jennifer had painted of Dylan that morning wasn't of a threatening, angry teenager. Except, he'd been through a lot. His father seemingly wasn't much to do with his life, his grandparents were gone, and he lived with his mum in the middle of nowhere. He was too young to drive and buses didn't go that way. There must be a lot of frustration in his life, even if Jennifer hadn't explained it in such a way.

There was also the fact that, despite the relatively short distance, there was a difference between the town itself, and the surrounding country. People *did* hunt and fish in the woods. People had legal weapons, though not somebody Dylan's age.

Still, it was a big jump from that to taking a gun to school.

'What did you tell Josh?'

That got a sigh. 'To keep it to himself for now. When he gets back from his mum's, we can talk about it more. I didn't know what to say.'

'Zac said Dylan was suspended from school for touching a girl's breasts.'

Ben blinked. 'That was him? I read the emails from the head but they kept the kids anonymous. I'd never really heard Dylan's name until this morning. There are so many kids in that year.'

Leah considered telling him that Zac had also said Dylan's father might not be his own. Maybe that was too personal? None of their business?

That boy had a lot going on in his life, and Leah knew what that was like for a teenager. She'd been through plenty herself at that age.

Even with that, Leah wondered what the girl would think

of it all. How she would feel about the concern and sympathy being offered to the boy who assaulted her.

'Do we tell someone about the gun?' Ben asked.

Leah wanted to turn the question around and ask him the same thing. Or find someone who knew what they were doing and ask them. She wondered if there would ever be a time in her life when she felt enough of a grown-up to make such decisions and feel confident.

'I've been with Dylan's mum at her farm this morning,' Leah said.

It was the first Ben had heard of it. He narrowed his eyes momentarily, probably wondering if it was some sort of joke.

'I didn't know you were friends,' he replied.

'We're not. I mean, maybe we are now? The police came to the house this morning, saying Jennifer had asked for me.'

'Why you?'

A shrug. 'Why'd you think? Who knows more about missing teenagers?'

It felt flippant, and certainly sounded it.

Ben seemed confused. 'What did you do there?'

'Nothing really. I didn't feel I could say no when the police asked if I'd go. I listened to Jennifer, then Mo's parents turned up for about fifteen minutes, before heading off. There's loads of police searching, plus they flew a helicopter around. I think they were going to send up drones next.'

They each had a drink and then stared off into corners, or through the window. Neither knew whether they should tell someone, or who to tell. Dylan's gun could have been some sort of air pistol, and have nothing to do with the fact he was missing. If the information got out, people would draw conclusions, that would never go away. Leah knew that. Even with the film, there were still people who believed she knew more than she'd ever said about her missing friends. Mud stuck and the town was too small to have it flung around.

Ben was thinking out loud. 'When Josh told me this morning, I was kinda hoping the boys would show up. That they'd gone on a trek in the woods, something like that.' He glanced at his watch, perhaps without meaning to. Somehow, the clock on the oven said it was already four o'clock. Where had the day disappeared?

The three boys had already been gone too long. If it was all a mix-up, one of them would've had phone signal at some point. Or they'd have simply returned to the farm. The longer things went on, the worse it was.

Neither of them wanted to say how ominous everything seemed.

'Are you OK?' Ben asked.

Leah couldn't meet his eye. Their relationship had happened largely by accident. They'd been spending moments together because their sons were friends. After that, it felt there was an inevitability to what developed. They talked a lot about other parents, and school politics. They drank their respective teas and protein shakes, then spent a lot of time in one another's beds.

There wasn't much beyond that.

They didn't talk much about their lives, or feelings. They'd never said the big L-word to each other. Ben had never asked about Leah's past, or her missing friends. He hadn't gone to the premiere, and Leah wouldn't have wanted him there. His lack of curiosity about the biggest thing in her life was probably why she liked him. Or, at the very least, didn't mind being around him. He was the opposite to almost everyone else she met.

Not everything had to be butterflies in the stomach.

The secrecy around their relationship was because they didn't know how their sons might take things – but it was also for them. Or, perhaps, it was for Leah. She liked not having to be public about things. She enjoyed the sneaking around. Her life had been all about secrets, and this was one more.

Ben must have realised he'd said the wrong thing because he moved on quickly, despite not getting an answer. 'Have you looked at the class WhatsApp groups?' he asked, although he already knew the answer.

'They're still on mute,' Leah replied. They largely had been since Owen had filmed part of his documentary at the school the previous year. Back then, it had felt as if everyone wanted to know Leah's opinion on it all – and she'd been determined not to give anyone the satisfaction.

'People are asking if they should keep their kids home,' Ben said. 'Some of the dads are already out doing their own search. Facebook's full of people offering to send up drones, or claiming there are paedos living down the road.'

It was expected, yet Leah still sighed. It was always the same. If people believed those Facebook threads, there was a paedophile in every other house.

Ben took that hint, too. Leah didn't want to talk about it.

'Are you gonna hang around?' he asked. 'I know you were coming over at eight anyway...'

It was tempting, and Leah almost took a step towards the stairs.

'Not today,' she said. 'I've hardly seen Zac all day.'

'I don't think he minds having the house to himself. I know I didn't when I was his age...'

'I'm not in the mood,' Leah said, even as she looked to Ben, who clearly *was* in the mood. 'Maybe tomorrow morning,' she added. 'You've still got the house to yourself then, right?'

Ben nodded, though it was clear from his expression that he was looking for more. In some ways, it was to be expected. Having an empty house for a few hours was what their relationship was based on.

The silence was awkward. Leah had no intention of explaining herself further, though it was the first time she'd ever told him no.

Ben dealt with it by washing up his shaker bottle, then Leah's mug, then a random fork that he seemingly produced from nowhere. Everything was dried and returned to its place, then the tea towel was hung neatly over the oven door handle.

'Have you decided what to do about Tuesday?' he asked.

Leah needed a moment to remember what he was on about. With the day's events, it had fallen from her mind.

'I booked the day off work,' she replied.

'A four-day weekend!'

Leah didn't match his enthusiasm. 'I've not figured out what I'm doing yet.'

'If you want company, I can come. We'll tell people I'm your neighbour, something like that.'

Leah shook her head. She wasn't sure if there would be a time and place to appear in public as something like girlfriend-boyfriend – but it certainly wouldn't be Tuesday. She found herself wondering if the missing boys would be back by then.

Ben had picked up his phone but, as he lowered it, there was something in his face.

'What?' Leah asked.

'It's just... on one of the parents' groups, someone's saying this is all happening because of the film.'

'Dylan and his friends?'

A nod: 'They're saying the town should've moved on.'

'It's not as if my friends going missing has created some sort of copycat. It's—'

Leah stopped herself, catching what she'd said, because the awful truth was right there.

What if it had?

EIGHT

Leah was riddled with guilt when she got home. It was largely for being out all day, even though she suspected Ben was right and Zac was perfectly happy being home by himself. He was fifteen, after all. Plus socialising had changed. When she was a teenager, she had spent a lot of time out with her friends; now there were mobile phones, the internet, online gaming, and video calls. Having friends didn't necessarily mean physically being with them all the time.

Leah wasn't sure how her younger self would have coped in a modern setting. She hadn't had much of a home life.

She asked Zac what he wanted to eat and ended up grilling him a cheese sandwich. He ate a lot of bread for a kid that didn't seem to put on weight.

After he'd taken his food upstairs, Leah ended up doom-scrolling on Facebook. There were hundreds of comments under the various posts about the missing boys: far too many to read. The general gist was that somebody should have done something to prevent the boys going missing, though nobody knew what. That somebody had to be to blame, though nobody dared say it was Jennifer. And that somebody should get out there and do something. There were at least some suggestions for that, what with the group of dads who were searching the woods.

As she was scrolling, Leah realised she was Facebook friends with Jennifer. She refreshed the page, figuring something must be wrong as she didn't remember accepting any request. She knew she wouldn't have sent the invitation, so it could only have come one way.

Except there had been a time a long while back, when social media was new, before everyone needed an opinion on everything, when it was about dog pictures and catching up with people not seen in years. Leah vaguely remembered accepting requests from old classmates when it had seemed fun – and, presumably, Jennifer had been one of them.

Leah clicked into the profile and stared at Jennifer's main photo. The other woman didn't post very often, though there were many public messages that day. All had a similar 'thinking of you' sentiment, along with notes asking if there was anything that could be done.

Further down the page, there were photos of Jennifer with Dylan. With all she'd heard across the day, Leah half expected some skin-headed tearaway but he was a normal looking boy. In one, he was wearing a wrestling T-shirt, squinting into the sun, with the ocean and a pier behind him. In another, Dylan was gazing uninterestedly out of shot as his mum grinned. Leah had an almost identical picture of her with Zac. It had been taken at a wedding to which neither of them particularly wanted to go. Zac had fidgeted all day in a suit that was slightly too big, while Leah had smiled and made small talk with the right people. Yes, the weather *had* held. No, the mother of the bride *didn't* need to give a speech. Yes, the bride *did* look lovely in her dress. No, she *hadn't* seen the four-year-old bridesmaid throw up because of too many sweets.

It was impossible not to see Zac in Dylan. They were the

same age, living in the same town. They even had that same distant gaze when posing for photos with their mothers.

Since Leah had found out the truth of what had happened to her friends, she'd become a little looser, more comfortable, at Zac heading out to do things by himself, or with friends. The town didn't have a big bad boogeyman out there.

Except, now... who knew what had happened?

Fifteen minutes had somehow passed, as Leah focused back on the page. She scrolled lower, to an earlier post in which Jennifer was asking for advice about the local agricultural college. Dylan was apparently considering going after his exams.

After that, there were the usual meaningless image-based slogans about love and kindness. About how cheese could solve everything. Nothing overly odd. At least, not for Facebook.

From what Leah could tell, it seemed as if Jennifer's husband had left a little over three years before. There were photos with the three of them as a family before that, but nothing after. The trio were at an agricultural show, with tractors and haybales, almost as if it had been set up as a cliché. The three of them were at a monster truck event, then on a sunshine holiday in Cape Verde. Dylan was playing football, with his father in the background; then the two males were sleeping side by side on a cramped caravan sofa.

Leah scrolled through years of photographs, with Dylan's life chronicled through his Mum's Facebook page. The younger Dylan became in the photos, the more Leah told herself to stop scrolling. It felt so morbid.

When her friends had disappeared, there had been none of this. The papers had written about her, and there'd been an awful *Crimewatch* reconstruction, but nobody *really* knew who she was. Her life hadn't been plastered across the internet.

Leah spent almost an hour telling herself to close the page. The intrusion was too much, but just... one more click. There might be more to see. She wondered if someone at the police might be doing the same. Maybe there was a clue.

Maybe.

Maybe.

Leah stopped. She stared. Because, out of nothing, there was a photo that was sixteen years old. Jennifer had an arm around a man who wasn't her husband. Who wasn't the same man that had been in all the photos with Dylan.

It had been taken a year or so before Dylan was born.

Jennifer was staring adoringly at the man, as he beamed at whoever was taking the picture. He definitely looked younger there, though still had the athletic build of a man who went running too often.

Leah knew him, because she'd spent the afternoon in his kitchen.

Ben.

NINE

Leah was up early the next morning. It had been hard getting off to sleep, given the theoretical conversations she was having with herself. She was trying to figure out how to ask Ben about the photo without *actually* asking. She had spent a couple of hours with him the previous day, largely talking about Dylan and Jennifer. Ben had never once said that he knew her, let alone that he was seemingly in a relationship with her.

Leah had scrolled through the rest of Jennifer's page – and Ben's – and there were no other photos of the two together. Not a single acknowledgement of them knowing each other, other than that they were Facebook friends. That didn't say a lot, seeing as Leah was also Facebook friends with Jennifer, despite not knowing her.

Then there was the timing. Zac had been told that Dylan's dad wasn't his real dad. The photo of Jennifer and Ben had been posted sixteen years before, and Dylan was fifteen.

Everything based on one low-res photo and a third-hand conversation. And yet...

It was five thirty in the morning on a Sunday and Leah was awake because she couldn't stop thinking about it. She'd been seeing Ben for ten or eleven months. He didn't know her biggest secret, and never would – but now she was wondering whether he had one.

Leah had saved the photo to her phone and knew every pixel. It wasn't a snapshot of a moment in which two people fell into frame at the same time. She knew the look in Jennifer's eyes as she gazed at Ben – and it was lust.

Even if he'd not said he'd once been in a relationship with Jennifer, Ben surely would have admitted to knowing her? Leah tried to remember what he'd said. She was sure she'd called her 'Dylan's mum' in the first place, but had she said 'Jennifer'... or had he?

Leah headed downstairs quietly and left a note on the fridge for Zac. They could text, but it wasn't the same. Rearranging the magnetic words to leave messages was their thing, and she liked that. Leah adjusted the words to read 'Had to go out. Back soon' and then grabbed her car keys. It was early and Zac would sleep until ten or eleven anyway. She'd likely be back before he saw it.

It was a long time since Leah had been out so early – or late – on a Sunday morning. She spotted a man in a bedraggled suit sleeping on a bench, across the road from the town's only nightclub. The place changed owners and names roughly every two years, and Leah had gone through an early twenties stage of spending most Saturday nights in there. That was when she was in her first proper relationship, with the man who became Zac's father. They'd spend their wages on luminous alcopops, then stumble their way home and spend all Sunday sleeping off their respective hangovers. That was how Leah coped with what happened to her as a teenager – except she was careful never to get *too* drunk. She had improved with age, but the alcohol still sent her to sleep.

As Leah slowed to drive past the man on the bench, that life felt so distant.

She continued past a lone woman, who was smoking next to the park gates. Somebody else was dragging a suitcase noisily along the street, presumably heading towards the train station. There was a mini homeless shelter underneath the railway bridge, with a mound of cardboard covering a series of tents.

It was hard not to picture the other tents Leah had seen that weekend.

She continued through the far end of town, following the same route as the day before, and parking on the verge.

The sun had cleared the trees as Leah moved carefully along the rocky path to Jennifer's farmhouse. The birds were having a party in the distance, which also sent Leah to another place. One time, when she really *had* been a good sleeper, they'd woken her up.

A single police car was parked at the end of the path. It was unoccupied, though Jennifer was sitting in a once-white plastic garden chair, staring into the distance as she smoked a cigarette.

As Leah neared her, she realised it wasn't tobacco at all, which was a brave move considering she was barely a couple of steps from the police vehicle.

Her eyes were ringed red, barely open, as she blinked in an attempt to take in Leah. She didn't get up.

'Constable Whatshisname said he was going to take a walk around the back and I had ten minutes until he came back,' Jennifer said. There was a conspiratorial hint in her voice, although it was largely masked by tiredness. She offered Leah the joint. 'Want a go?'

'Not for me,' Leah replied.

Jennifer had one final puff and then stubbed out the tip on the ground. She blew on the remains, cooling it, before returning it to a tin underneath the chair.

'Me either,' she replied. 'But I had a bad back the other year and a friend of a friend said it would help.' She smiled weakly, not meaning it. 'That's what I told Whatshisname anyway.'

There was nowhere to sit, so Leah rested on the back of the police car. She hadn't been tired, though suddenly she was, and a yawn rippled through her. She flapped it away, apologising, though only succeeded in yawning again.

'I thought about calling you last night,' Jennifer said. 'Or texting, I guess.'

'You should've.'

'I didn't want to be weird.'

It felt a bit late for that, given the way Leah had been escorted to the house less than a day ago.

Leah nodded past the house. 'Any news?'

'There were drones up all evening, though someone said it was just people from town. The police were trying to find out who it was, because they said it was hampering their investigation.' A pause. 'Whatever that means.'

'I heard some of the dads have started a search?'

That got a shrug and a yawn, although Jennifer barely opened her mouth. It almost felt as if she was too tired to manage such a thing.

'I don't know about that.' She nodded at the police car. 'They sent in sniffer dogs after you left, and they headed to the river.'

'Does that mean they think that's where the boys went?'

'I dunno. Dylan fishes down there anyway, so I guess they were always going to go that way.'

They waited as Constable Whatshisname appeared from the side of the building. He eyed Leah, though didn't question that she'd appeared at not long after six in the morning. He stopped at her side, next to his car, and she sensed him sniffing the air.

'Everything all right?' he asked, talking to Jennifer.

'Why? Are you gonna arrest me?'

The officer rocked almost imperceptibly from side to side. He ignored the question. 'My colleagues will be back by eight, just in case you, uh...' He poked his foot towards the tin underneath the chair, and the point was clear enough.

'Thanks for letting us know,' Leah replied, before Jennifer could say something silly.

The officer paused for a moment, tapping his foot, and then headed off towards the other side of the house again. Jennifer stared after him, top lip curled. Her anger was at the wrong person, though Leah wasn't going to tell her that. She knew the feeling.

'Matt and Zoe got back last night,' Jennifer said.

'Alfie's mum and dad?'

'Right. They were away for the holiday weekend in Inverness. Took them most of Friday to get up there, then they had to turn around and come back again.' She paused and, for a moment, Leah thought she'd reach for the joint again. 'What could I tell them? They were asking what happened, and all I could do was show them the tents. The police talked to them for a bit, then they went home.' Jennifer picked up the tin and held it on her lap. 'They think it's my fault,' she added.

'Did they say that?'

'They didn't need to. It was the way they looked at me.'

'I'm sure they don't blame you.'

Even as Leah spoke, she knew she didn't believe it. Of course they'd blame Jennifer, at least to some degree. They had left their son in the care of another parent, and now they didn't know where he was. When Leah had been a teenager she had never quite understood the suspicion directed at her friend's father when the girls had disappeared from his house. She got it now she was a mother herself.

Jennifer poked a thumb towards the back of the house, and the officer beyond. 'He got here about an hour ago but there's another inside. She said she's my liaison officer and she'll be with me until Dylan's found.'

'Did she stay over?'

'Yes. She asked if it was OK, something about it being the first night. I showed her the spare room but I don't know if she slept.' It sounded as if Jennifer wished she'd said no. 'Did you have a liaison officer?'

It was an innocent enough question, though it felt personal.

'Shirley,' Leah replied. 'I still see her now and then.'

That was an understatement. In the absence of real parents, Leah had leant on two women who'd shaped her as a person. One of them was Shirley.

'She was really helpful,' Leah added. 'We talked a lot last year, when the documentary was being made.'

Leah didn't add that Shirley had given her a copy of the police file about the girls who'd gone missing from her sleepover. She'd been told to burn it, though it was hidden underneath her bed. She couldn't quite part with it.

For a moment, it didn't feel as if Jennifer had been listening. She was staring past the car, towards the road. 'How was the premiere?' she asked. 'Dylan wanted to go. He applied for tickets but didn't get them. That's when I told him he could have his friends over. I saw a couple of photos on Friday night.'

There had been hours between Leah being at the community centre premiere and the boys disappearing. It felt such a long time before. So much had happened.

'It was good,' Leah said.

It didn't feel the time or place to say that it wasn't her thing – although a small part of her wondered whether Jennifer might understand better than anyone. Whichever way this ended – in however many hours, days, weeks, or longer – would Jennifer want her life plastered on screen? Who would?

'Have you seen what they're saying about me?' Jennifer said quietly.

Leah had. Most of the comments online had been supportive but there was always the ten per cent who couldn't shut their mouths. They'd been there a quarter of a decade back, albeit with only their immediate family and friends around to hear it. Now, they could broadcast to the world. Leah had seen the remarks saying Jennifer was hiding something, or outright insisting she'd killed all three boys herself.

'People are always going to have stupid opinions,' Leah said.

Jennifer didn't react. The tin containing the joint was now on her lap. 'I know what they used to say about you,' she said – and Leah had to fight away the shivers. Nobody spoke about this sort of thing to her. Nobody. 'At school, when it all happened,' Jennifer added. 'Girls would go around saying you must know where Vicky and the others went. There was this group in our geography class who got caught talking about it and the teacher kept them back. He said if he heard them saying stuff like that again, the school would have to send a letter home.'

She waited, possibly for a reaction, though Leah felt numb. She'd suspected, probably assumed, that's what people at school had said. It was the first time anyone had ever confirmed as much. Twenty-five years on and she shouldn't care.

Except she did.

Jennifer was still going: 'Remember Mr Snook? The history teacher who always wore that jacket with the elbow patches. There was a time after it happened when I was on my way to the library and he was at the back of the staffroom telling Mrs Campbell that he didn't think you could be trusted to be around the other girls.'

Leah was looking through Jennifer towards the house – and it felt as if someone was squeezing her insides. She couldn't get her breath. Mr Snook had been a kindly old man with a squeaky leather satchel. He brought his own sandwiches every day and had once taken the class on a school trip to a castle. He had somehow lost his glasses.

He was... normal.

Nice.

Leah had liked him. When someone had posted to say he'd died a few years before, she'd felt genuine sadness and affection.

Except, the whole time, he thought she should be kept away from other students.

'Really...?' It was Leah who spoke, though she could barely get the words out.

'Sorry,' Jennifer said. She gave a narrow, apologetic, smile – as if to say that *she* didn't think that.

Leah didn't want to hear more, but still it came.

'I remember seeing you in town once. I don't know what it's called now but it used to be Red Square.'

Jennifer was talking about the club in which Leah used to spend her Saturday nights, before she had Zac. It would have been seventeen or eighteen years back.

'There were these girls,' Jennifer added, oblivious to Leah's discomfort. 'You'd gone into the toilets and they were daring each other to go after you and start something. They were saying you were a killer, so it was fair game. One of them had these massive heels and she took them off. I didn't know them and didn't know what to do. I thought they were gonna, I dunno, hit you with them. Something like that. Then you came out and walked past them. Nobody said a word and that was it.'

The squeezing of Leah's insides tightened. This was a glimpse of a life that was almost hers but not quite. On the nights she had struggled to come to terms with everything that had happened, Leah had convinced herself that girls had been talking about her at school; that teachers had whispered and conspired, that people did think she was a killer.

And now it turned out it was all true.

Leah shifted her gaze a fraction, catching Jennifer's eye by accident – but maybe it was on purpose.

Here was somebody who knew how she felt. She had waited her entire life for such a person.

Leah shivered involuntarily, wondering if – maybe – this wasn't only about her being there for Jennifer, that it was Jennifer being there for her, too.

Sometimes when it was quiet, when Zac wasn't around, or when she wasn't in Ben's bed, Leah craved somebody to talk to about what had happened with her friends.

What had *really* happened.

Could she go the rest of her life and not say? It was such a big thing to keep to herself.

The two women remained where they were and time passed. Maybe a minute, maybe more. The trees were rustling and a trickling ripple of stones twittered across the drive.

'Do you want to come in?' Jennifer asked after a while. She pushed herself up, clasping the tin that had been on her lap. 'I've got coffee.'

Leah didn't reply, not properly, because Jennifer had already set off. She followed the other woman inside, into the kitchen, where Jennifer filled the well of a coffee machine, then dumped spoonfuls of brown powder into a filter. She pressed the button and frowned at the machine, before realising it wasn't plugged in. After trying again, it started to hiss.

They were alone, though Constable Whatshisname was pacing outside, past the window.

'They checked Dylan's room after you left,' Jennifer said. 'They took his laptop and some other things but said they were going to be back later today to go through everything again. I don't know what they think they'll find.'

Leah had been so lost in her past that she'd almost forgotten about Dylan's apparent gun. She wondered if the police would find it, or if they already had. Josh was still at his mum's – and all information was third-hand.

Should she say something? Would Jennifer know and be defensive about it? Would it be news to her? If it was real, then how had he got it?

As with so many things in the past day, it didn't feel the time to speak up.

'Can I use your toilet?' Leah asked instead. It was a way of escaping the potential conversation – at least for the moment.

'Upstairs, third door on the right.'

The banister of the stairs was wobbly as Leah headed up. Every step creaked and the wood was soft underfoot. There were spiderwebs in the corners, plus cracks along the ceiling and one in the wall. The landing was carpeted, though it was patchy and thin.

Leah turned towards the right but then stopped and looked the other way. A door was open, with a glimpse of Keanu Reeves on the other side. Leah knew she shouldn't but she'd already nudged open the door to take in the full *John Wick* poster. Keanu's face was in the centre, with a dozen or so guns circling his face. It would have seemed like typical teenage stuff if Leah hadn't heard that Dylan was concealing a weapon of his own.

Dylan's room was similar to Zac's, with a large television and a games console underneath. A controller was in the windowsill and the curtains open. The room overlooked the side of the house facing Charles the neighbour. There was nobody in sight; though, from higher up, Leah could see the scrapyard Jennifer had talked about. Charles' property had at least a dozen cars in various states of abandonment, and probably more that were out of sight.

Leah stared for a moment, before catching herself and turning back to the room. It was very much that of a fifteen-year-old boy: equal parts Lynx deodorant, gaming headset, and vaguely sexual posters. Aside from Keanu, there were others of women in various states of undress.

Jennifer said there had been a search, though it didn't look like it. The room was tidier than Zac's, although that might say more about her son, and her own child-rearing, than it did about Dylan or the police.

The floorboard creaked as Leah stepped towards the chest of drawers. It was ancient, with a scratched surface and uneven drawers that wouldn't quite close.

She shouldn't, Leah knew that, but there was a lure she couldn't avoid. Surely the police would have found a gun, if there was one? Even if they hadn't, it was better to leave it to them.

Except... Leah opened Dylan's top drawer to reveal... underwear. The teenager's boxers were folded neatly into rows, leaving Leah to wonder if he'd done that, or his mum. Zac was certainly not as tidy with his clothes. Leah checked the back of the drawer, though there was nothing there, other than more underwear.

Leah tried the other drawers, where there were games, an old phone, and what looked like some computer parts. Below that was Dylan's trousers and shorts, folded as tidily as his underwear. The bottom drawer contained T-shirts and tops. Dylan was a folder, not a hanger.

It was time to go, with Leah not quite understanding why she'd half-heartedly gone through the teenager's chest. There had been times in her life when she had felt drawn by fate, as if things were meant to happen.

Leah took two steps towards the door before she realised what she'd seen.

She reopened the second drawer, in which sat the computer parts, games and phone. Perfectly normal things for a fifteen-year-old to have. She closed the drawer and took another step towards the door, then turned again, to open the drawer a third time.

The phone *wasn't* normal for a teenager to have. It was an old Nokia, the sort of thing Leah had herself twenty years before, if not more. A fifteen-year-old likely didn't know this sort of device existed, let alone owned one.

Leah picked it up and it felt weighty compared to the phone in her own bag. The buttons on the front were chunky and solid. A relic, even though it had come into fashion – and disappeared – all within her own lifetime. It wasn't even the most recent device to do the same. There'd been Blackberries, then Motorolas. Everything moved so fast.

The creak came from nowhere, too sudden for Leah to get out of the room. Before she could do anything, a stranger was standing in the doorway, eyeing Leah with suspicion.

'Can I help you?' she said.

TEN

'I'm Leah. Jennifer's friend. I was here yesterday. You must be her liaison officer...?'

The woman was wearing dark trousers and a white top. Her clothes were crumpled and she had the air of someone who'd not slept much. That made three of them in the house.

She took a further step into the room and there was another loud creak. There wouldn't be much sneaking around in this place.

'Hannah,' she said, peering past Leah towards the window. 'Why are you in here?'

'I figured it was the best view of the neighbour's farm. Jen said she'd had loads of problems with him. I came over early to check on her...'

Considering she'd made it up on the spot, Leah was impressed with her own lie. The best fabrications were couched in truth, and the part about checking on Jennifer was real. She spoiled it somewhat with a small, stifled, yawn – although it was enough to set off Hannah, who erupted into her own drowsy slumber. She covered her mouth.

'Sorry about that,' Hannah said. 'I'm the liaison officer but you shouldn't be in here. We've got other officers coming later to do a full search.'

Leah stepped away, though nodded towards the neighbouring property. 'I didn't realise how many scrap cars was there,' she said.

Hannah followed her gaze but then winced. 'I really need a wee,' she said. 'Can you come this way?'

She ushered Leah out of Dylan's room and then closed the bedroom door behind them. She hurried to the third door on the right, and shut that door as well. Leah waited, listening to the squeaks from the bathroom floor. When she was confident Hannah was sitting, Leah removed the Nokia from her waistband. There were five dots in the speaker at the top of the device, then the green screen, with the keypad underneath.

Leah turned over the device, trying to remember how it turned on, before finding another button on the very top. She wondered if it would make a noise, or take a while to get going, so returned it to her waistband, while continuing to wait.

A short while passed until the toilet flushed and the taps ran. When Hannah re-emerged, wringing her hands, she blinked at Leah with confusion.

'I need a wee, too,' Leah told her.

They do-si-doed around one another as Leah headed into the bathroom. Inside, the bath was crusted with browny limescale. The toilet seat was cracked and the ceiling was speckled with black dots of mould. Everywhere Leah looked, the house seemed to be falling apart. It was easy to see why, given its age, size, the decline of the farming, and Jennifer's sole income. Maintaining such a place wouldn't be cheap, regardless of whether there was a mortgage.

On that, Leah realised she had no idea what Jennifer did for work. There had been no talk of work friends, or colleagues. Leah had gone through her Facebook but couldn't remember anything that didn't relate to the farm. In other circumstances,

Leah might simply ask – but it hardly felt appropriate. Besides, the most boring people were those who talked endlessly about their jobs.

Leah flushed, washed her hands, and headed downstairs. Jennifer and Hannah were both in the kitchen, though an awkward quiet hovered between the pair.

'I'm going to pop home for some clothes,' Hannah said. 'I'll check in with my colleagues and be back in a few hours. You've got my number if there's anything urgent. There'll also be people here shortly.' She waited for a reply that didn't come. 'Is that OK?'

'Fine,' Jennifer replied, though it didn't sound it.

Hannah glanced to Leah, who said nothing, and then she politely made her way out of the house.

Jennifer was sitting at the table, cradling her head in her hands. Her hair was greasy and beginning to clump.

'When she gets back, will you tell her for me?' she asked.

'Tell her what?'

'Ask her not to stay overnight. I don't like having someone in the house who's not Dylan. It feels wrong. Like, if he's not here, how's it fair that someone else is? Why haven't they found him?'

Leah understood the anger, although her experience of having a liaison officer had been completely different. She had been a teenager, with very few people in her life who would listen to her.

'If you don't want someone staying, I can talk to her,' Leah replied. She reached into her waistband and removed the Nokia. She placed it on the table and then sat across from Jennifer.

'What's that?' Jennifer asked.

'I found it in Dylan's room.'

Jennifer stopped tugging at her hair and looked from the phone to Leah. 'Why were you in there?'

'Because you'd been talking about your neighbour yesterday

and I was trying to get a better look at his land. I know you said it was a scrapyard over there – but it's bad, isn't it? Anyway, a drawer was open. I went to close it but this was right at the front.'

The lie felt like the truth now. Leah really *had* been in there to look at the neighbouring farm. Besides, she spoke quickly enough that the subject was back to the phone, not its location.

'I don't know if it's anything weird,' Leah added. 'But Zac's fifteen and I doubt he even recognises this as a phone. He's only ever known touchscreen. Is it the same with Dylan?'

Jennifer reached for the device and turned it over in her hands, much like Leah had done. 'I've never seen it before,' she replied. 'It's like the first phone I had when I was a bit older than him.'

'I think everyone had one. I did. You used to have to pay for every text.'

Jennifer nodded along as she poked at the main buttons and then the screen itself. Leah had done that once on her work laptop. It was hard to get out of the habit once used to touching the screens.

Nothing happened and Jennifer pushed the phone across the table. 'Do you know how to turn it on?'

Leah did – but only because she'd found the button while on the landing. She took the phone and gripped it hard at the top, then let go once black dots formed a rectangle on the right side of the screen.

'Why would he have that?' Jennifer asked, though it felt as if she was talking to herself.

'Do you pay the bill on his main phone?' Leah asked. She did for Zac.

'His is bundled with mine,' Jennifer replied. 'I don't pay for that.' She nodded at the phone in Leah's hand, where the screen was showing a fuzzy animation of hands touching, before the Nokia logo appeared.

It was another moment in time for Leah. A distant memory of viewing the same thing when she was a different person.

Leah's first phone, a replica of this precise device, had been given to Leah by Harriet's mother, Deborah, who had taken in Leah when times had been hard. Deborah had bought the phone and paid the bill. She had told Leah to send as many texts as she wanted, to whomever she wanted. She said that Leah could always call for help if she needed it.

Leah had somehow forgotten that.

It would have been a year or so after the three girls had disappeared. Back then, even though she was still a teenager, Leah didn't have a lot of friends. Her first contact added to the phone was Deborah and the second was Shirley: two grown adults. She couldn't remember much more after that. At some point, she had bought her own phones and paid her own bills.

Leah sometimes wondered how many other things she'd blocked out about that period in her life. Every now and then, small glimmers would creep through.

'Are you OK?'

Leah blinked back into the kitchen, still holding the phone, realising Jennifer was watching her.

'Trying to remember how it works,' Leah said.

The word 'Menu' was at the bottom of the screen and it took Leah a moment to figure out it was directly above the actual menu button. She clumsily fumbled her way around the options, and was baffled by the 'left' and 'right' buttons both being on the right side of the phone. A separate 'cancel' was on the other. So many buttons!

There was a moment of realisation as Leah pictured Mr Snook trying to figure out how the combined TV-VCR player worked, after wheeling it into a classroom.

Snook.

Leah's thoughts of him were now permanently tarnished.

More memories.

Leah focused back on the phone, eventually finding 'Phone Book', even though it was the first option. She clicked in and tried moving up and down. The up and down buttons were loose and well used.

At first, Leah thought her own competence was lacking, though she soon realised there were no contacts saved. She backed out of that menu and tried the next. 'Messages' contained more options, with 'Write Messages' and then 'Inbox'. It was another relic that texts never used to appear and back-and-forth conversations. Everything was individual.

Leah knew the device would be baffling for a teenager, though it was confusing for her as well.

It took a few missteps, but she eventually made it into the inbox, where there was a list of texts from the same 07 number. She pressed the top one and read.

'Oh.'

It was impossible not to appear surprised. More than that, really. Stunned.

Leah used the down button to read the full message and then moved up again.

'What is it?' Jennifer asked.

Leah passed her the phone and watched as the other woman started to read. Her eyebrows rose, her eyes widening. She had looked so sleepy a moment before but now she was awake.

'There's a separate outbox,' Leah said – and the two of them figured it out together as they worked backwards to view the message to which Dylan had replied.

'I didn't know he had a girlfriend,' Jennifer said.

Leah had thought the same thing initially. Except... 'Is that the sort of thing you text to a girlfriend when you're fifteen?' she asked. 'Or the type of thing a girl texts back?'

The two women eyed one another and Leah felt so old – and it wasn't only because of the phone.

There were so many more messages and Leah wondered if Zac was secretly messaging the same to some girl. She might be naïve, but she couldn't picture it. How could someone so young be sending, and receiving, such, well... *filth?* She wasn't sure she knew words like that when she was fifteen.

So old.

'Could he be hiding somewhere with a girl?' Leah asked. 'Maybe all three of them have secret girlfriends?'

It felt unlikely, even as she said it. One kid running off with a girl *might* happen. Three at once was very different. Besides, wouldn't someone have noticed the missing partners?

Jennifer was still holding the phone, though she had tilted the screen so Leah could see. 'We could call the number...?'

Leah faltered, wondering if she should have given the phone to Hannah after all. Let the police deal with it.

Too late. Jennifer was already tapping the number into her phone. She was about to press the green button to call when she stopped.

'I don't understand,' she said, angling the second device, so Leah could see the number already stored in her phone.

There was a name attached.

'It's his teacher,' Jennifer said quietly.

ELEVEN

The words 'Mrs Hawkins' remained ominously on Jennifer's phone screen as she and Leah read through the messages on Dylan's Nokia. The lengthy series of sexts were in reverse order and, from the sheer number, plus the alternating inbox and outbox, it took Jennifer and Leah almost forty minutes to catalogue the relationship. Everything went back for close to seven months – and the two were already on familiar terms in the initial texts. They had likely already been messaging before Dylan had acquired the ancient mobile.

Leah's initial thoughts that the relationship could all be hypothetical were dashed quickly, considering the pair had been sending specific times and places to meet. Most of the organisational ones were Mrs Hawkins arranging to pick up Dylan from various places.

There were small similarities in the way Leah and Ben would also go back and forth, telling each other times and places. Or they would use words like 'important', or 'urgent'. Still, they were adults – and never got anywhere close to being as explicit and Dylan and his teacher.

When they were done, Jennifer put down the phone and

stared at the wall. If things had been reversed, and Leah had been reading similar messages from Zac, she'd have been astonished her son was capable of such language. Soon after that, she'd have been furious at the teacher. Not too happy at her son, either – despite his age.

'Do we wait for Hannah to get back?' Jennifer asked. She shivered and Leah understood the ick.

The microwave said it was close to half-seven and officers were due within half an hour.

'I doubt Dylan's with her,' Leah said. 'Because where would the other two be?'

Jennifer didn't reply to that. She was still staring at the wall.

'It's always gone on to some degree.' She sounded preoccupied, which wasn't a surprise. 'Remember Rebecca Smith in our year? She was always hanging around with Mr Lewis.'

'The maths teacher?'

'Right. Do you remember Rebecca?'

Leah shook her head. 'I do remember Mr Lewis once commented on another girl's bra strap being pink.'

'That sounds like him. Everyone always said he and Rebecca were seeing each other out of school but it felt like a bit of a joke then. I don't know why it wasn't a bigger deal.'

That was true. That bra strap comment had stuck, though Leah was sure there had been similar ones about different girls from other teachers. It was normalised at one point.

'Are you in contact with many other people from school?' Leah asked. She was talking about back in the day, though Jennifer took it to mean the present.

'I'm in the WhatsApp groups but I never post. It's always the same lot trying to push things on everyone else. I keep them muted most of the time. I'd leave but every now and then, there's something worthwhile comes up.' A pause. 'You?'

It was eerily similar to Leah's own outlook on the group chat

– and she said as much. The more they talked, the more Leah felt drawn to the other woman.

'I know they've all been on yesterday, trying to be nice, but I think they look down on me 'cos I live on the farm,' Jennifer said. 'Especially the mums. They're the worst.'

Leah didn't disagree on that, either.

'You're not in that coffee club thing, are you?' Jennifer added, not waiting for a reply. 'They all meet at that Chai Don't You place after drop-off. I've never been invited.'

It was another grievance in among the many Jennifer had already listed. Her neighbour, her ex, the police, her parents, now the other parents. Every time Leah and Jennifer spoke, it felt as if Jennifer steered things towards the next group she was unhappy with.

Not that Leah was particularly enamoured with the coffee club lot, either.

'I don't think you need to be invited,' Leah replied.

Jennifer looked away from the wall for the first time in a while, focusing on Leah. 'Do *you* go?'

'I've been once or twice – when Zac's year was putting on *The Lion King* a couple of years back. There was that committee helping to make costumes.'

Jennifer rolled her eyes and Leah liked her a little more.

Leah's two visits had been dominated by the warring factions of the coffee club's passive-aggressive parents. Each was arguing over whose child deserved to be in which role. Nobody quite said they thought everyone else's kids was useless, most talking around it.

'I always got left out,' Jennifer added. 'When there were parties at school, things like that, I'd find out on the Monday.' She waited and angled away from Leah. 'I never got invited to your sleepovers...'

One more grievance.

Leah had been about to say something else about the other

parents but didn't get through the first word. The word 'sleepover' stuck. It had followed her for a quarter of a century, affecting every part of her life. The missing trio were 'the girls' and they disappeared at 'the sleepover'.

'We weren't really friends back then,' Leah said, truthfully. 'I didn't have a lot of mates. It was only really Vicky, Jazz, Harriet and me.'

Jennifer nodded shortly. It felt like she wanted to say something. Leah didn't know with whom Jennifer used to be friends.

'What about you?' Jennifer asked. 'Are you in with many of the parents?'

For the first time in a while, Leah thought of the photo with Jennifer gazing adoringly at Ben as they hugged one another. It was probably why she'd driven out to the farm so early. She'd tell herself and Hannah that it was to check on the confused mother – but, really, it was to try to find out what had gone on between Jennifer and Ben. She couldn't think of a good way to ask without coming out with it.

Leah did look for the reaction though.

'Mainly Ben,' she said. 'Josh's dad. Do you know him?'

There was a flicker of recognition... maybe. Jennifer shifted in her seat, though it could be because the chairs in her kitchen had no padding. After all that time scrolling through the Nokia, Leah had a sore arse as well. But it *could* have been a gentle moment of discomfort because Jennifer *did* know Ben. All that happened in barely a second.

'I don't think I know him,' Jennifer said – and that was the lie. Maybe it wasn't what she said, it was the overly confident way she said it. A definite lie, though.

'Josh and Zac are friends,' Leah pressed. 'We end up hanging around sort of by default. Either I'm dropping off Zac, or the other way around.'

There was a definite glimmer of... *something*. Jennifer pushed away a strand of hair and fidgeted again. 'I've probably seen his name in the groups,' she said. 'Didn't he host some foot-ball thing at the park when the teachers were on strike?'

'That's him,' Leah replied. She waited to see if Jennifer would add anything else but, instead, the other woman stood.

'It's stuffy in here,' she said, heading for the back door.

Leah found herself following, unsure what else to do. The Nokia remained on the kitchen table as they moved into the yard at the back. The officer who'd eyed the marijuana tin with suspicion was nowhere to be seen. Jennifer walked slowly towards the trio of tents, though stopped at the line of tape the police had put up. The ground was damp with dew, the silence booming. Even the birds had gone quiet. There was nothing except the expanse of land stretching to the trees.

Jennifer sighed and turned to stare back towards the house, as if expecting to see Dylan or the others there. 'Is this what it's like?' she asked. 'You wake up every day and don't know what to do?'

She looked to Leah and it felt important. That, maybe, this was why she'd asked for Leah yesterday. It was all about the one question.

Leah needed time, because how could a quarter of a centu-ry's experience be summed up into a comforting reply? The disappearance of her friends had played on her for twenty-four long years until she'd discovered the truth a year or so before.

The answer was yes. A person did wake up every day, not knowing what to do. People got on with their days. They had relationships and hobbies. They went to work; they smiled and laughed. But it never went. Never.

Except how could Leah look this woman in the face and tell her that? It had been twenty-four hours and, perhaps, it would soon be forty-eight. Then three days. Then a week. Then two. A month would be gone, then six. Then it would be the endless anniversaries. A year since the boys disappeared. Two. Five. The big one at ten.

Leah had lived through it all.

'I'm sure they'll be back,' she said, though the dishonesty was obvious in her voice. She didn't think she believed it, and she certainly didn't know that to be true. Misunderstandings with three missing boys didn't last a full day, let alone longer. Not now in the age where everyone had mobiles.

Leah had thought it might be the answer Jennifer wanted – but knew almost instantly she was wrong. The other woman had craved the honesty.

Jennifer was suddenly stabbing at her phone. 'Her name's Kylie, isn't it?' she said.

'Who?'

'The teacher. Mrs Hawkins. It's Kylie Hawkins.'

Leah didn't like where things were going. She was in a car heading full tilt towards the cliff's edge.

Jennifer was still poking the screen until she held it up triumphantly. 'There! Kylie Hawkins. She lives on that new estate. Her address is right here.'

Leah had no idea from where Jennifer had got an apparent address.

Jennifer started striding back towards the house and Leah had to rush to catch up. By the time they were side by side, Jennifer had grabbed a set of car keys from the counter next to the sink.

'Are you coming?' she asked, though it didn't feel as if she was waiting for a reply.

'We should wait for the police,' Leah said.

Jennifer opened the front door. 'I'm going either way...'

TWELVE

Leah wasn't sure what was worse: Jennifer's car, or her driving. The vehicle had lawnmower vibes with its howling engine – and there was also the way it bounced up and down, even over the mildest bumps. Leah knew nothing about cars, though even she could figure out the suspension was shot.

It didn't help that Jennifer kept crossing the centre line while doing sixty along the narrow, winding, country lanes. She barely slowed for corners, taking the turns with the delirious psychopathy of someone who knew the roads *too* well. Sure, she might be comfortable doing those speeds, but what if someone was coming the other way?

In among gripping the sides of the seat, and holding onto the door handle, Leah attempted to talk Jennifer out of whatever was about to happen. She pointed out that the police would be arriving at the farm any moment to continue searching. They would need to speak to her and would be concerned about her location. If not that, Jennifer could pass on the Nokia – and let them do their jobs.

Leah's lack of honesty in the back garden was really feeling

like a mistake as Jennifer barrelled across a four-way junction
without slowing.

'What if Dylan's there?' she said.

It felt even more unlikely, considering Leah realised – too
late – that it was 'Mrs' Hawkins, not 'Miss'. There would be a
Mr Hawkins somewhere, likely at the house to which they were
hurtling. It could probably be assumed he didn't know, so
rattling up to the house, early on a Sunday morning, was
unlikely to be a good idea.

Not that Jennifer was listening. She was muttering incomprehensibly under her breath and only slowed as they reached
the town's welcome sign. She still failed to give way to the right
on a roundabout, much to the fury of the bloke in his van.

Leah was trying to think of who to text or call that might
stop this – or, at the absolute least, be a calming presence. It
couldn't be Ben. If there was something in the past between
him and Jennifer, having him turn up unannounced wouldn't
help. It wasn't enough of an emergency to dial 999, although
the determined rage in Jennifer's face could turn it into one.

Leah did know *someone* close to that new estate, though.

'What's her address?' Leah asked.

Jennifer was seemingly too angry to wonder why Leah was
asking. She spat the location as she slowed for a red light and
eventually stopped. Jennifer sat drumming the steering wheel
and muttering 'come on' as Leah sent a text to a person who
would definitely be up this early on a Sunday.

'The new estate' was how it had been known ever since it
had gone up almost thirty years ago. Leah hadn't even been a
teenager when a bunch of fields had been converted into the
Big Asda, with an entire estate at the side. She remembered
the dusty lorries hurtling past the school, making the build-
ings shake. A girl in her class had ended up moving into one
of the new houses, which had everyone jealous of the novel
bounty that could be within. If all the old houses had stan-

dard stairs, what incredible invention might inhabit the new places?

As soon as someone reported back that the houses were much the same as the old ones, everyone lost interest.

Still, the new estate that was thirty years old.

Jennifer clearly knew where she was going as she drove past the supermarket and turned into the web of streets. She took a couple of rights, almost clipped a car that was parked half on the pavement, and then roared to a halt at the end of a driveway. There were two vehicles parked, and she blocked them in, leaving the car door open as she darted between them and thumped on the front of the house.

Leah didn't know what to do. A man walking his dog was on the other side of the street and had, unsurprisingly, stopped to stare. This was quality drama for any time of day, let alone a Sunday morning.

Bang-bang-bang-bang!

Jennifer hammered the door again as Leah closed in behind her.

A curtain flickered on the neighbouring property, though the blinds were drawn on Kylie Hawkins' house.

Bang-bang-bang-bang!

Jennifer kicked the door for good measure as Leah tapped her on the shoulder. 'Jen...'

The other woman shrugged her off and screamed 'Come out!' so loudly that Leah winced.

This time, there was movement from inside. The blind of the window above was edged to the side, though the glare was too much for Leah to see who was on the other side. Jennifer hadn't noticed and crashed a palm into the rippled glass of the door instead.

She might not have heard it, but Leah did. There was a shuffling of somebody on stairs from the inside.

Leah turned to see a couple of faces in the windows of the

houses opposite. The dog walker had crossed the road to get a better view. This was box office. Leah quickly checked her phone, where the message 'on our way' was waiting. At least backup was coming.

A man's voice came from the other side of the door, a weak and hesitant 'Who is it?' It was hard to blame the guy.

When Leah looked up to the window, a child's face was peering down at her.

Oh, no.

'Open up!' Jennifer shouted.

Leah tried tapping her on the shoulder but was again shrugged off. Aside from bundling Jennifer to the ground, she wasn't sure what to do.

The man did the worst thing he could, and opened up, as requested. He was stubbly, with genuine just-out-of-bed hair; wearing boxers and a loose T-shirt with '#1 Dad' on the front.

The poor sod.

'Who are you?' he asked, more bemused than angry.

'Where's your slut wife?' Jennifer shouted. She was angling around the man, trying to peep into the dark of the house beyond.

'Jen...' Leah said, not that anybody listened. The quiet worry of the morning before had turned into flat-out rage.

As if on request, the so-called slut wife appeared to the side of the man. She had messy brown hair and was in loose pyjama bottoms, with a spaghetti-strapped top that was probably too low-cut for the doorstep.

Leah recognised her from the school gates, though she wouldn't have known it was Mrs Hawkins unless someone had said.

When Leah risked a glance behind, one of the houses opposite had the front door open. A man was standing cross-armed in slippers, as somebody else stared from the window. At the house next door, it looked as if someone was filming on their phone from the top window.

Jennifer was pointing around the man. 'Your slut wife's been sleeping with my fifteen-year-old son.'

The man took this with a blink and then a frown. 'Sorry...?'

'You should be. Did you know?'

He looked between the two women, though Leah could see in Mrs Hawkins' face that the game was up. She was shrinking behind her husband.

The man started to say: 'I'm sure there's—', though he didn't get any further because Jennifer screamed, 'I've seen the texts!'

The teacher shuffled further behind her husband until she was almost out of sight.

'What are you talking about?' he asked.

Jennifer was still jabbing a finger past him, though – thankfully – wasn't making an attempt to burst into the house. 'Your wife has been sleeping with my son. He's in her class. He's fifteen.'

The man peered over his shoulder, to where Mrs Hawkins' was backing along the hall. 'Ky...?'

At that moment, Jennifer launched herself towards the doorway. The man turned at the sound of the noise, catching the other woman as Jennifer attempted to get past him.

'Slag!' Jennifer screamed. 'Paedo! You aren't getting away with this! Where is he? Is he in there?'

Leah took a step to try to help pull Jennifer away – but someone else got there first.

Deborah, her missing friend's mother, had been the woman who'd most shaped Leah as an adult. She'd been a surrogate mother, when no real one had been present. The other person in that household, the father whose daughter had disappeared at the sleepover, was Nick. He'd worked a lot but he'd always been kind to Leah. He was there now, moving confidently towards the door. He never laid a hand on Jennifer, didn't even get that close to her.

'Come on now, love,' he said.

And maybe, because he was older, or sounded firmer, or for any number of other reasons, Jennifer stopped wrestling. She rocked back and turned to take in the stranger.

'I know you're upset,' Nick said.

Deborah was beside him now. The parents Leah had never asked for but the ones with whom she'd ended up. They had lost one daughter but gained another.

'We're here, honey,' Deborah said – and Leah watched as Jennifer crumpled at the knees. She grabbed for Nick, who held on, wrapping his arms around Jennifer's back and supporting her weight.

As had happened so many times in her adult life, Leah had sent a text – and Harriet's parents had turned up.

'What do you mean?' Mr Hawkins said. He was turning between Jennifer and his wife, who was now out of sight inside the house.

Leah looked to where that poor kid was still staring down from the window above. His eyes were wide, cheeks red. The poor boy couldn't have been older than five and was terrified.

Over the road, more people were out of their houses, at least two filming on their phones. The dog walker stared open-mouthed as his pup lay on the ground.

'You're safe now,' Deborah said, as Jennifer cried on Nick's shoulder.

In the distance, a siren flared.

THIRTEEN

Leah and Jennifer were back at the farmhouse. Nick had dropped them off and headed away to check on Zac. In the couple of hours since their return, Deborah had remained and taken charge. Leah had largely watched and been there for emotional support, if it was needed. Sometimes, it was nice when a grown-up arrived and knew what to do.

That 'what to do' seemed to involve rustling up poached eggs on toast, while simultaneously cleaning Jennifer's kitchen. Leah had never quite been comfortable with the whole matriarchy thing, though Deborah appeared to relish it. She was one of those people who genuinely seemed to like cooking and cleaning.

As Deborah tidied away Jennifer's plate of largely uneaten eggs, Leah realised the wrong woman had been called the day before. *Deborah* was the person who knew what it was like to lose a child and still get by, not Leah. Perhaps all the cooking and cleaning had come as some sort of coping mechanism? Leah hadn't particularly known her before the sleepover. If anyone could answer Jennifer's questions, it would be Deborah.

Not that Jennifer had any questions. She had been largely

quiet after all the shouting. Leah suspected there was some embarrassment, though exhaustion as well. The out-of-context videos would be online somewhere already.

'Can I make you something else?' Deborah said. 'You need to keep your strength up, honey.'

'I'm not hungry,' Jennifer replied.

'I can probably rustle up some biscuits. I saw some oats and flour in the cupboard.'

Jennifer mumbled something that didn't sound like a 'yes', though Deborah took it as one. She turned on the oven and started sifting flour into a bowl. Leah had seen this so many times before that it felt natural. On teenage Leah's second day staying with Deborah and Nick, the two women had made oat and raisin cookies. Outside of a soggy pineapple upside-down cake at school – for which the teacher bought Leah's ingredients – it was the first time Leah had ever baked. At the time, Deborah had said they were Harriet's favourite – and here she was: still baking them for a daughter who'd never come home.

As she continued, Hannah entered the kitchen. She wasn't quite in a uniform, though her trousers and shirt were still smart. The shouting at the Hawkins house hadn't been referenced since Jennifer's return. In the meantime, the police had searched Dylan's room properly, taken the Nokia, and continued the hunt through the woods at the back of the house.

'Kylie Hawkins has been formally arrested,' Hannah said, which got no reaction from Jennifer – who was staring at the table. The officer focused on Leah, presumably hoping at least one person would be listening to her.

'Is that solely based on text messages?' Leah asked.

'For now. We're also pulling her phone records.'

Deborah was mixing dough in a bowl, with Jennifer cradling her head in her hands.

Leah figured someone should ask something. 'Has she said anything?'

'I'm not sure I can say a lot at the moment. The one thing she insists is that she doesn't know where Dylan or the others are.'

Jennifer abruptly pushed herself up from her elbows, glaring through red eyes to the officer. 'And you just take her word for it?'

Hannah was calm: 'Dylan definitely wasn't at the house but we're continuing to check alibis. If anything does come up, you'll be the first to know.'

Jennifer opened her mouth as if to say something but then decided against it. Instead, she slumped back onto the table. The momentary burst of anger settled back to resignation. Probably regret, as well.

Hannah checked her phone and then stepped towards the door. 'I'll be back in about ten minutes,' she said, talking to nobody in particular.

After she left, the only sound was the quiet crunch of Deborah mixing the dough.

Leah took out her own phone and sent a message to Zac, asking if he wanted to do anything that afternoon. It was somewhat wishful thinking as Leah wasn't sure when she'd get away. Her son replied almost instantly, saying he was fine.

Away from that, the 135 new WhatsApp messages were a bad sign. Leah checked the parents' group, largely so Jennifer might not feel the need.

It was as bad as Leah had suspected.

Someone had a photo of Jennifer's back as she was led away by Nick. They also had a couple of Mrs Hawkins being arrested by the police not long after. Some were wondering if the teacher had anything to do with the missing trio – though others somehow knew she'd been 'shagging at least' one of the boys in her year.

Then it had *really* kicked off.

If Leah was honest, she enjoyed the school drama when it was nothing to do with her or her son.

There were mothers wondering if they needed to talk to their sons about Mrs Hawkins, or other teachers. For every parent saying that was a good idea, there was another insisting it wasn't. Then there was disagreement over how best to raise the topic. 'Hey, son, was just wondering if you've had sex with your teacher' wasn't a good intro.

Someone said they thought Mrs Hawkins had put on weight and could be pregnant. Someone else wondered why it was a big deal, and was instantly shouted down. One person was correcting everyone's spelling.

As if the town didn't have enough scandals – and there were still three missing teenagers.

Leah kept picturing the little boy in the window of Mrs Hawkins' house. That poor kid. The husband, too. There would be ridicule and shame directed *at* him, plus anger *from* him. All that and he had a child to raise.

Perhaps Leah wasn't as into the drama as she thought.

As she was scrolling, a message arrived from Ben:

How are you?

It was loaded. He could actually be wondering how she was, or asking if she wanted to go to his house before Josh got back from his mum's. That was the problem with using code for everything.

If Leah couldn't ask Jennifer directly about a possible past relationship with Ben, she was going to have to figure out how to ask him.

Leah messaged Ben to say she was at Jennifer's – and that there was still no sign of Dylan. There was no instant reply, so she put her phone away.

Meanwhile, Deborah was at the stage of transferring the

rolled-out dough onto baking trays. She and Jennifer were making small talk about the farm, with Deborah saying that she and her friends used to ride bikes around the country lanes. It was one of the few topics in which Jennifer seemed interested. Something, at least temporarily, to take her mind away from the obvious.

That was until Hannah returned to the kitchen and everything went silent. It didn't feel like good news as she pointed towards the trees at the back of the farm.

'I thought you should know that there are people filming on the edge of your property,' she said. 'I'm afraid it's public land, so there isn't a lot we can do to stop them.'

'What are they filming?' Leah asked.

'They say the surrounding area for the search. There are privacy laws around taking photos of individuals.'

'Where are they from?'

'They're live streamers, so probably Twitch or TikTok. Beyond that, I'm not sure.' She eyed Jennifer, then Leah, probably weighing up how to put it. 'There are individuals on those sites who run channels looking into mysteries...'

Leah was only half surprised the town hadn't been inundated with that sort of thing because of the missing girls. The film's full release would likely change that – but a separate missing trio was bound to bring extra interest. The longer the boys weren't found, the more would come. Two missing trios, twenty-five years apart. People would never stop coming.

'That does bring me onto a related question,' Hannah added. 'We were wondering if you'd do a public appeal about Dylan.'

Jennifer glanced to Leah, as if asking whether she'd heard correctly. 'Like... go on telly?'

'It would be for the news channels and websites. We'd put it on YouTube as well. There'd be a script if you wanted that. Something nice and simple. You'd say something like how you

were missing Dylan and that you wanted him to come home.
We'd work with you on the language.'

'Just me?'

'We're talking to the other parents as well – but it is your
individual decision about whether you want to do it. If you all
want to, we'd have a joint conference this afternoon.'

Deborah's biscuits were now in the oven. She was leaning
on the counter, cradling a cup of tea as Jennifer turned to look
up at her.

'Did you do an appeal?' Jennifer asked.

The older woman was always so calm, seemingly ready for
whatever came at her. Except, for the first time in a very long
time, Leah saw that momentary freeze. The fixed stare into the
distance in which Deborah disappeared a quarter of a century
into the past.

It was there and gone in a blink. Her reply was upbeat, as if
talking about a pleasant car journey she'd taken. 'We did three
in total, across a month or so.' She caught what she had said a
moment after it came out. 'I'm sure you won't need that many.'

If Jennifer noticed the slip, she didn't say anything. 'Is it
hard?' she asked instead.

'I didn't want to do it – not the first one anyway. Nick did
the speaking but I was there.'

Hannah jumped on the opening: 'That's the thing, Jennifer.
If you want to talk, you can. We can work on a script, or you can
use your own words. There will be a teleprompter to help if you
need it. Or, if you don't want to speak, that's fine as well. It's all
about whatever you want.'

Jennifer turned between the two women – and Leah didn't
think she'd ever seen a person look more tired. Jennifer blinked
and it felt as if her eyes could stay closed.

The kitchen was beginning to fill with the sweet smell of
baking cookies and, even though Leah hadn't been hungry, her

mouth was starting to water. The sugar would at least keep Jennifer awake.

'Does it look bad if you don't speak? I've seen what they're saying about me.' Jennifer lifted her phone, stumbling over the words.

'I know we talked about this but I would strongly advise against looking at that sort of thing for the moment.' It sounded a little harsher than Hannah likely meant it and she immediately added in a softer voice: 'I realise it's hard to do that...'

Deborah picked things up: 'In truth, you're not going to change anybody's mind,' she said. 'The conferences aren't about that. It's for Dylan to see, or someone who knows where he is.'

Jennifer seemed far more convinced by Deborah than the liaison officer.

'Maybe I'll say something then...' She sighed and glanced to Leah – who knew precisely what she was going to ask next.

FOURTEEN

'Dylan's mum wanted you to be there?'

It was Zac who asked the question.

Although Leah and Ben were in a secret relationship, and their respective sons were best friends, the four of them were rarely in the same room together. Certainly for no longer than a couple of minutes here and there. This was a special occasion in the sense that all four were interested in the YouTube feed currently being streamed to the television.

The two teenagers were on the sofa, being boys and not sitting too close to each other. Leah was in one armchair, Ben the other.

Zac had his phone in his hand and it looked as if he was streaming the exact same thing as was on the main screen. For now, it was simply a holding message reading: 'Media Conference Starting Soon'.

'I would've gone with her,' Leah told her son. 'But the liaison officer said there were already too many people scheduled to be there.'

Hannah telling Leah there wouldn't be space had been something of a relief. Leah had been too young to do those sorts of appeal when her friends went missing. Despite giving a couple of interviews for the documentary, she didn't crave the attention, even though it had been with her throughout her life.

On screen, the message disappeared to reveal a desk that had a banner across the front, reading 'Police'. An officer was sitting up very straight in the centre: back rigid, as if strapped to a board. On one side of him sat Ali and Aisha; on the other was Jennifer; then Matt and Zoe. Three missing boys: five parents. Jennifer was the only single mum among them.

Jennifer was sitting low in the seat, wanting to be anywhere other than there. Someone must have helped with her make-up, because her eyes weren't as clouded by sleep as before.

Other than her, the other four simply looked... scared. They were all staring unfocused towards the camera, mouths slightly open. There was no sound from the feed but, as everyone looked away from the camera, it felt as if something was being said. Then, from nowhere, there was a clunk and the officer in the middle of the desk coughed.

He had the gravitas of someone in their nineties narrating a nature documentary. The sort of tone that would leave a person feeling it was fair enough if they needed a leg amputated.

The officer was some chief supersomethingoranother. He introduced everybody at the table and then laid out the time-line. Three boys had been camping in a back garden at the edge of town on Friday evening. They were last seen at around 10.50 p.m., but weren't there the next morning. There were no signs of a struggle in or around the tents and Jennifer, who was sleeping in the nearby house, hadn't heard a thing. None of them were answering their phones, with no devices recovered.

He went on to describe the area a little, talking about the tree coverage and difficulties with hilly terrain outside the town. There was something about the number of officers deployed – and then he handed over to the parents.

Zoe spoke first, though she started with a sigh. She said they desperately wanted Alfie to come home and that he wouldn't be in any trouble. At the mention of that, her husband sank into his seat, head dipped as he hid his face from the camera. The tears were easy to spot regardless. As soon as Matt began to cry, his wife gripped his hand.

Leah didn't know Alfie, nor his parents. They were the ones who'd travelled to Scotland and back in barely a day.

Leah risked a glance across to Zac, who was staring at the stream on his phone. There'd been a moment a year before in which he'd disappeared temporarily. She'd had a lot going on at the time and reacted poorly. This was far more serious and, probably sensing that, Zac looked up and met his mum's eyes. He gave a small smile, nothing more, which was enough to tell her that he understood. They both did. This was her nightmare – and three other sets of parents were living through it.

Ali spoke next. He reiterated much of what Zoe had said, finishing with: 'We just want you home, mate.' His wife stared blankly ahead, not reacting to anything.

It was uncomfortable to watch, though hard to look away. Leah couldn't remember a time she and Zac had been equally invested in something, let alone Ben and Josh as well. It struck her that, in the moment, it felt like their own little family. Zac and Josh might not be brothers but they got on and were the same age.

Leah and Ben were...

Jennifer sighed into her microphone. The chief police guy had introduced her and she'd taken a breath, then hankered it out. There was a silence, more silence, still more. It went long past the awkward stage and it was only when the officer reached towards her that Jennifer zoned back into the room. 'I just... I just... want him home,' she managed. Her stare was long and unfocused, a look Leah had seen plenty over the past day.

Leah was so focused on Jennifer's worried features that she forgot to turn and see what Ben was making of it all. By the time she did remember, the officer was back in shot. Ben had seemingly been watching without reaction. There was certainly no acknowledgement that he knew Jennifer, nor that they might have been an item around a year before Dylan was born. If Dylan missing meant anything to him personally, he wasn't letting on.

'As I'm sure everyone watching can understand, it's a very emotional time,' the officer said on screen. 'The searches will be continuing through the day. I would ask the public to avoid visiting the surrounding area and not to speculate online. We are currently following a few tips but, if you did see anything at all, or if you know something, the number to call should be on your screen. All calls can be anonymous. There's also an email address and a number you can text.'

The details appeared, plus a line to say it all would be in the video description. Someone who was presumably a media officer hurried into the shot before it went dark – and that was it.

'It's a bit late with all the speculating,' Ben said, though nobody replied.

Zac put down his phone and, for a short while, it didn't feel as if anybody knew what to say. It was all too close. For the boys it was their classmates; for Leah it was history repeating itself. For her and Ben, they each had children the same age. They all lived in the town.

Josh moved first, pushing himself up from the sofa and saying he was heading upstairs. Zac was a few paces behind.

'The police are coming soon,' Ben called after his son. 'Don't start playing something you can't pause.'

There was a mumbled reply, probably an 'OK', and then the boys were on their way.

'What time did the police say they were coming?' Leah asked.

'Any time this evening but you know what the boys like. All

the games used to pause when I was younger. Not like that now.'

Leah took his word for it, though it was true that Zac often called through a door, or downstairs, to say that he was doing something where he couldn't pause. Meals had gone cold, lifts to places had been delayed.

The police were visiting to ask Josh what he knew about Dylan's gun, though they understandably had a lot going on.

'How was the farm?' Ben asked – and Leah wondered if he was deliberately avoiding using Jennifer's name.

'Awkward,' Leah replied, honestly. 'But it was worse when we were at Mrs Hawkins' house this morning, I thought Jennifer was going to lose it. Like she might hurt someone. I didn't know what to do.'

The earlier parts of Leah's life had been lived with violence as a backdrop. It had been a long time since things had changed, though she still made a mental note of the exits when entering a place. There were constant mental calculations of the fastest way to get out. If not that, she'd analyse the furniture, figuring out if she could move things quickly to barricade a door. If all else failed, she kept one fingernail longer than the others.

A person never forgot.

Ben knew little about that part of Leah's past. Not many people did. They weren't there yet and Leah doubted they ever would be.

He nodded along anyway. 'What did Zac say about Mrs Hawkins?'

'Not much. We were in the car and I wasn't sure how to phrase it. I asked if he'd had much contact with her and he said he wasn't in her class.'

'Not *quite* a denial then.'

Leah gave him a look until the smile faded a fraction. 'What did Josh say?'

There was a smirk that Leah didn't much like. 'He asked

what was wrong with it. Fifteen, isn't he? Who's turning down sex at that age?'

'What did you tell him?'

'The usual stuff.'

Leah waited, fearing they might have different definitions of that.

Ben was still smiling but then relented. 'About positions of power and not being old enough to make adult decisions. Threw in something about the patriarchy for good measure.' He winked and, though Leah should've hated it, she took it as the joke she hoped was intended. 'Either way, he said he'd never had a one-on-one conversation with her, so I don't think it's a problem.'

Leah figured there would be parents across town asking similar questions, with teenage boys fidgeting in embarrassed awkwardness. Nobody, parents or children, wanted these conversations with one another.

As she was thinking about that, Leah realised she hadn't got around to talking to Hannah about not staying at the farm overnight. She wondered if Jennifer might change her mind and want someone around.

'You look preoccupied,' Ben said. He stretched from his chair and offered his hand. Leah gripped it and squeezed.

'I'm struggling to believe it's all happened again. Three girls, three boys, same town.'

It was slightly disingenuous, seeing as Leah knew what had happened to the girls. That meant that she knew more than anyone else that the same thing hadn't happened twice.

'You don't have to go to the farm...'

'I know.'

Leah had been telling herself the same, though it felt different coming from Ben. She wondered whether he was saying it because he didn't want her talking too much to Jennifer. Would his name come up?

Do you know Jennifer? I mean, do you really *know her?*

The question remained in Leah's head, along with other variations of the same thing. She wasn't actually bothered by whether or not they *had* been in a relationship, it was more the deception through omission.

As she continued to try to figure out the words, there was a sound from the stairs. Leah let go of Ben's hand and, seconds later, Zac entered. He waited in the doorframe, shuffling from one foot to the other.

'You all right?' Leah asked.

'Am I going to get in trouble if I tell you something?'

He wasn't making eye contact and Leah's instant assumption was that he and Mrs Hawkins had, um, well...

It might have been because Leah had paused, but Ben answered for her. 'Course not, pal.'

Leah hadn't known they had that degree of chumminess, not that she had time to consider it before Zac replied.

'It's just... Dylan told me where he keeps his gun.'

FIFTEEN

Athletics tracks were incomprehensibly large.

Leah had never bothered with anything like sports day, or even much of PE itself when she'd been at school. It wasn't as if she had a PE kit – and, because of her circumstances at home, the PE teachers tended to leave her alone instead of forcing her to take part. Leah would watch the other girls run around the track, some with boundless energy, others like the smokers they were, and she'd envy none of them.

Some things never changed, because the school field was still rock hard. Tufty patches of grass intermingled with what felt like concrete as their little party headed across from the road. Ben and Josh were at the front, quietly talking to the police officer as they walked. He had turned up to take Josh's statement about Dylan's gun and ended up getting Zac's as well.

Leah and Ben walked behind, not talking. The boys were still too young to officially deal with the police by themselves – even though Zac was taller than everyone.

The trio at the front were striding along the running track that was whitewashed onto the grass at the back of the school.

The boys were walking at their pace, which was far faster than anything with which Leah would usually be capable. She was sticking to lane one, remaining within the lines for a reason of which she wasn't entirely sure. Ben was walking with his hands in pockets, keeping pace easily, as Leah skipped to keep up.

It was after eight and the sun was starting to dip beyond the trees in the distance. Another day had passed and the boys hadn't been found. Any thoughts of a misunderstanding were gone.

They headed past the track and towards the hedge at the end. There was a thin patch, through which Zac ducked and pushed himself through. It happened with the speedy grace of a teenager who'd done the same many times before. Leah wondered if she needed to have words with him about skipping out of school after they got home, though there was little time to think of that as they reached the hedge.

Ben went first and held onto some of the spikier branches, making room for Leah to fit through. She ducked and pushed ahead, then emerged onto a dark, damp trail. The boys were a little further along, again seeming far too familiar with the surroundings for Leah's liking.

The verges were filled with discarded crisp packets, chocolate wrappers, small – presumably empty – gas canisters, plus disposable vapes. Trees had grown into one another, leaving everything soggy and limp.

They walked a short distance, following the line of the hedge until they reached a clearing. A black bin bag was overflowing with cans and other rubbish, while four tree stumps had been arranged in a circle.

Leah wondered if this area had been there when she'd attended school. If it had, she'd been left out of whatever happened here.

'It's here,' Zac said, talking to the officer.

The trees had dwindled and the ground was drier. Scuffed,

dusty footprints ringed the tree stumps, as Zac led Josh and the officer towards the back of the clearing.

Leah and Ben stopped at the edge of the trail and Leah took out her phone. There was a message from Jennifer.

Did you watch?

Leah tapped a reply to say that Jennifer had done great, even though it wasn't true.

An inevitable reply came back almost instantly.

Can you stay over tonight?

There must have been a sigh because Ben asked what was up.

'Jennifer's asking if I can sleep at the farm tonight,' Leah told him.

'Do you want to?'

'No – but it's not like I can say no. Dylan's still missing. She doesn't have anyone else.'

That wasn't strictly true. There had been the liaison officer – but it now seemed clearer why Jennifer didn't want her to stay. She preferred Leah. The time to say no to all this was the morning before, when the police had knocked on her door. Leah was too far in now.

'Can Zac stay with you tonight?' Leah asked.

'Of course.'

'I'll have to ask him.'

'I doubt he'll complain. They're off school tomorrow anyway.'

Leah had forgotten about the bank holiday. She wasn't at work either. She had lost track of days.

Across the other side of the clearing, Zac was pointing at a tree, saying something to the officer that Leah couldn't hear. They both looked confused.

'They seem familiar with this place...' Ben was stating the obvious, speaking quietly enough that neither boy would hear.

'Does Josh smoke?' Leah asked.

'I don't think so. You never know now, though. Vaping, laughing gas, smoking, who knows what else. I had the odd ciggie when I was his age. Everyone did, didn't they?'

Leah didn't respond to that. Her life as a fifteen-year-old was a lot different to other teenagers both then and now.

She couldn't hold out any longer. There was no point in trying to think of a way to ask around the question. She would just ask it.

'Do you know Jennifer?'

'Dylan's mum? How do you mean?'

'The way I asked it. Do you know her?'

Leah was trying to remain as chatty as possible. No hard edges.

She felt Ben turn to look at her.

'No,' he said.

So he was a liar too.

Leah took out her phone and loaded the photos, where she had the screengrab. She passed it to Ben, who stared at the image of his younger self with an adoring Jennifer's arm around him.

He pinched the screen to zoom in, stared, zoomed out again. Handed back the phone.

'We, uh...'

He didn't get a chance to finish the sentence because Zac crossed the clearing and headed past them towards a much larger tree stump. The officer was at his side, Josh a little farther back.

Zac stopped at the stump and turned slowly, before pointing towards a tree on which a carving of a bullseye was etched into the bark. Splattered, splintered dots circled the wood – and it looked to Leah like a speckling of shots that had missed the target.

'There,' Zac said, pointing at a clutch of mossy green past the stump, slightly into the treeline.

The officer pulled a glove from his pocket and stepped forward. He pointed to the green as he crouched, asking 'Here?' before pulling away a small pile of sticks. He crouched and peered into what looked like a small hole that had been dug in the soil. He reached in and then turned to look up at Zac. 'There's nothing here.'

SIXTEEN

The next hour or so was a blur of the officer taking more statements from the boys. Both now said they'd seen Dylan with a gun, although only Zac knew about the hiding space. Zac said Dylan hid it there because he didn't want his mum to find it at the farm. The fact the hiding place was empty felt ominous, though Leah didn't dare say so.

In among that, Ben never got past his 'We, uh...'

After a brief trip back to Leah's house, they left to go in different directions – Ben taking Zac and Josh to his, Leah heading to Jennifer's.

Leah was unsure what she should be most concerned about. There was Zac's comfort and obvious knowledge of that secret den, Ben's lies around Jennifer, three missing teenagers – and Leah's own developing friendship with Jennifer herself. It was a lot to think on – and that was without the parallels to her own past.

She parked on the verge outside Jennifer's place and headed for the farm. A text had arrived from Ben as she'd been driving, saying they could talk properly when she was free. Leah didn't reply, partly to leave him wondering about it, more so because it didn't feel as if they needed to do things face to face.

There was another message from Deborah, who always texted on a Sunday evening. That was their ritual and had been for a long time. Leah replied, telling the other woman where she was, though not *how* she was. Leah didn't know the answer to that.

Before Leah could continue towards the house, she realised a police car was parked at the top of the rocky path. An officer was inside and jumped out as soon as he saw Leah.

'You can't go down there,' he said.

'I think Jennifer's expecting me,' Leah replied, hefting her night bag higher to make sure the officer had seen it. 'She asked me to stay over.'

He eyed her suspiciously, the sort of look a traffic warden might give while pre-emptively writing a ticket for a car that was thirty seconds away from being overdue.

Leah told him her name and he radioed it through, never once taking his eyes from her.

'You can go down,' he said eventually – although he made it sound like he was doing her a favour.

It was dark as Leah hobbled carefully over the bumpy drive towards the house. There were lights on upstairs, none down, as Leah reached the front door. It was only as she knocked that the thought occurred this was a sleepover of sorts.

Nobody was going to call it such but that was only because of their ages. If teenagers slept at each other's houses, it was a sleepover. When adults did the same, there was no such demeaning term.

There was no answer at the door, so Leah knocked again. She called a curious 'Jen...?', which also got no reply.

Unsure what else to do, Leah tried the handle. It was unlocked, so she pushed her way into a hall. The pile of wellington boots and dirty shoes were unmoved, the beams close overhead as a narrow orangey glow came from somewhere upstairs.

'Jen...?'

There was no answer, though some sort of shuffling had Leah heading for the living room. Jennifer was in her armchair, sitting in the gloom. The only light came from the moon, drifting through the open curtains at the back.

As Leah slotted into the nearest chair and put down her bag, she noticed the bottle of Smirnoff at Jennifer's side. It was almost empty.

Leah didn't want to get too mumsy, especially with a near stranger her own age, though the 'Is that a good idea?' still came out as condescending.

'It was mainly empty already,' Jennifer said. 'I'm hoping it'll put me to sleep.'

She was picking at her nails. They had been purply-blue on the day Leah met her but were now natural and chipped.

'They get in the way,' Jennifer said, as she dropped another false nail into the bin. There were seven or eight in there and all colour was gone from her fingers.

'They looked really great with your hair,' Leah said, though it all felt a bit pointless now. Her son had been missing for two days.

'Charles won't let the police search his land,' Jennifer said quietly. 'Hannah said he's been arguing with the police all weekend about noise and trespass. She said they're going to get a warrant and come back tomorrow.'

'Why would he block them?' Leah asked.

'That's what he's like. I kinda thought he would. Same with the wind turbines. I think he just wants everything to be the way it was.'

She didn't add: 'Before his wife died' but Leah got it. She even understood it. There were a lot of times in which she wondered how life could be if things hadn't happened the way they had twenty-five years before. Would she still be friends with Vicky and the others? Would she have married her ex-husband? Would Zac exist? She doubted it – and, if that was the case, did that mean everything that had happened at the sleepover was for the best?

There seemed little point for Leah to comment on Charles. 'Have you heard anything else?' she said. 'You did so well at the press conference.'

Jennifer yawned and reached for the vodka bottle. She drank directly from it and then dried her mouth with her sleeve. 'They've been asking about a gun. Do I know if Dylan had a gun? Do I know where he kept it? Do I know if he uses it? Do I know if anyone taught him how to shoot? Do I know where he got it?'

It was unclear whether she knew the answers to any of the questions.

'Zac saw Dylan with a gun,' Leah said. 'So did at least one other boy.'

It was too dark to see where Jennifer was looking, though Leah didn't think it was at her. There was a solemn 'Oh...'

The silence of the house was punctuated by the groaning walls and creaking beams. It was as if the property itself had a voice and wanted to chime in.

'I don't know anything about a gun,' Jennifer said – and, exactly as it had been when she said she didn't think she knew Ben, it sounded like a lie. Leah wondered if she'd told that lie to the police, or if it was only for her. 'Do you want anything to eat?' Jennifer asked, even though it was gone ten – and she made no movement towards the kitchen.

'I can make something for you if you want?' Leah replied.

It felt as if Jennifer shook her head, though it was too dark to see. No reply came.

'Do you want a cup of tea?' Leah asked. 'I was going to make one for myself...'

Jennifer held up the vodka bottle, which was an answer of sorts.

Leah knew about how much caffeine was in tea, plus the times it should and shouldn't be drunk – except people were always going on about that sort of stuff. Don't eat too much chocolate. Don't drink too much. Don't drink tea in the evenings. A line had to be drawn somewhere against this sort of tyranny.

As Leah filled the kettle and eyed the lights of Charles' farm in the distance, she wondered if this was the sort of tyranny over which he was apparently annoyed. It was odd to not help out when a neighbour's son had been missing for two days. He could have simply let the police have a poke around and they'd have likely left him be.

Leah put the kettle on its stand and flipped it on. Deborah's cookies were on a plate and she took one, nibbling around the edges as she waited.

The parallels were impossible to ignore. Speculation was flying through the town and there was a sense of everyone and everything being on the precipice of something awful. The last time Leah remembered a sense of such doom had been twenty-five years before. Maybe that was why she felt so drawn to Jennifer? She didn't have to keep coming back.

And, now, somehow, Leah was close to the centre of everything once more. It wasn't her choice and yet here she was.

More time must have passed than she realised because the kettle clicked off. Leah jumped and wondered if she'd somehow fallen asleep momentarily while standing. It felt unlikely and yet the clock on the oven was two minutes ahead of where it had been. Her biscuit was also gone, with no sign of the remains. She must have finished it without quite realising.

Somebody – probably Hannah – had bought milk at some point. Leah made herself a tea and then headed back into the shadowy living room. Hot drinks and a dark space felt like an accident waiting to happen, but it wasn't Leah's house. She left the lights off and sat.

'Are you sure you don't want one?' Leah asked. 'You can have this. There's enough water for another.'

No reply came. Not at first anyway. When it did, Jennifer's voice whispered edgily through the night.

'Can I tell you a secret?'

It wasn't lost on Leah that her own son had asked something quite similar that evening.

'Of course,' Leah replied.

'I think my dad killed someone.'

SEVENTEEN

Leah knew she should say something but didn't know what. The mug was suddenly hot and she stretched to ease it onto the floor. There wasn't a table nearby.

This felt like a conversation far too big for her. There was a police officer literally outside. Where was he?

Too long had passed.

'Why do you think that?' Leah managed.

Jennifer picked up the bottle again and swirled it. Leah could hear the liquid glugging.

'After Mum left, he used to bring women back,' Jennifer said. 'He'd go out driving, though he'd never say where. Sometimes he'd pick up prostitutes. He thought I was asleep but I'd hear him with them.'

Jennifer let that sit, which was enough of a revelation. From what she'd said before, Jennifer would have been around twenty. Perhaps old enough to say something, not that Leah would judge a situation like that. Nor that speaking up would change things.

'Sometimes, it was like they disappeared,' Jennifer added. 'There was never anyone around the next morning. Dad was always up early anyway. He'd never got out of the habit from when he ran the farm. If he was still in bed at half-five, it'd be because he was ill. But I'd come down and Dad either wouldn't say anything, or – if I asked who he had over – he would say it was a friend who'd left early.'

'How do you know they weren't friends?'

A humourless chuckle. 'If they were friends, they were *really* good ones.'

Leah eyed the front window and the officer up the track. Couldn't he come knocking? Ask if everything was all right, so Leah could tell him they absolutely were not.

'Are you saying you think he killed some women?' Leah asked.

'And buried them in the fields. He kept all the farming equipment so he could easily have done the practicalities. I ended up selling the machines after he died – but he had them long after he needed them and I never understood why. He'd go out at weekends and check the engines, all that. Make sure they were working.'

Leah considered getting out her phone to record the conversation, though it would be impossible to do so without Jennifer noticing. Would she mind? Would this all be said again? Leah figured it was likely the vodka talking.

'Couldn't the women have left before you got up?' Leah asked.

'Maybe.' A pause and then: 'Not all of them. There were too many.'

It *really* felt like the vodka talking. Leah wasn't convinced Jennifer believed it herself, even as the other woman was saying it.

'Did you ever tell anyone else?' Leah asked.

There was a long silence this time, though the screeching, scraping house was trying to tell its own story. It felt as if the walls had a lot of secrets.

'Just you,' Jennifer replied – which, if true, meant she had been holding onto it for twenty years or so. Those long-cradled secrets got weightier and weightier. Leah wondered how many other people Jennifer had come close to telling.

'This is serious,' Leah said. 'If you *really* think this happened, you have to tell someone.'

No reply came, though there was a shifting of weight. Leah knew Jennifer was looking at her and, even though it was dark, she felt the eye contact. It made her shiver.

'Sometimes I wonder if he killed your friends...'

Leah breathed in, held it. It wasn't true because she knew what had happened to her friends – and it wasn't anything to do with Jennifer's dad.

'Why do you think that?' she asked, and it felt dangerous.

'He was out that night,' Jennifer replied. 'I was home and he didn't get back until maybe two or three in the morning. I heard the car and the lights swung past my window. Then he was up again at the usual time – five or so. I saw him at the edge of the field digging. A day or two later, he was helping with the search – but he took them the other way.'

It was so specific, that Leah wondered whether it was a lie. It was hard to know what it would achieve. If it was for Leah's attention, she already had it. Leah knew her friends were not buried beneath the farm's fields.

'I'm going to have to tell the police,' Leah replied. She still wasn't sure she believed any of it – but what if there was at least a grain of truth about the women? 'They'll want to dig up your fields. If this is some sort of, I don't know, joke, you have to say.'

Jennifer unscrewed the cap from the bottle and swigged. 'It's not a joke,' she said, although she didn't sound sure.

It could be the booze, or lack of sleep, so Leah tried again: 'I know this is all stressful and hard. We all want Dylan home safely – but, on this, are you telling the truth about suspecting your dad? There's no coming back if I tell the police.'

'Why would I lie?'

Leah wasn't sure how to answer that. There were always reasons to lie, especially for a lonely woman who wanted a friend. Leah wasn't naïve.

'Did you go through your dad's things when he died?' Leah asked. 'Was there anything in there?'

'His stuff is in the cellar,' Jennifer said. 'I keep meaning to go through it but couldn't do it by myself. It's been down there for years. I put it all down there after he died. Look if you want.'

'Weren't the police down there earlier? They would've found something.'

There was a murmured groan of what sounded like disinterest. 'It's mainly his clothes. They were looking for Dylan's things.' Jennifer yawned and lifted her legs onto the seat, where it looked like she had curled up. She yawned a second time. 'I might sleep here tonight.'

There was a soft clink as the bottle dropped a short distance to the floor – and then the house began to talk again.

Leah waited. She had her night stuff and she would presumably be sleeping in the room that the liaison officer had used the night before. She wasn't sure what she'd expected from the request to stay over – but it wasn't Jennifer telling secrets and then falling asleep in an armchair.

A few minutes passed as Leah sipped her tea in the dark. Her friends weren't buried on the farm, but what if other women were? A year before, her old liaison officer had told her that thousands of people disappeared each year and were never found. There would be families holding onto false hope – and maybe there were answers on this farm for at least one of them.

Maybe. She still wasn't sure whether she believed Jennifer, especially given the vodka.

Leah eked herself up, half a cup of tea in hand. She hovered, wondering if Jennifer might say something, though the only noise other than the house was heavy breathing from the armchair.

After moving the vodka bottle to the coffee table, Leah headed into the kitchen and tipped her tea down the drain. Deborah had cleaned up earlier, leaving nothing in the sink or the draining board. The kitchen was no longer a mess, so Leah washed her cup and left it drying.

She headed into the hall and closed the door, then turned on the light. There was a narrow threadbare rug in the middle of the scuffed wooden passage. As well as the boots and shoes near the door, there were coats in a mound. A single light bulb sat on the floor, not quite in the way – though close enough that it could easily be trodden on.

Leah moved to the stairs and opened the door underneath. It felt like an obvious place for a cellar – and cool air poured upwards as Leah stood at the top of a set of stony steps. A cord swung limply and Leah pulled it, sending a dim orange across a cramped, dank room.

Leah's footsteps echoed on the stairs as she headed down. The corners were gloomy, the air cold and damp; like opening a freezer at a supermarket. Leah held her arms around herself as she crept lower. She couldn't remember being in a cellar before. Her own house didn't have one and it felt like more of an American horror movie trope. Nothing good ever happened in basements.

As Leah reached the bottom step, she waited and took in the space. The single room wasn't the entire size of the house, and was perhaps around the width of the living room. A fake Christmas tree was abandoned in a corner, next to a box marked 'TINSEL'. There was a presumably empty box for a television, plus what looked like a broken fan. A mouldy large rucksack was on top of a camping chair, with a dog bed at the side.

So far, so landfill. Leah suspected that would be the

problem if she had a cellar – it would be too easy to toss every-thing down there, instead of into the bin.

Leah's skin bristled from the cold as she did a slow lap of the floor. She wasn't sure what she was looking for, if anything.

She found mouse droppings in the corner – or she hoped that's what they were, considering the alternative would be rats.

The thought persisted that nothing good could happen to her at night in the basement of a remote farmhouse. Yet she continued.

There was a set of suitcases next to the camping gear: three inside each other like Russian dolls, including a colourful child's case in the middle. Six black bin bags were full of clothes and, though Leah had no intention of looking through them prop-erly, the musty leather jacket and biker gear on top of one meant they all likely belonged to Jennifer's father.

Past those, in another corner, was a box of what turned out to be oils that were so essential, they'd been packed away for an indeterminate time. Next to that was another box, this one full of various skincare creams. They were all new and unused – which partially answered the question over what Jennifer did for work. At least some of it involved various MLM pyramid schemes.

Leah closed the boxes and moved onto a separate suitcase that was tattier than the ones in the other corner. It was made of soft yet squeaky leather, the sort of thing that would lead a person to saying they didn't make them like that nowadays. They also didn't put asbestos in walls nowadays, but nobody brought that up.

The case was heavy as Leah dragged it towards her. She sat on the camping chair as she unzipped the case to find... bits. It looked like someone had emptied a chest of drawers or a bureau into a case. An old passport was on top, with the name 'Gary Hook' inside. Jennifer's father was a man sporting sideburns with a head that was otherwise bald. It was a brave look, though not one he'd managed to pull off. He looked like an egg with sandpaper glued to the sides.

His birth certificate was underneath the passport, along with discharge papers from the local hospital. He'd been admitted more than forty years before and had kept the admin for some reason. Four sets of reading glasses gave the air of a man never quite sure where the TV remote happened to be.

Leah wondered if these were the sort of things people kept after a parent died. She'd lost her mother, though had never been sure what had happened to her things. If there was a passport, Leah had never seen it. There must have been a birth certificate somewhere, though that was absent too. As for her clothes, they'd all gone in the bin. It wasn't as if there was anything valuable left. If there was, it would have been sold long before.

Underneath that was an ancient, faded Tesco carrier bag, with an old logo. The sort more usually found under a hedge. It was heavy and, when Leah looked inside, there were piles of newspapers. Old people loved their old news.

Leah almost shoved the lot back into the case, until she realised it *wasn't* newspapers as such, it was a collection of black and grey craft paper, with articles stuck to them. There was no binding, though it was unquestionably a scrapbook of sorts. Pictures of kids falling over at sports day, or someone finishing third in a pub darts competition.

Or not...

THREE GIRLS MISSING AFTER SLEEPOVER

Leah stared at the clipping. She'd seen it before, and it might even have been in Owen's documentary – except someone here had cut it out and kept it.

The page underneath was similar.

POLICE SEARCH WIDENS

Leah skipped through the pages, which seemed to be a day-by-day account of her missing friends and the search. The headlines weren't particularly new, and many had appeared in the documentary, but Leah had never seen a collection quite like it. There was everything from those first articles, through the early anniversaries. It had all been cut from the newspaper and glued to a page, then filed in order.

It was almost as impressive as it was creepy. Why would Jennifer's father have such a collection. Leah *knew* he hadn't done anything to her friends – and yet…

Leah jumped as something slapped on the stair behind. She turned quickly, expecting a mouse or worse. Instead, Jennifer stood over her, sleepily yawning towards the opened suitcase.

'Told you,' she said.

EIGHTEEN

Jennifer's spare bed had a mattress with the consistency of Brie left in the sun. Leah had sort of slept on it, though slept *around* it was a better description. By the time she got off, it was time to wake up again. There was somebody knocking on the front door and Leah slumbered onto the landing and then down the stairs. She opened up to find Hannah on the other side.

There was no news, other than that the search was starting earlier that morning. This non-revelation felt like something that could have waited, though Leah left Jennifer upstairs, sleeping off the hangover, as she sat in the kitchen with the liaison officer.

It was one more throwback, because Leah had spent so many hours sitting in kitchens and living rooms with her own liaison officer. It was incomprehensible that it could all happen again – yet here they were.

Hannah busied herself, putting on the kettle as they watched the sun rise through the window. Officers were dotted around the trees for the third day running and Leah wondered what they were hoping to find that they hadn't before.

There was no easy way to start the conversation, so Leah simply went for it.

'Jennifer told me that she thinks her dad might have killed at least one young woman,' Leah said. She wasn't sure she believed it but it didn't feel like something to keep to herself. If she told the police, they could deal with it.

Hannah was close to Leah's age, maybe a little older. They didn't know one another and the officer raised an eyebrow, perhaps wondering if it was a strangely timed joke.

'She'd been drinking,' Leah added. 'But she said that, after her mum walked out, her dad used to bring back prostitutes. She says they were always gone the next morning and that she thinks her dad buried at least one on the farm.'

Hannah had been leaning on the counter, but now reached into a pocket and took out a notebook. 'She said this?'

'Last night.'

'Did you believe her?'

'I don't know. Maybe. She said she'd never told anyone. It would've happened about twenty years ago, maybe a little more. She reckoned her dad kept all the ploughing or digging equipment, long after the farm went out of business. It was a bit unclear.'

Hannah said she was going to have to make notes – and jotted something into her book. It was a small act but suddenly felt official. No going back.

'Do you think she was drunk?'

Leah had been thinking about that overnight. 'No,' she replied. 'Maybe tipsy – but more down than up with it. I told her it was serious, that I'd have to tell people and she carried on. It felt like something she'd been wanting to say for a long time.'

Something more was written in the book and Leah remembered another interview, another notebook, a living room. She'd only been fifteen then.

'I looked in the cellar,' Leah said, and it came out far more ominously than she meant.

Hannah had been writing but her gaze shot up. 'What did you find?'

'Junk, mainly. A lot of her dad's stuff. But there was a scrapbook from years ago, with pages and pages about my missing friends.'

Leah stood and opened the cupboard next to the oven. She removed the faded Tesco bag and placed it on the table. Hannah crouched, peering without touching at first, before removing the top page and reading the headline.

'Are they all like this?' she asked.

'Years and years of it, up to about the fifth anniversary.'

Leah could see Hannah doing the mental calculations. It was roughly the time Jennifer's father had died.

The next part was the thing Leah had spent the most time considering. The thing that was definitely wrong. Would this be wasting police time at a moment where they needed all their resources?

Leah said it anyway: 'Jennifer thinks her dad might have had something to do with my friends going missing...'

Hannah had been writing, though her pen stopped on the pad. 'Jennifer said that?'

'She said her dad was definitely out that night and came home late.' The officer scribbled something quickly into her book as Leah added: 'I don't know if she really believes that.' A pause. 'Or me...'

When the notebook snapped closed, Hannah turned to look at her colleagues in the distance, then towards the front of the house. Leah didn't know much about police ranks but this felt like a big piece of information for one person to have.

'I'm not saying *I* believe it,' Leah added, knowing she

couldn't say why she didn't believe it. Without knowing she'd done it, Jennifer had forced Leah to lie.

'Is she awake?' Hannah asked, glancing upwards.

'She wasn't.'

Hannah was nodding, mind made up. She muttered, 'Let me just—' and then headed for the stairs.

There was an opening of doors and the sound of muffled voices, before Hannah reappeared a few minutes later. She poked her head into the kitchen, though was angled towards the front door.

'I'm going to have to make a call,' she said, not waiting for a reply before disappearing along the hall and out the house.

Time passed. Leah texted Zac, asking if he'd slept well. The sort of nothing question people used when they weren't sure what else to say. She messaged Ben to say something big had come up and she might be some time, then sent another to clarify that the boys hadn't been found.

Jennifer arrived downstairs, wearing the same clothes she'd had on the day before. If she'd slept, it didn't look like it. The rings were so deep, it looked as if she had a pair of black eyes. She hadn't seemed particularly old when Leah had met her, yet she had seemingly aged a couple of decades over the weekend.

Time passed. They talked, though not really about anything. Jennifer nibbled at a cookie from the day before but otherwise didn't eat.

By the time ten o'clock rolled around, the farm was all go. The search was continuing through the woods, and one of the officers had said something about dogs working the area near the river. While that was happening out of sight, some sort of machine that scanned beneath the ground had been brought in to examine the surrounding fields. Hannah called it 'a sort of X-ray device' that was to look for traces of Leah's friends, or anyone else that might happen to be buried. Hannah said it wouldn't normally happen so quickly but told Leah quietly that they were already planning on scanning the ground in the coming days. Presumably, that would have been for traces of Dylan and his friends, though Leah hadn't wanted to ask.

As well as that, more drones had been sent up to circle the trees – plus a different officer came to tell Jennifer that three live streamers had been intercepted after heading over a fence near the trees. They had said they were there to 'help with the search'.

In the meantime, against her better judgement, Leah had been keeping an eye on the class WhatsApp group, in which a second parent said his son had also admitted an affair with Mrs Hawkins. With the trio of missing boys and the 'Teacher sex claims', local news had never had it so good. Their awful website, with the adverts that appeared over the top of stories, before asking for cookies to be accepted, and then wanting people to enter their email address, would be doing huge numbers.

Through all that, Leah had hung around and made small talk. She assured Jennifer she was right in voicing her suspicions about her father and continued to lie and say she thought everything would turn out fine with the boys. It was becoming harder to say, given they were now onto day three. If she was bold enough, Leah would have said she wanted to leave. She had spent almost none of the bank holiday weekend with her son.

Instead, as they continued to drink tea and coffee and sit glumly around the kitchen table, Leah dropped hints. 'I'm back at work tomorrow,' she said.

That got an airy 'Oh' and an eventual: 'What do you do?'

'I'm a community support worker. I visit people who've had, or are having, problems in their lives.'

Jennifer had been largely staring into her coffee, though she looked up at this. 'What do you do for them?'

'Lots of things. Sometimes, it's more of a chat. Or I'll help with paperwork or admin, applications and forms – that sort of thing. Occasionally, it's helping with washing, or making sure they've eaten. Everyone's different.'

'Does that make me one of your patients?'

Leah didn't correct Jennifer that they weren't 'patients', but, in reality, she wasn't wrong. This wasn't *that* far away from what Leah did day to day – although never quite so serious. Also not quite as personal.

'What do you do?' Leah asked.

For a moment, it didn't feel as if Jennifer was going to answer. She was staring into the distance, as she'd done so many times since they met. 'A few things,' she replied quietly. 'I sell oils and creams. If you have eczema, I know just the stuff. I've been doing the farmers' markets now and then because I grow strawberries out back. I did some temping in town for an agency, plus a bit of classroom assistant stuff when Dylan was younger. I thought about going for teacher training but I was already feeling a bit old for that.' She took a long, wistful breath. 'Did you always know what you wanted to do?'

Leah almost laughed at that. She could hardly explain the things she'd seen and gone through as a teenager.

'Shirley helped me,' she said. 'My liaison officer. I had no idea what I wanted to do but she knew a few people around town and I ended up doing a few bits and pieces, before I started in the office. It all sort of spiralled...'

That was true. People talked about not being what you know, but who. There was a lot of talk about privilege and access. She sometimes wondered if that counted for her. She hadn't got her job because of any qualifications, or experience beyond her own life. There were probably other people out there who had that – and she'd gazumped them because a friend had put a word in. Was it different because of where she started?

Leah felt edgy talking about Shirley around Jennifer. Best-case scenario was that she wouldn't need someone like Hannah in her life. The longer a person had to get to know a police liaison officer, the worse things had become.

They sat for a while and perhaps Jennifer had figured that out for herself. She stood abruptly, chirping: 'Do you want to go for a walk?' Her mind was seemingly made up as she strode into the hall and grabbed a pair of walking boots from the pile, leaving Leah to wonder how far they were going. She only had her regular trainers, which were scuffed with little in the way of sole.

Not that she could say no. She felt tied to the other woman, now. They understood one another.

There was a chill to the air that hadn't been there in previous days. Steam was rising from the fields, creating a thin, dusky mist. Officers in dark clothes were roaming the back end of the field, with what looked like an oversized iPad but was probably the ground scanner. Meanwhile, a drone buzzed over the top of the trees.

'This way,' Jennifer said, leading Leah away from the search and towards Charles' farm. They stopped a little short of the boundary and followed the line of the hedge towards the trees. There was a thin patch, that looked suspiciously similar to the one Leah had seen the day before at the school. It was likely the shortcut Dylan had been caught taking by the neighbour – though Jennifer didn't reference it. They soon reached the corner and entered the trees, where it was colder still. The ground had a hint of stickiness, with frosty embers clinging to the darkest verges.

Leah wasn't the sort to go hiking, or slumming it up hills on a miserable Saturday while wearing a supposedly waterproof jacket. She understood the teenage urge of Dylan and his friends to sleep outside as something different and got the appeal of festivals and the camping that came with it. Beyond that, she had a perfectly good roof over her house, thank you very much.

Not that she complained.

There was a series of rustles in the distance and a faint echo of voices. The police were out of sight somewhere, still searching, still presumably getting nowhere.

Jennifer walked with the purpose of somebody who'd done the same thing many times before. She had grown up on the farm, after all. This was her territory.

The faint, far-off, trickle of water was steadily getting louder as Jennifer led the way through the trees. She talked about adventures with friends when she'd been young. They'd tried to build a raft for the river out of scrap wood, but it hadn't floated and she'd ended up wet. There had been a rope swing, from which her friend had slipped and cracked her head on the rocks. There was blood and panic, ahead of a hospital trip that had revealed a dislocated shoulder. Her younger self had tried to make a bow and arrow out of twigs but only succeeded in shooting one of those branches into her own eye.

None of it was a life Leah recognised, though they'd been in the same year at school, and lived a handful of miles from one another.

The faint trickle became more of a rush, though not really. With talk of rafts and rope swings, Leah had expected something vast and powerful from the river. The reality was a gentle wash of something that could be described, at best, as a stream.

'Is this where they fish?' Leah asked. The confusion in her voice was unintentional but obvious.

'The water seems to get lower every year,' Jennifer replied. 'It used to come up to my waist when I was a girl.'

It was far from that now: the water was barely above Leah's ankles and she suspected she could walk through it. There were footprints in the dirt around the riverbanks, most seemingly from big feet. Paw prints, too. Leah supposed they belonged to the officers and dogs who'd been searching.

'Do you really think they came here the other night?' Leah asked.

Jennifer had crept down the sludgy bank and was standing so close to the water that it was nudging the end of her toe. For the first time since Leah had met her, the other woman seemed comfortable in her surroundings. While Jennifer bounded confidently across the uneven ground, Leah constantly felt as if she was in danger of going over on her ankle.

'Maybe,' Jennifer replied. 'Dylan came out to go night fishing sometimes. I always figured there was nobody around, so what was the harm? Just him and a friend. Or it used to be his dad.' She stopped a moment, then added: 'His dad always used to say the bigger fish came out at night.'

Leah assumed the water must have been higher back then too, unless local fish had legs.

Jennifer patted the edge of the water with her toe, probably judging its depth, before scrambling back up the bank. In the distance, the voices of the search party reverberated around the trees. Birds chirped in annoyance as a drone buzzed somewhere nearby. There was peace among the noise.

After crouching to untie her shoes, Jennifer sat on the part of the bank where the grass met the mud. She removed her socks, wriggling her toes, and then lay back. 'Do you wanna sit?' she asked.

Leah didn't, though it felt rude to say so. She'd never been one for peer pressure, yet the past few days had been a steady stream of agreeing to things she didn't particularly want to do.

The spot Leah picked was slightly further up the bank, entirely on the grass – and she kept her shoes on. The barefoot-in-the-woods thing felt a bit kumbaya for her liking.

'Thank you for all this,' Jennifer said breezily. 'I know you didn't have to come. I know the other parents are going through it as well but they have each other, don't they?'

She unexpectedly stretched a hand and Leah took it. They held hands momentarily but, this time, Leah didn't feel pressured. It was her choice. She squeezed the other woman's fingers gently until they released one another.

'Do you really think my friends are in your field?' Leah asked, knowing it was dangerous, and knowing the truth.

'I don't know.' A pause. 'Maybe.' Another pause. 'Probably not.' She turned away, back towards the water and crossed her arms. 'I don't know why I said all that.'

Leah wondered if the other woman was trying to push that connection between them. One lonely person wanting to be friends with another. 'Did you tell anyone at the time?' Leah asked.

Jennifer was quiet. The voices had gone, so the search party must have moved on. The drone had silenced, leaving only the murmuring trees and the quiet babble of the water.

'You're a mum, aren't you?' Jennifer asked, though she knew the answer. 'It's only me and Dylan here. I thought about saying something so many times. But he was my dad. I didn't want to believe it. Then I got older and this place became mine. And I had Dylan. You don't want to lose that.'

She stopped and it felt as if she wished she had stayed quiet the night before.

'They're going to dig everything up,' she said. 'And then what do you think the kids at school will say to Dylan if they find something? This is the only home he's known. What if they take it?'

'I don't think they're allowed to do that.'

It didn't feel like the sort of thing that could happen, though Leah was guessing. What if Jennifer's father was some sort of mass killer? What if the field was riddled with bodies, with more underneath the farmhouse's foundations? It sounded obscene, yet bleaker things had happened. It also felt unlikely. Did Jennifer *really* believe her father was a killer? Had she *really* sat on it for so long? Could it all be put down to the vodka Jennifer had drunk? Something didn't feel right, yet Leah wasn't sure what. At least the police could do their thing now.

Leah leaned back onto the grass, propping herself on her elbows and closing her eyes. She was so tired that her thoughts were cloudy. She had to get home and have a shower, if nothing else. Check in with Zac, too. When she reopened her eyes, the sky swam and greeny-pink stars swarmed. The shadows from the trees swayed and bobbed from the breeze. This place was far more peaceful and comfortable than Leah had imagined. Perhaps she'd been doing things wrong forever and spots like these really were a haven for that cherished peace.

Except...

Leah pushed herself up into a sitting position, then standing. She brushed away the dirt from her palms as she crept towards the nearest tree.

Etched into the bark, above eyeline and probably eight or nine feet up, a bullseye was carved into the wood.

Jennifer was on her feet, too, a pace or two back.

Leah stretched on tiptoes, running a finger across the markings, making sure they were real. She'd seen the same thing in the clearing the day before. The one Zac had led them to.

'What is it?' Jennifer asked.

There were no chips in the bark on this tree, unlike the previous one.

Leah lowered herself and looked around, wondering if there might be another target somewhere. If there was, she couldn't see it.

But she did see something else. The previous day, the officer had removed a small pile of sticks and rocks from the ground, revealing an empty hole underneath.

Now, there was another pile of rocks and sticks, a handful

of steps from the tree, largely hidden next to a clump of mossy foliage.

Jennifer's 'What have you seen?' went unanswered as Leah crossed to the pile and started pulling away the sticks. There was dust and dirt on her palms as she pushed them to the side, before doing the same to the rocks.

And there, sitting in a tiny cubby dug into the soil, sat a pistol.

NINETEEN

Leah and Jennifer were back at the farmhouse. There was an odd triumph in the sense that the search party had spent three days combing the woods in vain, while Leah had bumbled in and found a gun. Not that she felt much in the way of satisfaction.

She hadn't touched the weapon and it had been taken by an officer to be examined. Jennifer had said very little since the discovery, perhaps fearing the worst.

Back in her kitchen, and Constable Evans had returned. This time she had a notepad and was sitting on one side of the table, with Jennifer on the other. Leah was leaning on the counter. It felt as if they'd been playing musical chairs in the room for three days.

'Do you know whether Dylan owned a gun?' Evans asked.

'How do you mean "owned"? It's not like you can just buy one.'

'I suppose I'm asking if he *had* a gun?'

The shrug seemed to give away a lot. 'My grandfather did. It was an old one from the war. He showed it to me when I was six or seven. That's the only gun I've ever seen.'

'Was it the same gun that was found in the woods?'

Jennifer had withdrawn since the walk with Leah. Her arms were folded, body hunched. 'I don't know,' she replied, with a yawn.

Evans's pen was a blur, though Jennifer probably realised how unconvincing she sounded.

She quickly added: 'I don't know a lot about guns. I couldn't tell the difference between them – plus it's a long time since I saw Granddad's.'

That sounded more likely, though Leah still wasn't sure whether she believed the other woman.

'Do you know what happened to your grandfather's gun?'

'I've not seen it in thirty-odd years.'

'Did your dad inherit it?'

'Maybe – but he never said. Dad's stuff is downstairs but I don't remember it being there. He'd have probably sold it, if it was worth anything.'

As Evans continued to write, Jennifer suddenly sat up straighter and turned towards the window, with the fields and trees beyond.

'How do you know what was found in the woods belongs to Dylan?' She was angry. 'Anyone could have left it there.'

'We don't,' Evans replied calmly. 'But there *are* witnesses who say he was seen with a gun. There is more than one report of him showing it to people at the school. It was also found close to an area that you yourself say he visits regularly. We're simply trying to establish who it might belong to, and why it's there.'

'That doesn't mean it's his. You're guessing – plus why aren't you looking for him. What are you trying to say? That he shot the others?'

'Nobody's saying that. But the more information we have about the boys, the more chance we have of piecing together what happened.'

The constable was walking a tightrope with her choice of

words – and was saved by a buzz on her radio. She excused herself and headed out back.

Jennifer had slumped again. 'You could've left it,' she said – which was as close to a cross word as she'd had for Leah, who didn't respond.

There was no follow-up because Constable Evans was back inside, a curious look on her face.

'Someone who says he's Dylan's father is at the top of your driveway,' she said. 'What would you like us to do?'

Jennifer spun to take in the officer, who'd entered the kitchen behind her. 'Steven's here?'

'I believe some of my colleagues have been in contact with him at his main residence, though he didn't tell anyone he was planning to come here. We can send him away if you want...?'

'I can't believe he showed up.' Jennifer shrugged, as if to say it didn't matter much. 'Send him down, I guess.'

Evans headed back outside to pass on the message, as Jennifer pushed herself up.

'He's got a cheek,' she said. 'Last time he was here, he was packing his stuff. I, uh...' She glanced away. 'I cut up some of his stuff and then we shouted quite a bit.'

'Was Dylan here?'

A nod.

There was a knock on the front door, which then opened. A man's voice called 'Jen...?' and then Steven appeared.

He wasn't what Leah expected. The Steven Bailey she remembered from school was skinny, with a shaved head and bumfluff moustache. He had lost or killed the class rabbit, depending on who was believed.

Even with that, when Jennifer had talked about Dylan's father shagging someone from work and running off to a water-front flat, Leah had pictured her own ex. Their stories weren't entirely the same, though they weren't that far off. A year before, Leah's former husband had taken money to tell stories about her. He was rarely out of his work jeans – unless he was off to the football at the weekend.

This Steven was in a smart, fitted suit, with an open-neck collar. That shaven head had been replaced by something swept-back and glossy, as if he'd stepped out of a magazine. Leah's immediate impression was that she couldn't imagine this Steven living on a farm.

He didn't acknowledge Leah as he stood in the doorway, looking to Jennifer. 'Why didn't you call?' he said. 'I had to find out from the police on Saturday. I've been trying to get news on Dylan for two days but you're not replying to texts, or answering your phone. I didn't know what else to do, other than come here.'

This was absolutely not what Leah had expected. Jennifer had said he and Dylan didn't see much of each other, painting the picture of some sort of deadbeat.

'You made your choice,' Jennifer said, spitefully.

'He's still my son.'

'Why walk out on him then?'

'I didn't walk out *on him*.'

It felt like an argument that had been had many times before; one which would never see a conclusion. They couldn't help themselves, even when their son was missing.

Steven was still going: 'I've had to drive all the way out here to try to get any sort of update. It's—'

'That's farther than you normally drive to see him.'

'What do you mean by that?'

Leah knew these signs. She'd had similar arguments, knowing exactly which buttons to push when she wanted to wind up her former husband. She saw the glint in Jennifer's eye.

'You're only bothered now the police are involved,' she sneered. 'Now it's all over Facebook and everywhere else. Now people are saying how useless you are as a dad. Then, suddenly here you are, wanting to be the big hero.' She mockingly waved jazz hands-style at him.

'I'm his dad,' Steven replied, firmly. 'I only found out Dylan went missing from the police turning up to ask if I'd seen him. I've been reading updates off the internet because nobody is telling me anything.'

'Nobody's telling you anything because you moved out. You can't have it both ways.'

Steven shook his head furiously. 'You let him go fishing at night again, didn't you? I told you about that before.'

'It was your idea!'

'It was my idea when I was *with him*. He's only fifteen. You can't let him do things like that by himself.'

'He wasn't *by* himself!'

Constable Evans had entered the kitchen as the final barbs flew. She glanced between both parties, mouth slightly open.

'Is everything all right?' she asked, which almost made Leah laugh because of the understatement.

'Can you make him leave?' Jennifer said, talking to the officer. 'I want him to go.'

'I just got here. I'm trying to find out what happened to my son.'

The officer stepped around the table and reached a guiding hand towards Steven. He didn't resist as she led him back towards the hall. 'I'll have someone brief you fully outside,' she said.

For a moment, it felt as if that would be that – except, before he was fully through the doorway, Steven turned. He was taller than anyone present and aimed an accusing finger at Jennifer from over the top of Constable Evans' shoulder.

'You know *she* did it, don't you? Probably killed all three of them. Ask her why we split up.'

Evans was having none of it, continuing to walk, which made Steven back away.

'Cos you shagged that slag from work.'

'More like 'cos you're a psycho.'

'He hit me, do you know that? And Dylan.' Jennifer was louder now.

'That's a lie.' Steven was at the front door, still shouting along the hall as Evans reached around him to open it. Daylight beamed behind, casting him in shadow. 'That's a lie,' he repeated, more firmly. 'She knows it's a lie.' He pushed himself even higher, again pointing over the top of the officer. 'You know it's a lie.'

The door closed, though it was unclear who shut it, leaving Leah and Jennifer in a momentary calm. Steven had been there for three or four minutes and it had caused a tsunami – not that it had all been his fault.

'That's what he's like,' Jennifer said, lowering her tone, though with a manic twitch to her eye. 'He can't take responsibility for walking out on his own son. Only wants to see him when it suits and wants to blame me instead. As soon as he gets home, he'll be off on some rant on Facebook, or wherever.'

Leah wasn't sure who she believed, though suspected there were problems on both sides. The allegation of Steven being violent was something different and more serious. Leah's instinct told her that Steven's denials were so instant and vociferous that he was telling the truth – but she'd seen manipulation before. The only thing that seemed clear was that he'd left her, not the other way around. And that Jennifer hadn't wanted him to go.

The question was reluctant and as non-judgemental as Leah could manage. 'Was there another reason you split up?' She quickly added: 'I'm not saying I believe him – but it sounds like that's what he's telling people. That's what he'll tell the police if they ask.'

'He can tell people what he wants. He knows what he did.'

'What *did* he do?'

Jennifer's stare was fixed, her jaw as well. 'I need to get out of here.'

Leah knew the feeling – she was sick of the kitchen and it wasn't even hers.

There was a moment of déjà vu as Jennifer hurried into the hall and started picking through the pile of shoes and boots. The same thing had happened not long before when they'd ended up near the river.

'Where do you want to go?' Leah asked.

Jennifer seemingly couldn't find the shoes for which she was hunting. 'This is gonna sound silly but I just...' She stopped and plopped herself onto the floor. 'You're going to think I'm an idiot.'

'Why'd you say that?'

'I visit a psychic healer. She's really good. She once told me to avoid silver cars and, later that day, there was a crash on the roundabout going into town that involved a silver car.' She held up her hands, indicating, well, everything. 'It's not like this is working.'

Jennifer had a point, even though Leah didn't think a psychic healer – whatever that was – could be the answer.

'Can you drive?' Jennifer asked, likely because the last time she'd driven was that mad dash to confront Mrs Hawkins. Her car had been left blocking the teacher's drive, and an officer had brought it back.

And so, once again, Leah agreed to do something she didn't want to do.

TWENTY

The psychic healer turned out to be a normal-looking woman in a normal-looking semi-detached house. There was a plastic slide in the small front garden, plus a yippy little dog on the other side of the front door. The psychic introduced herself as Claire, which was fair enough, though seemed somewhat plain compared to what Leah had pictured.

Claire led them through a ridiculously normal living room, cluttered with toys for both dog and toddler, into a separate side room that was more like it. Dark, translucent curtains covered the walls, with dreamcatchers and other related market tat hanging from the ceiling. The room had that in-between smell of possibly being incense, though it might also be weed.

'I was wondering whether you'd come,' Claire said, as she pushed Jennifer into a wooden chair. Claire sat in something that was similar but on a step, making it a few inches taller. She waved Leah towards another wooden chair. It looked like something retrieved from the bin at the back of an antiques auction.

With little option other than to sit, Leah did precisely that and failed to get comfortable.

'I was hoping you would,' Claire added, before: 'Who's your friend?'

'This is Leah,' Jennifer replied.

Claire nodded knowingly, as if she'd known that the entire time. 'Leah. Of course it is.' She turned back to Jennifer. 'You have such dark energy today.'

'I know, that's why I'm here.'

'Shall we start with some of the usual?'

Jennifer pushed herself up from the chair, seemingly agreeing, as Claire pulled away a curtain to reveal a massage bed. If she'd added an excited 'ta-da!', Leah wouldn't have been surprised.

With the bed unveiled, for a moment, Leah thought her new-found friend was about to strip off. Instead, Jennifer lay front-down, fully clothed.

'Do you want to watch?' Claire asked, though it took Leah a moment to realise she was the one being asked.

'Depends what I'm watching,' Leah replied, failing to hide how uncomfortable she was finding things.

Claire seemingly took that as a yes. She pulled out a blanket and covered Jennifer in it, then held her hands around a foot above the other woman.

As best Leah could tell, the psychic healer spent the next fifteen or so minutes swishing away, well... air. She said things like 'Can you feel that?' and Jennifer replied to say how nice it was, even though nobody had touched.

After a while, Claire said that the dark energy had been 'temporarily' dispersed, and Jennifer clambered down from the bed. She insisted that she felt refreshed and, in fairness, that air of sleepiness had disappeared. She returned to the chair and stretched high.

'You should try it,' she said, talking to Leah.

'I'm good.'

'I do sense dark energy persisting in the room,' Claire said, which sounded as if it could be an insult. Leah said nothing, which left the healer to turn back to Jennifer. 'I feel as if you're due a reading.'

'That's what I was hoping for. It's been a while.'

Claire opened a drawer on her side of the table and drew out a stack of cards. Leah had seen Tarot on television but not in person. There was always the odd reader with their booths at the seaside – but Leah had ignored them in the way she ignored the chuggers on the high street who wanted her bank details.

'Why don't you go first?' Jennifer said, turning to Leah.

It took Leah by surprise as she stumbled over a way to say no. 'I don't think it's for me,' she managed.

'How'd you know if you've never done it.'

Claire was calmly shuffling the oversized deck. Leah hadn't said she'd never gone for a reading, though it must have been obvious. As if taking the decision for her, the healer handed Leah the cards. 'Here,' she said. 'You can shuffle.'

Leah didn't know how to shuffle a regular-sized deck, let alone something bigger. Some people could work magic with a thumb and there would be that tidy riffling sound. Leah always felt as if trying the same would lead to the cards flying in all directions.

She couldn't think of a polite way to decline, so folded the tarot cards a few times and then returned the stack to the table.

'Hold the cards,' Claire said, so Leah did – and then she was told to shuffle them again. After putting them back on the table again, Claire took the top card from the pile. She placed it facing Leah, with the card showing a mournful woman in a cape, half turned away.

Jennifer let out a soft but shocked 'Oooh,' which wasn't a good sign.

'This is the five of cups,' Claire said. Her voice had seemingly lowered a fraction. 'This speaks to your past and represents sadness and loss. Perhaps a sense of loneliness?'

She phrased it like a question and, though Leah wanted to think of the whole thing as nonsense, the card felt a little too close. If she owned a cape, the image could have been of her.

'I told you she's good,' Jennifer said, which wasn't particularly welcome.

'I didn't realise cups was a suit,' Leah replied, though nobody laughed. 'I'm not particularly lonely,' Leah added, though it felt as if she was trying to convince herself. She had Zac, Shirley and Deborah. A son, a police officer and a mother stolen from her missing friend. She wasn't sure what she felt for Ben, though doubted it was love. Besides, if the card was to represent the past and only that, it was hard to deny her history was filled with loss, loneliness, and sadness.

Still, one card. Anyone could fluke that. Plus what was cups supposed to be as a suit? What would come out next? Plates?

Claire reached for the next card and flipped it, then placed it next to the five of cups. The new image showed a man in a fez carrying a pile of swords by their tips.

Jennifer was nodding, possibly in agreement, though Claire seemed much more thoughtful. Her lips were pursed, gaze focused on the card.

'That's interesting,' she said. 'This is your present, your now. It's the seven of swords and shows there's dishonesty and deceit in your life. Perhaps someone close to you is guilty of manipulation?' She looked up and it again felt like a question, an invitation for Leah to reveal the person responsible for all the dishonesty.

Too close. Two for two. There was an awful lot of deceit in Leah's life, the vast majority of which was only known to her. She carried it every day but it wasn't as if she could say that.

She shuffled in the chair, caught herself, and forced her body to be still. 'Not that I know of,' she said.

'You wouldn't know, though, would you?' Jennifer chirped

– and she was either being deliberately unhelpful, or it was coming naturally.

Leah couldn't quite remember how she'd ended up having the reading.

From somewhere else in the house, there was a clunk, though the other two ignored it.

'Is someone else here?' Leah asked, though she didn't get a reply.

There were footsteps from overhead as if to confirm the question.

Claire turned over a third card and put it down next to the others.

'This is your future,' she said, ominously.

The card showed what looked like a yellow sun rising over two pillars, with a pair of dogs on a beach below. The words 'The Moon' gave away that it wasn't a sun.

'This shows fear and anxiety,' Claire said. 'Maybe a sense of risk in your life?'

'Isn't everyone a bit anxious nowadays?' Leah said it with a forced laugh but it wasn't reciprocated.

It was, somehow, three out of three. The dishonesty of Leah's present meant her future was always going to be filled with the fear of being found out. A concern of what might happen to Zac if things came out.

'I don't know what it means,' Leah said. From the bag at her feet, there was a buzz of a phone. Though she ignored it, there was at least a break in the tension. 'I think it should be Jennifer's turn now. I don't want to take up her time.'

Claire smiled thinly, removing the three cards from the table and returning them back to the deck. She shuffled them effortlessly and then passed them to Jennifer. They went through the routine of shuffling, holding, then shuffling again until the stack was returned to the table. Jennifer angled forward, keen for whatever to come. Leah wondered if the other woman believed there might be answers to the location of her son. She herself had been sceptical – and still was – though it had been hard not to be rattled by what had been revealed for her.

Jennifer's first card was a king on a throne. Almost.

'This is the Emperor,' Claire said. 'We've seen him before. Your father figure was a large presence in your life...?'

Jennifer bowed her head a fraction, though it didn't feel as if this card was a surprise. When she spoke, it felt like it was more for Leah, as if she and Claire had been over this.

'I was always scared of him,' she said. Leah had to sit on her hands to stop herself picking at her nails. This card could have been hers. 'He'd lock me in my room and leave me for hours. Sometimes an entire day. I never knew when he'd let me out, or what he'd do next.'

Leah hadn't known what to make of Jennifer saying she believed her father had killed people – but this felt genuine. There were so many differences between them but, not for the first time, Jennifer had said something that felt real for Leah. Their parallels made her ache. Her own father had spent close to twenty years in prison for various offences, until his recent release. He now lived across town, though they didn't have much in the way of contact.

It felt as if Jennifer wanted to talk about her dad, and nobody stopped her. She told tales of his drinking and the anger when he couldn't pay bills and the farm went out of business. She said that he forced her mum to leave and then moved onto bringing home random ladies in the early hours. No mention was made of any potential consequences for those women.

When Jennifer stopped, Claire asked if she wanted to continue with the reading. After a short nod, the Page of Pentacles was revealed. It showed a figure in a short green robe holding a giant coin embossed with a pentagram.

'This is a new one for you,' Claire said. 'Something for your present. It means you're sticking to goals, that you're loyal.' A pause. 'It's what you're going through now, isn't it? You're desperate to find sense in what's happening in your life.'

Jennifer was nodding. 'I just want Dylan home.'

'The cards say that, if you keep doing what you are, then you *will* find him.'

Jennifer touched her heart as Leah held back a gasp at the brazenness of it all. Not 'might' find, not 'could': a definitive 'will'. She'd felt guilty about remaining positive – but this was the meaning of false hope. It felt reckless – not that Jennifer minded. It was what she wanted to hear, and probably why she'd come. Regardless of which card had come up, Claire would have found a way to make it mean Dylan's homecoming was around the corner. Just keep visiting every few days, pay the money, get that hope.

'Let's move onto your future,' Claire said, as she flipped the third card and placed it next to the second. The image was simple enough: a heart, with three swords plunged through it.

Jennifer's reaction was instant. She rocked back in her chair and whispered, 'No...'

'It's the three of swords,' Claire said, calmly, and then: 'I'm sorry.'

'What does it mean?' Leah asked. In the moment, it didn't feel as if Jennifer could speak.

'Grief,' Claire said. 'But this is the future, not the present. It doesn't necessarily mean what you think it might.'

Leah's phone had been quietly buzzing on and off for at least ten minutes. She'd ignored it, though it felt like now was the time to stop whatever was going on. Leah didn't agree with offering false hope, but she certainly didn't think indicating Dylan was dead was a good plan, either.

She stretched for her bag and pulled out her phone, where there were four missed calls, all from a mobile number that wasn't in her contacts. If it was one of the usual scammers or spammers, they'd have surely given up after one attempt.

'I should take this,' Leah said, pushing herself up from the table and hoping Jennifer might follow. When she didn't, Leah weaved her way back through the house to the front garden. She leant against the frame of the slide and pressed to dial back the number that had called.

A woman answered on the first ring. 'Leah…?'

'Who's this?'

'It's Hannah. Are you with Jennifer?' She sounded panicked, the words all feeding into one another.

'I can be,' Leah replied. 'What's happened?'

'It's Dylan. We've found him.'

PART TWO

TWENTY-ONE

Leah drove too fast, which was something she almost never did. Jennifer was in the passenger seat, frantically texting and talking the entire time. Leah only got one half of the conversation – though it sounded as if, somehow, miraculously, Dylan was alive. It was barely comprehensible. He had disappeared somewhere in the early hours of Saturday – and, now, more than two full days on, he had reappeared.

As they neared the destination, Jennifer started to relay directions from the person on the phone. Leah was told to ignore the signs for the police station and instead take a route that led to the back entrance. There was a high fence but someone waiting outside. As soon as they saw Leah's car, the gate opened and Leah eased through. The officer motioned for her to wind down her window and, when she did, he told her to park next to the main door ahead and that someone was on their way.

Even as they got out of the car and headed for the doors, Leah couldn't quite grasp this as real. In her mind, she'd already assumed Dylan and the others were dead. She hadn't admitted that to herself, let alone Jennifer, but she'd been readying herself to be that shoulder to cry on.

And now... he was alive?

Where had he been? What about the others?

Leah had so many questions as they rushed up the steps and through the door, into the back of the police station.

'Is he really here?' Jennifer asked, speaking to an officer who was apparently waiting for them. There had been so many police roaming around the farm in recent days, though this person hadn't been one of them.

'This way,' the officer said. She was carrying a clipboard, and hurried them along a series of corridors until they ended up in a large room with a trio of sofas in a U-shape. There was a rug in the middle, along with a coffee table. A large mirror was on one of the brightly coloured walls.

Jennifer edged ahead, looking around non-existent corners for her son.

'If you wait here, we'll bring Dylan along in a minute or so. It won't be long, promise.'

'But he's here?' Jennifer asked.

'He's definitely here.'

The officer exited, leaving Leah and Jennifer alone in the room. It was more like a living room than anything usually associated with the police.

'What is this place?' Jennifer asked. She probably hadn't expected a reply, though Leah knew.

'I was interviewed in a room like this,' she said. 'When Vicky, Jazz and Harriet disappeared. They talked to me at the house and then I came to the police station. They couldn't get hold of my mum, so Harriet's sat with me. There were a couple of sofas, and the mirror. No table, but more rugs. They said it's where they talk to young witnesses.'

Jennifer wasn't really listening. She was pacing from side to side, tugging on her sleeve, then her hair. 'I told you Claire was good, didn't I? She said that my present was the Page of Penta-cles. That if I kept believing, everything would be OK.'

That wasn't *really* what the psychic healer had said, not that Leah was going to point it out. She remained standing close to the chairs as Jennifer did a lap of the room.

'How long did they say?' she asked.

Leah eyed the mirror, wondering if there was already some-body behind. She'd learned some things about policing from Shirley. Reading that police file about her missing friends a year before had taught her more. She wondered if the issue wasn't Dylan being brought up from wherever he was but, instead, someone wanting to observe Jennifer's reaction before he appeared. It was hard to figure out without knowing what had happened to Dylan.

Jennifer's pacing was getting quicker and she was rubbing her hands together, though that anxiety was surely under-standable.

'A minute or so,' Leah replied, knowing a minute had already passed – although the 'so' was ambiguous.

Then the door clicked, opened, and revealed the boy from the photographs.

It felt unreal. Mother and son momentarily stood a few paces apart. Dylan had greasy dark hair and the merest hint of stubble on his chin. There was a cut close to his hairline and he was wearing a large puffer coat that likely wasn't his. He hugged his mum – and there was an awkwardness that Leah recognised. A proper teenage boy hug, one arm limply on his mother's back, the other loose at his side. Leah had instigated plenty of hugs like that in recent years with her own son.

An officer in a suit was a few paces behind Dylan, which felt somewhat ominous. No longer the realm of uniformed offi-cers, this case was now one for the detectives.

Not that Jennifer noticed him. She took a half step away

from her son, took him in from head to toe, then hugged him
again. This time, he patted her back.

'I'm fine, Mum,' he said.

No big tears, no massive reunion. Leah wasn't sure what to
make of it. How were people supposed to react to this sort of
thing?

'Where are the others?' Jennifer asked.

There was the merest shake of the head, perhaps a
narrowing of the eyes. 'I don't know,' he replied, in a way that
sent Leah spinning decades into the past. 'I don't know where
they went.'

TWENTY-TWO

The suited officer introduced himself as Detective Inspector Bryan – or 'Call me Ashley'. He shook Jennifer's hand, though her gaze never left her son. Leah hovered near the door, unsure what she was supposed to do. She'd not had a chance to text either Zac or Ben to tell them that Dylan was found. It still felt surreal he was there.

Ashley held out an arm, indicating that everyone could sit on the sofas. As he moved, Leah noticed that Dylan was bigger than he seemed in the photos. It wasn't height, more a presence. There was a lumbering sense about him, not quite a hunched back, but not far off. The coat was massive and he shrugged it off, revealing a long-sleeved dark T-shirt underneath.

'They gave me this,' he said, as if answering an unanswered question.

'What happened to your clothes?' Jennifer asked, which was quite the mumsy response.

'They took it all.'

Dylan sat first and, as he did, he took in Leah for the first time properly. She was still standing across the room, near the door.

'You're from the movie,' Dylan said curiously.

It was true and yet it was strange for Leah to be described that way. She was a mother, a community support worker, a secret girlfriend. Not a film star.

She supposed it was natural when anything happened in a small town in which people were used to nothing. There wasn't a single place on the planet Leah would be called someone 'from the movie' – and yet, here, it was sort of true. Even for young people who didn't necessarily read the news, it would have been impossible to miss the year of coverage for Owen's film. Leah knew it was a documentary that *might* get a release in the arty cinemas. It *might* limp onto a streaming service at some point. The people in the town had somehow convinced themselves it was going to be some sort of blockbuster that would be selling out multiplexes.

'This is Leah,' Jennifer said. 'She's my friend. She's been there the whole time since Saturday. I wouldn't have got through this without her.'

Leah was still angling for the door. This wasn't her reunion.

'Do you want to sit in?' Ashley asked. 'You're welcome to. We're going to have a bit of a debrief, so it's entirely up to you.'

He spoke with a casualness that Leah didn't completely believe. 'Debrief' made it sound like someone's monthly numbers were a bit off – and a bunch of boring people in suits were going to spend an afternoon going on about it. In reality, two boys were apparently still missing – and Dylan's own absence had caused a county-wide search. Not only that, if the police had been wanting to interview Dylan – which they definitely would have done – they wouldn't have been able to do so without a parent or guardian present.

Whatever was going to happen wouldn't be a casual 'debrief'. Leah considered all that, while concluding that reading and re-reading that stolen police file had driven her slightly mad.

Jennifer had placed herself on the same sofa as Dylan, who'd angled away from her. She nodded to the free sofa and Leah found herself crossing the room and sitting.

Ashley pointed up to a camera in the corner. 'Just so you know, everything in here is recorded but that's as much for your own benefit as anyone else's. Before all that, do any of you want a drink? We've got tea and coffee, or there's a vending machine.'

Dylan's gaze lingered on the camera for a moment until he turned back. 'Can I have a Coke?' he asked.

'We can sort that. Anybody else?'

It was all very calm, considering a missing boy had reappeared after two days. There were no takers for the offer, though Jennifer reached to take her son's hand. He shook his head and frowned a fraction. There was very much a *not now* vibe.

Nobody had moved to fetch a drink but Ashley didn't seem bothered. 'While we wait, I wanted to emphasise that we don't *have* to do this now.' He was talking to Dylan. 'But time might be crucial to finding your friends, so whatever you can tell us might be important.'

'He understands,' Jennifer said.

Dylan side-eyed her momentarily and then added: 'OK.'

A moment later and there was a tap at the door. A female officer entered, can of Coke in hand. She smiled as she placed it on the table, but didn't say a word before leaving.

Dylan twisted in his seat to look at the mirror. 'Are people watching?' he asked.

'There are,' Ashley replied. 'It's so we can act quickly if you have anything to say about the location of your friends.'

'I don't know where they are,' Dylan replied.

'I understand – which is why I was wondering if you could tell me what happened on Friday night. I believe you were camping...?'

Dylan squinted and stretched. He didn't appear as tired as

his mum, though there was an air that he could yawn at any moment. He was seemingly unfazed by the way the officer had twice steered the conversation to the present.

Over the next few minutes, he told the officer more or less what Jennifer had told Leah. He had arranged with his mum for his friends to come over for a sleepover. The weather was decent, so they had set up their tents on the edge of the field at the back. They'd started a small fire and warmed up cold pizza on skewers – then Dylan had texted his mum to ask her to bring out crisps.

That detail got a hint of a smile from the officer. 'What happened after that?' he asked.

'Alf wanted to try night fishing. He'd not been before.'

'What time was this?'

'I don't know. After it got dark, maybe eleven? A bit later.'

'Do you regularly go fishing at night-time?'

Dylan glanced to his mum, with a general sense that he didn't want her there. 'Not regularly.' A pause, with another glance to Jennifer. It felt as if he was speaking specifically to her. 'Sometimes.'

'And where do you go?'

'There's a river at the back of the house. You head through the trees and it's right there.'

'D'you catch much?'

A snort: 'Have you seen it? There ain't many fish there.'

'So it's not about catching fish?'

There was a confused shrug, as if to say that of course it wasn't about catching fish. Why would a person even think that?

'If it's not about catching fish, why did you go?'

Another shrug: 'You just hang out and stuff. I film videos and put them up. I've got about three-hundred subscribers now. I—'

'The moon makes everything look like daytime, doesn't it?' Jennifer prompted. 'That's what your dad used to say.'

Nobody replied, leaving a couple of seconds of awkward silence. It felt like a pushy mother encouraging a child to show off that they'd learned their twelve times table.

'Did anything happen while you were fishing?' Ashley asked.

Dylan glanced to his mum on one side, then the mirror on the other. 'We were just sitting there—'

'Yourself, Alfie and Mo?'

'Right. We were sitting there and this bloke sort of... appeared. He had a rifle under his arm.'

'How do you mean "appeared"?'

'I don't really know where he came from. I didn't hear him. He said something like, "All right lads?", and we all sort of jumped.'

'What did he look like?'

'Dunno really. Tall. A bit fat.'

It took a bit of pressing, though they managed to settle on the man having short, darkish hair, and wearing a black jacket that wasn't leather.

'What was the rifle like?' Ashley asked.

Dylan eyed his mum again, largely speaking to her. 'The sort of thing they use on the pheasant shoots.'

'So a long barrel?'

'Right.'

'What happened with the man?' Ashley asked.

'He told us he had a van at the end of the trail. We were all like, "So...?" Then he kinda picked up the rifle properly. Locked the barrel in place and flicked it on past the trees, like he wanted us to go that way.'

'Did he say that?'

Dylan held out both hands, palms up. 'I can't— It's sort of hard to explain— I don't think he did but I can't remember. We all knew what he meant but it felt like a wind-up. You hardly ever see anyone out there during the day, let alone that late.'

'And you'd not seen this man before?'

'No.'

The officer paused for a moment. 'What happened then?'

Dylan reached for his drink and cracked the ring pull. He'd been speaking confidently but started to fidget.

'We can do this another day,' Jennifer said, though her son didn't acknowledge she'd spoken. Even though he'd been missing for two days, he still had an air of embarrassed teenager.

'We didn't know what to do,' Dylan said. He was avoiding eye contact, looking at the floor instead. 'Then he pointed the gun right at Alf. We all put our hands up, like it was instinct. He flicked the gun past the trees again, towards the road.'

'And you went?'

'I guess.' He shrugged. 'What were we meant to do? I kept thinking it was a joke. Maybe he was someone's dad from school, and it was a wind-up.'

Ashley took another moment. 'Did the man say anything?'

'I don't remember, not properly. I think he said to leave the rod. I said something like that it was expensive.' Dylan's voice cracked a fraction and he looked to his mum again. 'I saved for ages to get it but he just said "leave it", so I did.'

'It's at the house,' Jennifer told him and, for the first time since they'd reached the sofas, Dylan acknowledged his mum. It was a gentle nod, though with a little more behind it.

Leah knew that look and she knew what it was like to grow up poor.

The first major thing she'd ever bought herself was a pair of comfortable trainers. The only shoes she'd had growing up were hand-me-downs that seemed to appear from nowhere; or charity shop finds that didn't cost her mum very much. They rarely fitted to the point that Leah didn't know what size foot she had until she was into her teens.

After getting her first job, Leah had saved a little each week until she had enough to pay for the pair of Reeboks which had thirty per cent off at the local sports store. They hadn't been anything like top-of-the-range, though they still gave more comfort to Leah's feet than she had ever known.

Even after so many years, even now she actually had a savings account, the idea of having to leave those shoes behind left Leah cold. A person never forgot poverty and it was impossible to explain to someone who'd never known it. Small things mattered.

Maybe the officer understood, too, because he left it a moment more.

'Did the three of you walk together?' he asked eventually.

A nod. 'Sort of side by side, except when it got narrow.'

'Where was the man?'

'Walking behind but close. It's hard to describe. It didn't feel like it was happening. Like I was watching myself. I was thinking I should run but when I looked back, he was still pointing the gun.'

'He was aiming it at you?'

A nod. 'All of us, I guess.'

Leah was watching from the side, taking in Ashley on one side, then Dylan and his mum on the other. Dylan had slipped deeper onto the sofa, folding his arms across his front. She understood what he meant when he said things felt like they were happening to someone else. She'd had a similar experience of feeling like she was watching herself twenty-five years before.

She thought about Zac, wondering how he'd have handled it had he been part of the camping trio. Would he have thought about running? Was it even an option?

'Where did he direct you to?' Ashley asked.

'When you follow the trail, you eventually get to the road. It's further along from our house.'

'So you ended up on the road?'

A nod. 'There was a van there. Mo was at the front and the man told him to open the back. Mo couldn't figure it out for some reason and the man was calling him stupid. Saying he just had to pull the handle.'

'Can you describe the van?'

'Sort of dark, maybe black or blue? There was hardly any light.'

'What sort of size?'

Dylan held his hands out, as if to indicate the width. 'Like a work van. The ones where you see three people in the front.'

Ashley's gaze flickered momentarily towards the mirror. 'Did Mo manage to open the back?'

'Yeah.'

'Then what happened?'

Dylan took another sip from his can and stopped to look into the mirror. Leah wondered how many people were on the other side and what they were making of it all. She wasn't sure what *she* was making of it. There was a definite sense of disbelief, but not necessarily at Dylan himself. The story of a random man in the woods with a gun felt unlikely, and yet there was that statistic Shirley had told Leah the year before. Thousands of people went missing every year. They had to go somewhere.

'He told us to get in,' Dylan said.

'And you did?'

Dylan glanced to his mum again. 'He had the gun right there. What would you have done?'

Ashley didn't flinch, and didn't invite confrontation. 'I'd have got in.'

Dylan had unfolded his arms but not for long. Ashley's reply seemed to surprise him.

'Nobody's judging anyone here,' Ashley added.

'Oh...' Dylan pushed back onto the sofa and had another drink, before putting down the can. 'There were handcuffs in the van,' he said, holding up his arms to show the reddened marks around his wrists that Leah had missed.

Jennifer reached for him: 'Are you hurt?'

That got a shake of the head. 'We had to cuff each other, with our hands behind our backs,' Dylan said. 'Then he took these black hood things out of his coat and put them over our heads.'

'Who did you cuff?'

Dylan had zoned out a fraction. 'Huh?'

'You said you had to cuff each other.'

'Right, um... Mo. He did Alf, Alf did me. The man stood there the whole time, pointing the gun and telling us what to do.'

'And you did it?' Something about the way Dylan's stare turned to steel led Ashley to add quickly: 'No judgement. I'm just asking.'

'Yeah,' Dylan said quietly. 'We did it.'

It felt like a natural break and the officer asked Dylan if he wanted anything else to eat or drink. That got a shake of the head.

'Let's finish,' he said, which didn't get a complaint from the other side.

Leah was still stuck in a state of disbelief. She knew what it was like for people to openly question that. Some still did, even after so many years. Unlikely didn't mean impossible. Dylan's telling was riddled with ums and ers, full of hesitant pauses and coughs. None of that meant much, especially considering his age.

Leah was desperate to know what those on the other side of the mirror were thinking. Had they already started to look for a van? A man with a jacket? There wasn't a lot to go on. She had so many questions of her own. Had the man known there could be people by the river? The boys specifically? Had he simply been in the area? Why would he do such a thing?

'What happened once you were all in the van?' Ashley asked.

'He told us to sit.'

'Were there chairs? Cushions?'

A shake of the head. 'Just metal. It wasn't comfy.'

'Then what?'

'I don't really know. He sort of drove. I couldn't see anything but you could hear the engine and it was really bumpy. That's how I got this.' Dylan pointed to the cut on his head that had scabbed over.

'Because you were cuffed?'

'Yeah, everyone was bumping into each other. I think I hit my head on the side of the van.'

'Do you know how long he drove for?'

'It felt like ages. Half an hour?'

That seemed very much like a guess.

'What happened when he stopped?'

Dylan yawned and cricked his neck. He said sorry but immediately yawned again, which started his mum off. It took a good minute for the pair of them to stop yawning over one another. They both apologised together and then Dylan answered.

'We couldn't hear each other while he'd been driving. When it was quiet, Alf asked if we were all right. I said I'd hit my head and I think he had, too. Mo was really quiet and said he'd hurt his arm. He left us in the back for ages. We were like, "What do we do?" Alf said he'd got his blindfold off and then the doors opened.'

'Could you see anything at this point?'

'I couldn't even stand.' Dylan put his arms behind his back and started to wriggle. 'It was like being a worm, or something. I couldn't push myself up.'

'Did you get up in the end?'

'He sort of pulled me up. I think he did the same with the

others. There were steps at the back of the van and he counted us down to the ground.'

Leah realised she'd moved her hands behind her back and was trying to figure out what it was like to walk while being off-balance. Even with full vision, it wouldn't be easy.

'We ended up going down some steps,' Dylan said. 'I think I was at the back. He was counting those stairs, too, until we were at the bottom. Then he took off the blindfolds really suddenly. I didn't even know he was close until he'd moved away.'

'Did you get a good look at him?'

Dylan waved a hand in front of his face. 'I couldn't see very well. It had been dark for so long and then it wasn't.'

The questions had largely been short and to the point. Pure efficiency over anything else. For the first time proper, it felt as if Ashley stopped to consider what should come next.

'Do you know where you were?'

Dylan let out a long puff of breath. He reached for his can and, after picking it up and realising it was empty, put it down again. 'Just a dark room. I think it was a basement. There weren't any windows. It was kinda damp.'

'What happened then?'

'He kinda left us. I don't really remember him going but I don't remember him being there either.'

'What do you mean by that?'

'I don't know. Lots of things were happening at the same time, then it was just the three of us in there.'

'You were all still cuffed?'

'Right. We just sort of walked around, looking for a door. I was wondering what had happened, where we were. I think Mo was shouting but nobody came. Then Alf spotted a camera high in the corner.'

Dylan turned to look at the camera that was also in a corner. The way he'd asked whether they were being watched before suddenly had a new context.

'How big was the room?'

Dylan turned and took in the space. 'Probably about this size. The door opened and he called down, telling us to face the wall and that, if anyone turned around, he'd shoot us all. He left us some bread and crisps. Alf asked what he wanted but he just said to keep looking at the wall.'

'Did you recognise an accent?'

Dylan thought on that and yawned again. He seemed exhausted, which could be understood. 'I don't think so. Just kinda normal.'

'Did he ever tell you what he wanted?'

Dylan stopped and his gaze flicked sideways to Leah. A chill shot through her that came so quickly she couldn't hide it.

'He said he was going to kill us like he killed those girls.'

TWENTY-THREE

Detective Inspector Bryan, of Call Me Ashley fame, had been calm throughout, giving nothing away. He had told Leah she could stay, while giving no indication he knew who she was.

He definitely did, though.

The three people in the room all turned to look at Leah, who wriggled awkwardly on the sofa. It was probably only a second or two until Ashley turned away, followed by Dylan. Jennifer's stare lingered a little longer. Nobody spoke.

And then everything continued as if Dylan hadn't said what he had.

Leah listened, though she felt absent.

Dylan said that the man had left the sleeping bags and brought them food. He barely spoke, but held the gun as he made them drink a liquid that made them all feel sleepy. The boys would pass out for what felt like hours. When they woke up, they would talk quietly of escape, while always being conscious of the camera and wondering if the person on the other side was listening, too.

He added that, one time, he drank the liquid and then woke up outside. He didn't know where he was, that it was some sort of wasteland. He was dizzy, thirsty, and could hear cars. He walked towards the noise and found a road. Somebody stopped – and said, 'You're that missing kid,' and that pretty much got them to where they all were.

Leah was not completely taking it in.

He said he was going to kill us like he killed those girls.

'Were you ever told why you'd been let go?' Ashley asked.

She had plenty of her own questions that weren't going to be asked.

That got a shake of the head. 'I didn't even know I'd been moved,' Dylan replied. 'I was on one of the sleeping bags and then outside.'

The officer glanced to the mirror and it felt as if things were wrapping up.

'I do need to ask you something else,' he said, turning back to Dylan. 'Some of your classmates say they've seen you with a gun. It was found near the stream close to where you were fishing...'

There wasn't quite a question there. Dylan eyed his mum and, probably for the first time since he'd entered the room, he seemed surprised. He started a reply and stopped, then tried again: 'It's an air pistol,' he said. 'I shoot rabbits sometimes.' A pause. 'Or try to.'

Assuming that was true, the police would know what it was. Ashley didn't react either way. 'Why hide it by the tree?' he asked.

'Because that's where I fish, so I don't want to carry everything all the time.' There was a definite schism of annoyance as he looked back to his mum, presumably wanting her support. On this occasion, Jennifer was silent and, if anything, her folded arms made it seem as if she was annoyed. 'Why are you asking?' Dylan added.

'Because you've been missing for three days and there've been a lot of questions asked and tips acted upon. The issue of your gun came up. We could've asked at a later time but, seeing as you're here...'

That got a shrug that was pure petulant annoyance.

'Do you have any idea where Mo and Alfie might be?' the officer asked.

'I told you I didn't.' This response was borderline spat. Jennifer reached a hand onto her son's knee, which he pushed away. 'Not now,' he added, before turning back to the officer. 'When can I go home?'

Ashley waited a moment and it felt as if he might have some bad news to deliver. Then he stood quickly and brushed down his hands. 'It won't be long, Dylan. I'm going to leave you a few minutes and then we'll see where things are.' A pause. 'Are you sure you don't want anything from the vending machine?'

'I just wanna go to bed.'

Ashley asked Jennifer the same, though she shook her head.

A moment later and it was just the three of them in the room. Well, the three of them plus whoever was watching.

'Are you OK?' Jennifer asked, talking to Dylan.

He was fidgeting in the seat, scowling towards the door. 'Shoulder's sore.'

'I've got that heat pack at home. Remember when you bumped it playing rugby?'

Dylan didn't respond, he simply stared at the door. It was easy to judge him, and Leah was, but she also knew what it was like to be asked the same questions over and over. She understood the desire to get away from an interview room.

A minute passed, maybe two. Jennifer never stopped staring at her son as he studiously ignored her. Leah felt as lost as a third wheel. She had no official connection to anyone in the room and had no idea what to say. She wasn't quite sure why she'd remained, though she was glad she had.

The door opened and Ashley was back. Dylan stood but it

was his mum on whom the officer was focused. 'Can we have a word out here?' he asked.

Jennifer stood hesitantly.

'It'll only take a minute.'

Dylan's mum followed the officer into the hall and the door closed, leaving Leah and the teenager alone. They were on separate sofas and, though he'd been glaring towards the door, he stopped to look at her.

'I didn't know you and mum were friends,' he said.

'We're not,' Leah replied, probably too quickly. 'I mean I suppose we are now. We weren't before. An officer came to my house on Saturday and asked if I'd visit your mum. I suppose she thought I could help.'

Dylan bit his lip and started to nod slowly. He glanced to the mirror and then back. 'Is this what it's like?' he asked.

'What do you mean?'

'You just... I don't know. You wake up and don't know what's going on?'

It was a question at odds with the hunched way he was sitting. There was vulnerability and, perhaps, a small amount of fear. Not only that, Leah was sure his mum had asked almost the exact same thing the day before. She couldn't quite remember the wording but it felt similar.

Jennifer had gone too long without answering, so he added: 'What was it like when your friends went missing? When you woke up and didn't know what had happened?'

That was a question Leah could answer with absolute truthfulness. 'Confusing,' she replied.

'Right...'

Leah eyed the door, figuring Jennifer could be back any moment. If she was going to ask Dylan what she wanted, without his mum around, she'd probably only get this chance.

'What was it the man said?' she asked. 'When he talked to you about "those girls"?'

Dylan blinked at her, having not expected the question. He stumbled over the reply. 'Um... It was something like he was going to kill us like he killed those girls.'

'Did he say *which* girls?'

His eyes widened a fraction. 'No... I mean, I thought... with you and everything.'

Leah pressed back in her seat, letting it sit. Which other girls could it be?

Except she knew this random man with the dark jacket, the shotgun, and the dark van didn't kill her friends.

It was a definite lie – except who was lying?

Perhaps the man was trying to frighten the boys to make them do what he wanted. Everyone in the area knew about Leah's friends disappearing at the sleepover. They had long been presumed dead, despite Owen's documentary and the recent coverage.

Dylan had turned away and was eyeing the door. His glare had relaxed, though he was tapping his foot anxiously.

Was his story true? Teens did go missing and there were bad people out there. Everything Dylan had said sounded unlikely, though plausible. As far as Leah could tell, he'd been consistent and hadn't contradicted himself.

Leah watched Dylan.

She knew a thing or two about lying to the police and couldn't figure out whether he had done the same. There was a time that she had rehearsed what to say, and maybe Dylan had as well.

Because 'those girls' was a lie – and if it hadn't been invented by the unknown man, that meant it had definitely been told by Dylan.

TWENTY-FOUR

Ashley's minute had taken longer than that. Leah had shifted to watching the door herself. There was no way to tell people she knew a lie was being told without giving herself away.

But there were still a pair of missing boys. Either Mo or Alfie could be Zac. There were two sets of parents worried about their children.

There was one other person who would know this had to be a lie – and Leah was already trying to think of the best way to bring it up with her.

A silent minute passed. Ashley's timekeeping was appalling, unless he'd deliberately removed Dylan's mum from the room to see what her son might say when she was away.

When she looked to him, Leah realised Dylan had been watching her. If it had been Zac, he'd have turned away, though Dylan was less intimidated by adults.

'You OK?' Leah asked.

He pursed a lip, perhaps weighing her up. 'Can I ask you something else?'

'Go for it.'

Dylan shuffled to the edge of the sofa, and leaned closer. He lowered his voice in a way Leah suspected meant those outside wouldn't be able to hear. 'Did you ever see your friends' bodies?' he asked. He must have seen a degree of horror in Leah's face, as he added: 'I know what they say happened but did you wake up and see them, like... *dead?*'

Leah couldn't answer. She could barely believe he'd asked it.

'I get why you'd say you didn't see them...'

There had been plenty who'd alluded to similar things in the past. That Leah must know her friends were dead, that she had to know more than she said. This was a different question, something far more sinister and direct.

'Why would you ask that?' Leah replied.

She could have spoken louder but kept her tone the same as his. This was their secret and a part of her wanted it that way.

'Mum talked about it,' he said. 'I didn't know you were friends but I wanted to go to your premiere. I couldn't get tickets. She was saying it would end up at the cinema, or we could wait for Netflix. Everyone's been talking about you all year, so I suppose I wondered if you actually woke up while they were still there.' He shrugged. 'Never gonna get another chance to ask, am I?'

It was perhaps true, in the same way Leah had taken her moment to talk to him.

'I won't tell anyone,' he added.

'There's nothing to tell,' Leah replied, though even she heard the gentlest waver of her own voice.

For a teenager who had recently been through a trauma, Dylan didn't *seem* very traumatised. But then people said the same of Leah. She seemed to think that a lot. The parallels with her and Jennifer, now her and Jennifer's son, were borderline creepy.

'Where are your friends?' Leah asked.

'I don't know,' Dylan replied, holding her stare. It felt like a challenge, although he almost immediately broke into a yawn – and the confidence was gone as quickly as it had come. He was suddenly tired and vulnerable. He looked like a teenage boy, desperate to show that he wasn't confused or scared. Leah had seen Zac do the same when he'd come into the kitchen to tell her three boys from his year were missing. She wondered if she'd misread Dylan's masked confidence as something more sinister.

The door clunked and Jennifer was back. She was flustered, stumbling over her words as she approached Dylan, who had stood.

'They need to talk to you about your phone,' she said.

'What about it?'

'Your hidden phone. They found it and saw the messages between you and your teacher.'

Dylan's sleepy eyes widened as he gulped. 'They... what?'

'You know what it's about. I don't want to get into it now. They're going to talk to you about that now. After that, they've cordoned off the farm but they'll let us go back to grab some things. They're going to sort us a hotel room. I'm going to text your dad now but, when we get there, you can call him.'

'Why can't we go home?'

Jennifer looked to Leah and it was clear something bad had happened. Something *new* and bad.

'First,' she said, turning back to her son, 'they don't want the media or anyone else coming to take pictures of you.' A pause, a breath. 'Second, they've found bones in the field.'

TWENTY-FIVE

Leah waited in her car outside Ben's house. She'd driven there from the police station alone but for the relentless sprint of her thoughts.

Bones had been found on Jennifer's farm.

Because of what Jennifer had said, the police would first think they belonged to Leah's friends. She knew they didn't – but they were definitely from someone.

As soon as she had left the station, Leah had started to doubt everything she thought she had seen in Dylan. She was judging him by her own standards, which was an unfair thing to do with any teenager.

Zac must have been watching for her because he came out of the house and crouched at the passenger side, making her jump. Leah got out of the car and rounded it, finding herself hugging him as he pulled away. 'What's up?' he asked.

'They found Dylan,' she said.

'What? Where?'

'It's complicated but the other two are still missing.'

Leah looked past her son, to where Ben was standing in the doorway.

'I know I've abandoned you all day – but do you mind if I have two minutes with Josh's dad? You and I can have a proper talk on the way home.'

Zac turned to look at Ben and there was a hint of confusion on his face. From his point of view, Leah and Ben talked in the way parents did when they dropped off children with each other. Shame about the weather, and all that. Nothing serious.

'OK,' he said, although he wasn't convinced. He headed back to the house and said something to Ben as the pair swapped places. Leah watched her son head inside and close the door.

'What's wrong?' Ben asked.

'They found Dylan.'

'Oh.' He reeled a little. 'That's good news, right?'

'The other two are still missing – but that's not what I need to ask you.'

There was curious confusion on his face, perhaps even mild panic, as if she might do something mad like get down on one knee.

'How do you know Jennifer?' she asked.

As Ben looked to her, Leah realised how little she knew him. He was the father of her son's best friend, he was pretty good in bed – but, beyond that, who was he?

She watched him trying to figure out how much she might know. Whether it was worth trying to turn the question around before giving anything anyway.

'We hooked up a couple of times,' he said. 'I don't know how to put it any better than that – though it was so long ago that we wouldn't have called it that.'

'How long ago?'

He puffed a long breath, like a plumber about to tell someone they needed a new boiler. 'Fifteen years? Sixteen? Ages. We met in a pub in town. She said she was divorcing her husband, because he was cheating on her. Me and Jill were always on-off. You know that. We were "off" at that time – so Jennifer and I were two single people looking for a bit of, um… company.' He fumbled for the final word, though it was a better choice than other options.

Ben had told Leah that he and Jill, Josh's mum, had always been on and off. From what he said – even though he hadn't laid it out quite so clearly – he'd never had a full-on relationship. Leah hadn't thought a lot about it, and had spent the past few months living in the moment. Now she wondered if it was more him than the other women.

More him, than her.

'Jennifer and I had a night together,' he added. 'Then a couple more – then I got back with Jill. That was it.'

It felt like it was probably true. Leah seemed to spend a lot of time attempting to figure out whether people were telling lies.

'Why did you say you didn't know her?'

He let go of a long breath, which felt a little dramatic. 'It's not a complete lie. I've barely spoken to her in fifteen or sixteen years. Maybe once or twice around school, or at the petrol station. Neither of us were parents back then. I don't *really* know her.'

He knew it was nonsense, even if it was truthful nonsense.

'Fine,' he said, almost immediately, likely because of Leah's disbelieving expression. 'It's because I like you and didn't want to have a conversation about the women I've been with in the past. I figured it didn't matter too much.'

'You could've just said that.'

He laughed gently. 'I know. I regretted it the moment I said I didn't know her but it was already too late. I couldn't change my mind and say I actually did. Can I say "Sorry" now, and we carry on like before?'

Leah thought on that but not for too long. There weren't a

lot of non-teenagers in her life with whom she spent time. 'It's OK,' she said.

'Is it really?'

Leah had already moved on. There were bigger issues to address. 'Did you ever get weird vibes from her?' she asked.

The change in tone had Ben frowning in confusion. 'Weird? Jennifer?' He blinked and shrugged at the same time. 'I don't know. I'm not going to get into details but it's not as if we were having lengthy conversations.'

That was fair enough, though his interest was obviously piqued.

'Are you finding her weird?'

Leah dismissed the question with a shake of the head. 'I can't believe I'm going to ask this – but were you, um, *careful?*'

Ben was a fraction slow on the uptake. As he figured it out, his eyes almost popped out of his head.

'Dylan's fifteen,' Leah told him.

'Right, yeah, um. Yeah. I mean, of course we were.' A beat. 'Wait, did you think Dylan might be my, um...?'

Leah enjoyed the couple of seconds in which he was wriggling. Served him right for that little lie about Jennifer.

'He looks nothing like you if it's any consolation,' she added.

'It's not the right timeframe,' he said.

'So you did check...?'

He squirmed again and she smiled to let him know she was teasing.

'Thanks for taking Zac.'

He calmed, though likely realised he had messed up: 'Are we definitely all right?'

'We're good.'

Leah meant it. There was too much real drama in her life for an old relationship to cause more.

There were footsteps from the stairs and then Ben and Zac swapped places once more, before Leah started driving them home. The momentary oddness over his mother wanting a chat with Ben was apparently forgotten, because all Zac wanted to talk about was Dylan being back. Not that Leah blamed him. His phone was in his hand and she suspected he'd already messaged everyone he knew. It was exciting to be in the know.

As she drove, Leah gave Zac the abridged version of everything the day had brought. Dylan had returned, though Mo and Alfie were still missing. Dylan's gun had been found, though he said it was an air pistol. She decided to keep her scepticism to herself and tell Zac that a man in a dark van with a shotgun had abducted the three boys.

Zac reacted as she would've expected – with a mixture of bemusement and concern. Events like those described didn't really happen – and, if they did, they definitely didn't happen in their town.

Except, when everyone else found out, they would assume something similar had now happened twice, twenty-five years apart.

'Do I still have to go to school tomorrow?' Zac asked.

Leah laughed at that. Teenagers were ever the opportunists.

'Yes,' she told him, which was when she noticed the clock. The day had gone – and, with her at work and him at school, it was time for their respective beds.

By the time she sent Zac up to bed with a sandwich, Leah realised she had forgotten to tell him that the farm had been locked down because the police had found bones in the field. That news would likely be out by morning – and the entire town would go into meltdown. The two biggest news stories in its history were colliding.

Leah went up to her own room, though she didn't change. Just because it was time for bed, didn't mean that's where she was headed. She sat, waiting for the gentle din of Zac's videos to go silent.

She waited a while longer and then sent the text. Fifteen

more minutes and Leah crept downstairs and left via the back of the house.

The only street lights were over the top of the fence and beyond the next house, leaving a gentle orangey-white among the gloom. Leah was a shadow in the night as she hurried along the path and through the back gate. She followed the lane past the darkened neighbouring houses, keeping her head down and moving quickly in case anyone might be watching.

There was a street light at the end, so Leah stopped a few paces away from the junction and shrank into the shadows.

It didn't need to be a clandestine meeting, though nobody else in Leah's life knew about the occasional meets she would have to unload how she was feeling.

An electric car glided to a silent halt and the headlights were switched off. A woman got out of the driver's seat and pulled her jacket tighter.

Only one other person knew where Victoria, Jasmine and Harriet had ended up – and, seconds later, she was standing next to Leah in the dark.

'We have to stop meeting like this,' she said.

TWENTY-SIX

Leah had last seen Esther Merrivale at the premiere of Owen's documentary. It had been at the start of the long weekend, which was now almost finished – yet Leah had to remind herself it was only seventy-two hours before. It felt like so much longer.

'It's freezing out here,' Esther said.

Leah somehow hadn't realised. She wasn't wearing a coat and the desire to tell someone what she knew was somehow enough fire to keep her warm.

'Sorry, I had to wait 'til Zac was properly in bed. He's had an unsettled few days.'

Esther nodded along the lane. 'If we can't do this indoors, can we at least do it in my car? If some nosey neighbour thinks we're doggers, I'll live with it.'

Leah laughed at that, then followed the other woman to her Tesla. Considering the size of their town, a car such as Esther's stood out to the extent that most people knew it was hers. She was a partner in a legal firm in the centre, posh glass-fronted office and all. Sitting and talking in her car kind of spoiled the whole stealthiness of their chat, although, as Leah thought that over, an involuntary shiver told her that it really *had* got cold.

Esther often dominated their conversations and wasn't accepting no for an answer. She unlocked the doors and Leah clambered into the passenger seat. They waited for the lights to go off and then sat in comparative darkness.

'Still in the work suit...?' Leah said.

'I started late, so kept going for a bit.'

'Sounds like something a workaholic might say. Especially on a bank holiday...'

Esther snorted, though there was a serious point in that Leah rarely saw the other woman out of her work gear, no matter how early or late they met.

'I do worry about you,' Leah said, meaning it – even if it was for selfish purposes.

Esther didn't know the entire truth of what had happened to her sister a quarter of a century back – but she knew more than anyone except Leah. They could talk in a way that was impossible for Leah to manage with anybody else.

That didn't mean their friendship was outwardly public, nor that either of them necessarily relished their secrets.

'That's probably the nicest thing anyone has ever said to me,' Esther replied. She laughed, though Leah wasn't convinced it was a joke.

It took a while but Leah told Esther everything she remembered from the past few days. The police had come to her house and asked if she'd go to the farm. She had met Jennifer, whose son was missing.

'You get involved in everything,' Esther teased, which felt a little too close to the truth. Then: 'I heard they found one of them.'

'I was there when they interviewed him,' Leah replied, which got a perplexed sideways stare. Esther was used to being with clients and listening to statements. Leah not so much.

'It's a long story,' Leah added. 'But the thing is, Dylan's story is off. He said the three of them were taken by a man with shotgun who said he was going to kill them "like he killed those girls".'

Leah turned to take in Esther's confused gaze.

'*Which* girls?' Esther asked, wondering if she'd missed something.

'Vicky and the others.'

'But they weren't killed by some mystery man with a shotgun.'

It was stating the obvious and Esther turned to face the front. She drummed her fingers on the steering wheel and the jokey air was gone. This was business Esther. Leah wasn't about to interrupt.

'Someone's lying,' she said, making the same calculations Leah had hours before. 'It might be this guy with a shotgun? He wants to scare them, so he brings up Vicky?'

'Maybe...'

'You think the kid's lying...?'

Leah couldn't make up her mind. She'd been convinced he was, then decided his teenage bravado was clouding her judgement. Now, with Esther at her side and those few hours further on, she was questioning Dylan again. Leah couldn't quite say he was lying, but failing to deny it was enough for Esther.

Leah knew it would be. It's why she'd texted her.

'Why do you think he's lying?' Esther asked. Her legal head was on, with that rat-a-tat of short questions. Leah knew it well.

'I don't know,' Leah replied. 'But there was something else. There were a few minutes when it was just me and him in a room. He asked, "Is this what it's like?" I think he was talking about the police and the attention. He knew who I was.'

'That sounds like a normal question for someone who's been through what he says he has.'

'I know – but his mum asked the same thing a couple of

days before. I think it was word for word. I suppose I felt...'
Leah wasn't sure how to put it, but Esther knew.

'You felt like they'd talked about it together?'

'Exactly.'

Leah knew the direction in which her thoughts had been
heading. She'd tried to push it away but she knew why she
wanted to talk to Esther. She knew how the other woman's
mind worked.

'You think they planned this?' Esther said. 'Mother and
son...?'

Leah didn't think that. Except maybe she did. There was so
little to go on: a similar phrase coupled with a lie that nobody
else could know was a lie.

Beyond that, it was a feeling. One liar spotting another.
Possibly two others.

'I don't know,' Leah replied. 'But something doesn't feel
right. The police are digging up Jennifer's field right now.
They've found bones. Until they've checked them properly,
they're going to think they belong to Victoria, Jasmine and
Harriet. Someone's probably going to be in contact with you
tomorrow to ask about it.'

That made Leah remember that she had to set an early
alarm to get up and call Deborah to tip her off as well. She was
going to spend at least a few hours thinking the remains of her
daughter were in a place they definitely weren't.

'Why would they think those bones belong to Vicky and the
others?'

'Because Jennifer *also* said she thought her dad killed them.
That was among saying she thought he might have been a serial
killer of young women.'

Esther wasn't easily confused, though she asked Leah to
repeat herself, before replying: 'So there are two different
versions of what happened to Vicky and the others? The mother
says the girls are buried on the farm, the son says they were

killed by this stranger who took him?' A pause. 'Neither are right.'

She had summed it up far more neatly than Leah had managed.

'Right.'

Esther was drumming her fingers on the steering wheel again and making a gentle popping sound with her lips. Her thinking face.

'It's going to be very interesting to find out whose bones they've found,' she said, before adding something about talking to a police friend Leah didn't know. 'Do you know if the police are suspicious of Dylan's story?' she asked.

'It's hard to say. There was only one guy asking the questions and he kept a straight face the whole time.'

'I suppose they wouldn't make it obvious – plus it would've been a first interview. It's all information at that point. They'll be worried about the two lads still out there. They're the priority.' A pause. 'Do you know what's interesting? If Jennifer knows something's buried at her farm, why would she want the police to dig there?' She barely stopped a beat before adding: 'They'll know that, of course.'

Leah was already changing her mind: 'It could be that everything she told me about her dad was true. She said she was scared of him and that, after her mum walked out, he would bring home prostitutes.'

'Hmmm.'

Esther didn't sound convinced but neither did Leah. She was blinded not only by her own secrets but by her relationship with her father. Which reminded her.

'Tuesday,' Leah said out of nothing.

'Sorry?'

'It's Tuesday tomorrow.'

'Is that a problem?

'No, it's just... I've got things on.'

Until a few days before, Tuesday was going to involve one of the biggest decisions Leah had ever made. She still had to make it, even though it had fallen from her mind. Not only that, she'd spent the past few days thinking she was back at work, but she wasn't. She had booked Tuesday off. Despite all that, Leah had somehow forgotten until that moment.

She recovered enough to finish another thought. 'Sorry for dumping on you. I didn't know who else to tell.'

Esther nodded her acknowledgement. She wasn't much for sentiment but this was their pact. If either needed to talk about what happened with Vicky, Jazz and Harriet, the other would be there. What that meant in reality was that Leah messaged Esther once every six weeks or so to have a chat. There was never any complaint, never a 'no' – but it only worked one way.

Leah reached for the handle, though she could never remember how the doors worked on Teslas. As she was fumbling, Esther unexpectedly touched her arm. 'Lee...'

'What?'

'If you're saying one or both of them are dangerous, you've got to be careful.'

'I think that's the nicest thing anyone has ever said to me,' Leah replied, with a laugh that was unreturned. 'I've been alone with Jennifer a lot,' she added. 'I don't think she's dangerous.'

It felt ridiculous even to be saying it out loud. She was the mother of a missing boy. The daughter of an abusive killer of a father. Jennifer was a victim.

But Leah knew better than anyone what victims were capable of.

'We need the police to find those two boys,' Esther said, stating the obvious.

'What if they don't?'

Esther's reply to that was silence, which always worried Leah. If Esther didn't know the answer to that sort of thing, who would?

It was almost midnight, almost Tuesday and the day Leah had been dreading. She found the door handle and opened it. A light pinged on just as Leah's phone buzzed with a message. It was too late for anyone she knew to be messaging – yet Jennifer's name was on the screen.

Leah read the message, then read it again.

Esther wasn't one to pry, but she must have noticed something being off. 'You all right?' she asked.

'It's Jennifer,' Leah replied. 'She says the police have found the van that was used to kidnap Dylan.'

TWENTY-SEVEN

Leah made the early call to Deborah, who'd already been up for almost forty-five minutes. She and her husband were one of those couples who thought the best part of the day was half-six in the morning, or something mad like that. They were usually in bed by eight at the latest, and then up by six. It would have felt madder if Leah's recent existence hadn't had her waking up at a similar time but then staying up until midnight. Something had to give.

Deborah was as kind and understanding as ever. She'd seen rumours online about bones being found on the farm, and people had been commenting to say it might be Victoria, Jasmine and Harriet. She appreciated the call and would wait to see what the police said. All very gracious, yet Leah had heard the hesitation in her voice, perhaps the hope. It had been a long time for her without answers. Considering everything she'd done for her, Leah knew it wasn't right to keep her in the dark.

Not that she could ever say what she knew.

Before Zac came down for school, Leah read the update on the local news website. There were pop-ups to shut down, notifications to ignore, email address requests to deny. It was a wonder anybody visited the places – but the page was full of justifiable hyperbole.

TWO STILL MISSING IN HUNT FOR BOYS

BONES FOUND ON MISSING BOY'S FARM

TEACHER HELD IN STUDENT SEX SCANDAL

That was a lot of juicy stuff to spread across a year, let alone a weekend.

Leah read the story about the missing boys, which had been updated in the early hours. The dark van used for the kidnapping had been found a little out of town on a piece of derelict farmland. It sounded similar to Jennifer's own place, though was a couple of miles away. From the description, it seemed like the sort of thing that might go unnoticed, or get blamed on kids, if it hadn't been for people hunting for that precise vehicle. The search was ongoing at that farm, apparently.

With all that, the class WhatsApp group had reached seven-hundred unread messages, with Leah again putting it on mute. How did people find the time?

She'd been wrong, then. If the van was real, then Dylan's story surely had to be? That's what Leah had been telling herself when she eventually fell asleep the night before.

She wondered what Esther was thinking of her and her judgement.

Leah switched from reading similar variations of the same news to checking her emails. Because there wasn't enough happening, a message marked 'Emergency' had been sent from the school at 6 a.m. It had been written so hastily by someone on the board of governors that Mrs Hawkins' last name had been spelled three different ways. It said the board was aware of rumours and reports over the long weekend. Blah, blah, blah. Investigation into the conduct of one of our teachers being carried out by the police. Blah, blah, blah. Teacher currently suspended and, if there was a need for any further investigation, it would occur in due course.

For a group of people overseeing the school, Leah often thought someone on the governors' board could do with taking an English class themselves.

When Zac came downstairs as hungry as ever, Leah told him there was going to be an all-school assembly later in the day that would address the events of the weekend.

Leah got her things ready and then drove Zac across town to school. She would usually leave him on the corner, except, as Leah neared the drop-off area, it was impossible to miss the commotion. Or the reason for the seven-hundred WhatsApp messages.

Leah parked a street away and followed her son to where a group of parents had blocked the road. Someone had painted 'Paed-No' on a sheet and a couple of the dads were holding it up while a photographer took pictures. The black paint hadn't fully dried, with the 'a' and 'e' running into each other, and making a protest against a sex offender seem more like a typographical display.

One of the mums, who seemed to run most things extracurricular, was giving an interview to the TV news, with the backdrop of the school. It would have had more impact if not for a different parent holding the 'Honk if you hate paedos' sign. Passing drivers were drowning out the interview with a constant series of beeps.

As all that was going on, a woman on the other side of the blocked street was handing out flyers to anyone who'd take them. There was a consistent stream of parents taking the paper, glancing at it, and then depositing it in the bin that was a dozen steps away.

This was why Leah didn't get involved with the WhatsApp groups.

Everyone's heart was broadly in the right place. There were two missing boys and a teacher who'd been sleeping with at least one student. It was no wonder they were concerned and wanted to do something – but they could've at least settled on *one* thing.

Leah hadn't walked Zac to the gates in a long while, though there was a line of students trying to get into the school. As Leah trailed the teenagers towards the entrance, she realised there were teachers with clipboards, checking students into the grounds one at a time.

Zac said goodbye and traipsed off to join the queue – but it had triggered a memory for Leah. When her friends had disappeared, she hadn't gone back to school for close to a month. Things had never quite been the same for her, largely because her mates, the people with whom she hung around, weren't there. Some of the other girls tried to make friends, though Leah was always suspicious of their intent. Did they *actually* want to be friends, or were they trying to get in with the girl everyone knew? Were they going to ask about the *real* story?

There was no widespread email back then, though there had been letters home about children's safety and some sort of mass assembly. It didn't stop kids sneaking out for a smoke on their lunch break, but it was the last time Leah could remember anything close to this level of security and worry.

People were starting to notice Leah. There had always been a low-level of interest around her as the girl who was left after the sleepover. That ramped up at various anniversaries, with even more attention over the past year because of the documentary. Now, with more teenagers missing and bones being discovered, it was going to be too much.

The parent who organised everything had either finished or given up on her TV interview. She was heading across towards Leah with a big smile and wide, hospitable arms. She was eager to welcome her into the road-blocking fold. One false word and Leah would end up on the summer fete committee, in charge of baking cupcakes.

Instead, Leah gave a classic hello-goodbye wave and then turned and hurried in the opposite direction, away from her car. The direct route would have taken her through the protest, so Leah walked fifteen minutes out of her way, before doubling back.

With the almost forgotten day off work, and no plans for the morning, Leah drove aimlessly for a while. If she stopped for too long, she'd end up overthinking why she'd taken the day off. She had a decision to make and the clock was ticking.

By the time she arrived home, wondering how she was going to waste the following few hours, Leah had a message from Jennifer. It named the hotel she and Dylan were in and added 'Nice room'.

There was a clear implication that Leah could head over, though Leah was deliberately trying to put distance between them. The discovery of the kidnap van made it much more likely that Dylan, and therefore Jennifer, was telling the truth – but Leah still wasn't sold.

Then the thought occurred that, if Jennifer was at the hotel, she wouldn't be at the farm. There would be a search going on anyway, following the discovery of those bones – but there was another person to whom Leah could talk.

She drove with purpose, following the now familiar route

out of town and towards Jennifer's house. Leah barely saw another vehicle as she reached the country roads – until she reached the farm itself. The same police car from the other day was blocking the rocky drive by the gate, but a slew of vans with satellite dishes on top were parked along the verge. No reporters were allowed onto the property, though plenty were set up with the police car as the backdrop.

Leah slowed but kept driving. She remembered those satellite trucks and the rows of reporters, filming from slightly different camera angles. Past Jennifer's, but not by far, Leah parked on the verge, next to a large sign that had been nailed to a post. The message of 'NO TRESPASSERS' was impossible to miss as Leah walked past it and headed carefully down a muddied drive towards the scrapyard she'd seen from Dylan's upstairs window.

There wasn't a single vehicle on Charles' farm that looked like it worked. As well as the piles of tyres and the three separate rusting exhausts, there was a front half of an old Mini sitting next to the back half of something else entirely. Other vehicles sat abandoned with windows down, doors open, moss growing on the bonnet, or a combination of all that and more.

Leah walked slowly, sticking to the centre of the driveway and doing her best to appear friendly. When she reached the farmhouse, there was no sign of a bell, so she knocked hard on the door. She waited, taking in the wooden plaque above the door that read 'Garrison Residence'. It was scratched and faded, along with the door and frame itself. Everything could do with a good coat of paint.

After waiting a minute or so, there was no answer, so Leah tried the glass at the side.

At first, she didn't think anyone was home, though when she took a step backwards, the door opened. It happened so abruptly, that Leah yelped with surprise.

'What are you doing here?' Charles snapped. He was in

browny-green trousers with a shirt far too big for him. Like the after photograph in a weight-loss campaign.

'I'm Leah,' she said. 'I'm—'

'I know who you are. What do you want?' His voice was a growl.

'I was wondering if I could talk to you about Jennifer.'

TWENTY-EIGHT

The answer was so direct and short that Leah almost laughed.

'No.'

Charles took a step backwards and put a hand on the door, as if about to close it. 'It's non-stop with you lot, isn't it? The police with their questions, now you. Don't you know what "No trespassers" means? Is it the "No" part you're struggling with?' He waved a hand towards something behind Leah, adding: 'Look at the mess they made.'

When Leah turned, there was certainly a mess – though she didn't think it had been caused by the police.

Charles started to close the door, so Leah spoke quickly. 'What did you mean when you said you weren't surprised Dylan ran off?'

The door froze in place and then reopened a crack.

'I know what it looks like,' Leah added. 'I know I was with Jennifer the other day when you came out – but we aren't really friends. She asked me to help because Dylan was missing. I couldn't say no.'

It did sound, and feel, as if Leah was abandoning the other woman. There was an air of suspicion about the way Charles was looking to her, though she was telling him what he wanted to hear.

The door opened a fraction further and Charles leant on the frame, as if about to step outside once more. 'Why'd she ask you to help?'

'She said she'd thought I would understand because I'd lost people as well.'

Leah could see the recognition in Charles' face. He would have probably read the recent stories about her. He was her dad's age and, if he lived locally back then, it would have been impossible for him to not know her name.

Charles pushed himself up, cupping a hand to shield himself from the sun as he gazed past her towards Jennifer's farm on the other side of the hedge.

'I heard they found him?'

'Last night. But the other two are still missing.'

The man's expression didn't change. He had the sort of face that meant winning the lottery or being told he had incurable cancer would be treated with the same scowl. A second or two passed and then he pushed his door wider. 'You coming in then?'

Leah figured she wasn't going to be asked twice, so passed under his arm and then waited for Charles to close the door.

The inside of his house was little surprise compared to the outside. Random car parts littered the hallway and, though Leah didn't know what much of it was, the wing mirrors, front grille and unattached steering wheel were easy spots.

Charles muttered an irritated 'in there', and Leah ended up in a living room cluttered with piles of football programmes, and at least seven televisions around the perimeter of the room. From the caked-on dust, Leah assumed most – if not all – of them weren't working. The curtains were drawn at both ends of the room, the only light coming from a dim lamp in the corner. There were two individual armchairs, each covered in a sheet.

'I suppose you want tea, or something?'

Leah had paused in the middle of the room, wondering if she should sit. She had a vague recollection of someone at school a long time back, telling her that their grandparent put sheets over everything in an attempt to keep things new.

'I'm not that—'

'I don't have any milk, so you'll have to make do.'

Charles didn't wait for the reply, instead disappearing through the house, banging doors on his way. The sort of person who grumped about doing any job, even when nobody asked them to do it. Every office had one.

Leah's mouth felt powdery and dry, like waking up with a hangover. The house didn't need a simple vacuum, it needed some sort of tornado to deal with the dust.

She did a small loop of the room, stopping to take in the display unit at the back. It was one of those antique wood things so solid it could only be moved with a forklift. A series of frames sat on top – which were the only items in the room that had been dusted at any point in the previous decade. There was one of a young boy sitting on a tractor, legs dangling over the side, one hand shielding his eyes from the sun. A second had the same boy leaning on a shotgun in a way Leah didn't think looked particularly safe. It had 'Boy blows off own head' written all over it. The lad couldn't have been older than seven or eight. In a third photo, the boy was sitting in an old-fashioned race car. A man was standing next to him, wearing overalls that were unzipped to his belly button. A rug of chest hair battled with bronzed skin for attention.

There was a shuffling of movement behind Leah and, when she turned, Charles was standing a pace or so too close. Her instinct was to step away, though there was nowhere to go. He was oblivious to her discomfort anyway, instead handing her a tea, while sloshing hot liquid onto the carpet.

Leah took the cup and scooched it around in her hand to avoid the boiling water.

'Is this you?' she asked, indicating the boy in the photos.

'Who else would it be?'

Leah ignored the grumpy annoyance. 'Is that your dad?' she added, pointing to the man with the half-zipped overalls.

Charles leaned in for a closer look. 'That's James Hunt,' he replied with the irritated air of a person explaining that grass was green.

Leah flinched a fraction. Her father used to talk to her in a similar way, though she didn't want to show that Charles was getting to her.

She pointed to the photo of a young Charles on the tractor. 'Have you always lived on this farm?'

This was apparently a better question, seeing as Charles didn't immediately snap at her. He still had no sense of personal space, stepping around to the point that he more or less barged Leah out of the way. He picked up the photo and held it up for her to see more closely.

'I've never lived anywhere else,' he said – and, for the first time, the edge in his voice was absent. 'Dad used to have a milk float. He and mum would take bottles around town and I'd sit on the back.'

He batted her away from the drawers and opened the one at the top, before hunting through a new pile of photos. The one he thrust at Leah was black and white, showing a milk float sitting on a patch of faded grass at what looked like a summer fete. That was the sort of thing that counted as entertainment back in the day.

'I remember,' Leah said. 'When I was young, I used to wave at the float when I was walking to school.'

In truth she wasn't sure if it was *this* milk float to which she used to wave, but there was definitely one. She might've been five or six.

Charles snapped the photo away and returned it to the drawer, ushering her towards the sheet-covered chairs at the other end of the room.

Leah clasped her tea as she sat, fighting the urge to cough as a dusty cloud puffed around her. Not that Charles noticed.

He sat in the opposite chair. 'It's all long gone,' he said, on a roll now. 'There's loads of history in this farm. I tried to talk to the council about setting up some sort of town museum but they wouldn't know a good idea if it kneecapped them.'

Leah had never heard the turn of phrase before, though she was letting a lot go. 'What sort of history?' she asked.

He was interested now, clearly talking about something in which he was interested: 'This whole area was a bombing target in the nineteen-forties because of the food produced on these farms. This area fed over a million people at one point, so the people who worked here were war heroes.' He paused. 'Dad lived through it but we all used to do bomb shelter drills. This farm was his dad's before him. I've been petitioning the Home Office to get him a posthumous medal for service to the nation – but you never get a reply back.'

A pattern was emerging of a man fruitlessly writing a series of letters and being utterly furious at the lack of enthusiasm for his ideas. Still, the stuff about feeding the nation was something Leah hadn't known. At heart, despite his outward grumpiness, he and Jennifer shared something in the sense that he wanted someone to listen to him.

'Does this all mean you knew Jennifer's dad?'

Charles probably didn't have too many one-on-one conversations – and he certainly didn't like anybody else attempting to steer the subject. His eyebrow twitched and Leah had a sip of her tea in an attempt to show that she appreciated his efforts. In reality, she hadn't wanted the drink in the first place, plus he'd made it without milk and with sugar. It tasted like something that had been left in the cupboard for fifteen years with the lid open.

'Been loads of problems since *she* took it over,' Charles said, nodding towards Jennifer's place. 'No issues with her dad. He was a good bloke. Always used to swap Christmas hampers with him.'

Leah didn't point out that the police were currently digging up the neighbouring property, with the assumption that the 'good bloke' had killed at least one person and buried them in the field.

Charles was still going, having seemingly waited a long time for someone to bring this up: '*She's* got no control. No respect. Doesn't want to listen to anyone.'

Leah nodded along, giving him the platform, though not openly agreeing. It wasn't difficult to see why a younger woman wouldn't want to take advice from a grumpy older man. He was annoyed because he thought he knew better; she was annoyed because she didn't think her farm was any of his business.

Charles had been pressing forward, poking an angry finger towards his neighbour – but, in a moment of self-awareness, he leaned back onto the sheet. 'You probably think I'm an old moaner, don't you?'

'I don't know you,' Leah replied, taking the safe option.

Charles was shaking his head, though his furious momentum had been replaced by something quieter and, perhaps, more reflective. 'It's not just that,' he added. 'That boy is on my land all the time. You let the little things go if the big ones aren't left to rot – but he set off fireworks one time, aiming them at the house. That was back when we'd not had rain for a month or so and everything was dry. He could've sent the whole thing up.'

He waved his hands in the air, making a *whoosh* sound to imitate the fire.

'His mum said nothing of course. That's what parents are

like these days. They all want to be friends with their kids and not have to discipline. She said the fireworks came from somewhere else, even though I watched him do it. The little scrote. She won't hear a word against him.'

Leah could believe the last part, though she wondered if the parenting jibe was fair. At least some of those past methods involved repeatedly belting a child until they did what they were told. It hadn't been *that* long ago.

'They're always playing loud music. I mean, look how far apart we are. How loud does it have to be for me to hear indoors? And the bonfires! It's every week sometimes and I swear they wait until the wind's blowing this way.' He shook his head. 'Nobody wants to listen. The council won't even take my calls any more – and the police are a waste of space. Now they want something and they're here every day. I told 'em to get lost. See how they like it.'

Leah understood his frustration. As part of her job visiting people in the community, Leah heard over and over how neighbours were terrorising each other with loud music, barking dogs, revving engines, motorbikes at stupid times of the morning, and any number of other things. It was true that the council told people to talk to the police, who told people to talk to the council. One big circle of nobody doing anything.

'I heard they got a warrant,' Leah said.

'The cheek of them! Came back with all the papers and then went through all my cars, looking for God knows what. You can't do anything on your own land nowadays. I've been onto Channel Four news, trying to tell them what's been going on. Nobody cares.' Charles threw his hands up in exasperation as he started to work himself up again. 'Have you seen them all digging up the field over there? Who knows what they're looking for!'

'They found bones,' Leah told him, amazed he didn't already know.

Charles had been so animated he was almost out of his seat – but he froze, halfway up, 'They what?'

'There were bones buried in the field.'

He lowered himself back into the chair and scratched his chin, before turning to look in the direction of Jennifer's farm. Not that anything could be seen with the curtains closed.

'They found *bones?* Are you sure?'

'I don't know who they belong to.'

'Huh...' Charles wriggled in his seat, pulling on his sleeve, then his hair. He stood and opened the curtain, sending a flood of light into the room and making Leah wince from its sudden appearance. 'It's her,' he said. 'I'm telling you that right now. She's trouble. I've always said it.' He turned back to Leah, though again pointed a finger in the direction of the neighbouring farm. 'You mark my words, when this is all figured out, everyone will know what she's like.'

TWENTY-NINE

Leah left Charles' farm with an even greater sense of confusion than before. She'd had plenty of her own doubts about Jennifer and Dylan, though it felt a bit much for her neighbour to openly say he thought she was capable of burying human bones in a field.

The satellite trucks and the manic reporters remained unmoved, waiting to see what the police might have to announce. Leah continued into town and almost out the other side, before stopping at the one hotel that didn't look as if it might have a series of health violations hanging over it. Among the two-star chains, with their five-star mice problems, sat a single spa and hotel in the centre of town. It had been built around ten years before, after a good three or four years of local opposition. Nobody ever wanted anything built and then, when it was, everyone shrugged and broadly admitted it was fine.

Leah parked in the hotel grounds and sent Jennifer a message to say she was there. A reply came, telling her not to bother with reception and instead head to the back. Leah followed the directions along a tidy paved path, through a gate marked 'residents only' until she reached a courtyard. There were rows of doors on the surrounding sides, with a pair of benches in the middle of a small green.

Jennifer was sitting on a bench, wearing a towelled white hotel dressing gown. It was the sort of thing that usually sat untouched in the back of a wardrobe. Her hair was wet, knees crossed, and she was flicking porridge oats towards half a dozen pigeons.

She smiled as she spotted Leah and then stretched high. 'I finally slept last night,' she said.

Leah wished the same was true for her.

'I bought these for you,' she replied, passing the other woman a packet of Jammie Dodgers.

Jennifer mumbled a 'thank you' and then tore at the corner, sending a flurry of crumbs onto her lap. She licked her finger and patted the specks.

'I can't leave and you can't get anything here,' she said, indicating the biscuits. 'The police said there are photographers outside the gates.'

Leah hadn't seen them, though it didn't feel worth pointing that out.

'How's Dylan?' she asked, taking a seat on the bench.

'Tired. He was up for breakfast and then went back to bed. The police let him bring his games console from home but he can't get online with it. The Wi-Fi's awful, and he's never known a world without the internet. Other than that, he's as well as you'd expect.'

Jennifer reached into a cereal bowl at her side and tossed another handful of oats towards the birds.

'They wouldn't let us go to the main buffet, so the staff put on a mini one for us,' she said. 'There was way too much to eat but I took everything back to the room anyway.'

Leah smiled kindly. It was that thing about growing up poor. What if another meal *didn't* come along? What if the money ran out? Might as well eat everything that could be fitted in a stomach and take the rest for later. Leah had done something similar for a long time – and, in a way, she was still doing it. Her freezer was full of Deborah's batch cooking.

'Have you seen much of Hannah?' Leah asked.

'She's been around. She said we could order room service and use the minibar as long as we don't go mad.' A pause. 'I wanna go home.'

From the view Leah had of the farm earlier in the day, she wasn't sure that would happen any time soon. It felt as if the police were going to scan and dig up the entire field, just in case.

'Any news on Mo and Alfie?' Leah asked.

'I was going to ask you the same thing.'

'I don't know,' Leah replied.

They sat quietly for a moment – and Leah thought this sort of space must be the difference between those two-star hotels and this type of place. The private residents' garden was quiet and peaceful. She watched as one of the birds finished the oats and then trotted towards Jennifer, as if to ask for more.

'I emailed the school and they said they might send Dylan some work,' Jennifer said. 'I've not told him yet.'

Leah chuckled at that. What did a kid have to do to get out of schoolwork? Even an apparent kidnapping wasn't enough.

A quarter of a century back and her own return to school had been managed differently. Her mum had told Leah she was sick of her being around the house all the time. That wasn't long before things really fell apart and Leah ended up living at Deborah's.

'He admitted the relationship with his teacher,' Jennifer said, from nothing. 'He says she started it about a year ago. She kept him back after class. He thought he was in trouble but she asked what he did after school. She ended up driving him out to car park in the middle of nowhere. I didn't ask for details after that.'

Jennifer shivered at the ick.

'Did he have to tell that to the police?' Leah asked.

'Yes, they talked to him here. They've got all the texts anyway. He's fifteen – and a boy. I don't think I blame him. Her, on the other hand...' The sentence wasn't finished and probably for the better.

Leah had read that Mrs Hawkins was out on bail but no longer staying at her house. At the absolute least, she was going to end up fired and on the sex offenders' registry.

'They should bring back hanging,' Jennifer said, which felt like some people's solution to everything. Burglary? Hang them. Parking outside the lines? Hanging. Walking too slowly? Definitely hang.

Leah didn't reply and they sat watching the birds for a few moments more.

'Hannah gave me the number of a therapist for Dylan,' Jennifer said. She had the air of someone with a lot to share but, until now, nobody to tell.

'Because of his teacher?'

'Everything, I suppose. I don't think he'll be back at school this year. The head already said they can figure something out for his exams but I don't know how that will end up working.'

She stretched, uncrossing and recrossing her legs, showing a bit too much flesh for Leah's liking. Jennifer grabbed another handful of oats and flung them towards the birds. More had appeared over the minutes Leah had been watching and they jumped on top of one another in an attempt to get first dibs.

'Have you heard from Mo's or Alfie's parents?' Leah asked.

'Not directly.' Jennifer was focused on the birds and spoke distantly, as if the missing pair of boys had no connection. 'Hannah said they left a message to say they're glad Dylan's back. They've got a lot of questions but the police are apparently handling that.' She fingered a Jammie Dodger from the packet and nibbled around the edges. 'I think they want to talk to Dylan directly,' she added.

Leah understood that. Everything they would've been told was second- or third-hand. Their sons remained missing and they wanted to hear things for themselves, especially as Dylan had disappeared at the same time.

'Is that going to happen?' Leah asked

The biscuit was now only the jam circle and Jennifer popped it in her mouth. She sucked on it as a way of not replying. Leah had the feeling Jennifer didn't want anyone talking to her son unless it was absolutely necessary. That could be simple protective instincts, or a greater desire to stop him slipping up by telling his story too many times. Leah swerved from believing him to not.

'The police talked to me about the bones this morning,' Jennifer said, changing the subject. 'They've not been able to analyse them too much but they think they date from twenty to thirty years ago.' She paused a beat, removing another biscuit from the packet and holding it in front of her. 'They could be your friends...'

It was almost as if she wanted the bones to be Vicky, Jazz and Harriet, even though Leah knew they weren't.

'Who do you think they belong to?' Leah asked.

Jennifer didn't reply at first. She was focusing on the biscuit, probably considering the answer.

'One of those women Dad brought home,' she said, lowering the Jammie Dodger and not biting it. She didn't sound convincing. 'I keep thinking I should've told someone sooner.'

'You weren't to know for sure.'

From nowhere, Jennifer turned to look at Leah. Her stare was so intense that Leah found herself shrinking away. 'Do you believe in karma?'

'I, um—'

'I know you're gonna think I'm some hippy weirdo, with the healer and now this – but I wonder about the whole what-goes-around-comes-around thing. Maybe what happened with Dylan is payback for whatever Dad did?'

'I don't think—'

But Jennifer was on a roll: 'If you don't believe that, then bad people get away with doing whatever, don't they?'

The stare continued for a couple more seconds until Jennifer returned her attention to the birds. She popped the biscuit into her mouth and bit it in half.

Leah *did* believe in fate, though she didn't think it was the same as karma. There had been times in her life when she felt guided towards an inevitable outcome. If it hadn't been for that, things would have been very different with Vicky, Jazz and Harriet.

'You can't think about it like that,' Leah said. 'This is all separate. Whoever took Dylan couldn't have known there were bones on your farm. It's unrelated.'

Jennifer didn't reply, and seemingly wasn't convinced.

The conversation had gone in a direction Leah hadn't anticipated. From her talks with Charles and Jennifer, she wasn't sure she'd achieved anything. She still had no idea whether Dylan had invented his story of an abductor. She certainly had no clue about the location of the two missing boys, or whose bones were in the field.

Leah stood and stretched, with various body parts creaking and cricking. She had massages in town once a month from a woman with thumbs like mallets. Every time she had one, it felt like a luxury she didn't deserve. Something by which her younger self would be perplexed. Either way, it felt overdue – and the lack of sleep wasn't helping.

'I've got to go,' Leah said.

Jennifer stood abruptly, still clasping half a biscuit. Her features had slipped into disappointment. 'Oh. I thought you might stay a bit longer. I can get free teas and coffees at the bar, if you want anything?'

'I can't,' Leah replied. 'I've taken today off work and I have things to do.'

'Like what?'

It could have been a rude question, considering Leah hadn't volunteered the information first time around. Despite the time spent together, she also wasn't sure they were actually friends.

But the wasted morning, the conflicted ideas on who was telling the truth, and those missing boys had clarified one thing for Leah. There was one demon in her past from which she wouldn't run.

'It's my dad's wedding,' Leah replied.

THIRTY

Leah went home and changed into what was more or less her work clothes. She wore dark trousers and a dark jacket, with a light blue shirt, after remembering that it was a wedding after all. Only psychopaths and brides wore white, though sometimes they were one and the same.

The town's register office was essentially a door at the back of the town hall. There were remnants of sodden rainbow confetti underneath a large 'DO NOT THROW CONFETTI' sign. Someone had scrawled 'Don't do it' in black biro on the sign listing the opening hours. If Leah's own experience of marriage was anything to go by, the graffiti writer knew what they were on about.

The inside of the office had crematorium vibes. A row of neat chairs was against a wall, as soft organ music buzzed in the background. Someone with a painted-on smile asked if Leah was there for the 'Pearce party' and the sound of Leah's own last name in a place such as this felt wrong.

Leah barely got out an answer before a delighted squeal sounded from a line of chairs around the corner. Leah had missed them at first but a blonde woman in a cream dress was on her feet, arms welcoming and wide.

'You came?! I was hoping you would. I know you said you had a lot on but it's brilliant you made it. I was just saying a minute ago that you could be on your way and here you are.' She turned towards the man in an ill-fitting suit, who hadn't stood. 'Wasn't I just saying that she could be on her way?'

Mandy was the sort of person for whom the word 'bubbly' was invented. Her relentless positivity and, well, niceness was borderline exhausting. She was impossible to dislike and the reason Leah had come.

Leah allowed the other woman to hug her and then nodded to her father. He nodded back and that was as emotive as they got. He was a piece of work, after all.

'You look lovely,' Leah said, talking to Mandy.

The other woman took a step back and brushed the non-existent creases from her dress. 'That's so kind of you. I know it's neither of our first times, so I didn't want to go over the top. I found this in the Oxfam in town. It was hidden at the back of a rail. Only forty quid, if you can believe that. Fitted perfectly.' She turned and pointed to another woman, who was sitting on the row of chairs. 'Gloria was with me and tried to haggle them down – but I didn't mind paying it. You only get married twice, after all!'

Mandy laughed at her joke, and Gloria joined in. It felt as if Mandy had been telling it for weeks to anyone who'd listen.

'We don't need another witness,' Mandy added, once she'd stopped laughing. 'I knew you'd be here but we did have a backup plan. Harry lives next door and he said he'd do it. You might know him because his daughter Lucy works at the car wash in town and she says she once did a Zumba class with you?'

Leah nodded along, as she often did in conversations with Mandy. The other woman had a seemingly compulsive need to link every person she'd ever met to every other person. Forget Kevin Bacon with his six degrees, Mandy would have it down to two at most.

As Mandy talked, Leah looked past her, towards her father. He was sitting towards the front of his seat, elbows resting on his knees. She didn't think she'd ever seen him in a suit, though he'd likely worn one for his multitude of court appearances. He'd shaved and looked a little younger than the only time Leah had seen him in the past two decades or so. That had been in prison around a year before, when he was nearing the end of his sentence following a lifetime of crime. He had been a dick then and Leah didn't doubt he was still one now. She couldn't understand what Mandy saw in him. They had met when Mandy had been writing letters to prisoners.

Seemingly following Leah's gaze, Mandy turned to look at her husband-to-be. She raised an eyebrow, like a mother silently telling a child not to jump in the mud.

He stood and crossed, forcing a smile that didn't suit him.

'Thanks for coming,' he said, which was probably the only time he'd said such a thing to Leah. She returned it with a narrow smile that she didn't mean.

'How was your journey over?' Mandy asked. 'We were worried because of those roadworks out by the Shell garage. They've been doing alternating lanes for the last week, so...'

Leah tuned out. Impossible to dislike but also impossible to spend much time around. Mandy had an innate ability to talk non-stop without actually saying anything. Leah gave a few 'yeah, I know' replies, as Mandy talked about the weather, the bike lane plans in town, how they hit every red light on the way over, and how awful everything was around those poor boys.

Leah's father had long since returned to his chair, while fiddling with what seemed to be a very itchy suit. It looked like something he'd had for a long time, probably the sort of seventies thing that was more flammable than petrol. Get within five metres of a lit match and up it would go.

As Mandy talked about how Alfie's mum's cousin's friend once lived three doors away from her, a head popped out from the nearest door.

'We're ready for you,' she said.

Leah's dad was instantly on his feet, striding towards the room. Gloria had been hanging around, chipping in with her thoughts about the diversions, roadworks, bike lanes, red lights, and the rest. She clapped her hands together and squealed in gleeful anticipation.

Mandy suddenly seemed nervous. She spun on the spot, still brushing the invisible creases of her dress. 'I guess it's time,' she announced.

The office itself had a table at the front, plus rows of four chairs on either side of a central aisle. There was space for twenty or so guests to sit, plus a handful more to stand – though Mandy and Paul had only themselves plus their two witnesses. The room had that freshly vacuumed, air-freshener vibe, with a maroon carpet and soft red seats.

Leah had never been to a register office wedding before. There had been a friend's at a church, a colleague's at an old water mill, a different friend's in a giant marquee at the back of a pub. Everyone had been lashed at that one by the time the bride got anywhere near the venue.

Her own had been in the restaurant annex of a country hotel. There was a bay window, where silhouetted photos were taken of her and her ex saying vows neither of them kept.

Him especially.

There was no preamble to this ceremony. The registrar checked everyone supposed to be there was present – and then they were into the vows.

Leah sat on one side of the aisle, Gloria on the other. Mandy was shaking as she stood next to Leah's father. She stumbled over her words, apologising after each time, as the registrar calmly said it was fine.

Leah's dad was gruff and direct with his vows. When asked if he took Mandy to be his lawfully wedded wife, he replied 'Yes', before correcting to 'I do.'

Then it was done.

Mandy began crying as they were declared husband and wife. Gloria leaped into action with a crumpled packet of tissues from her bag. There were the formalities as they signed the register, with Leah carefully printing her own name in block capitals. Her job was listed as Community Support Worker, and it all felt a bit final. One label that would forever sum her up in the moment, as if no changes could ever be made.

Leah saw her dad's name listed alongside Mandy's, and it was impossible not to think of her actual mother. Her real mum. It wasn't as if she'd been a good parent, though Leah suspected many of her failings were down to her choice of husband. It had been more than twenty years since she'd killed herself and now, all this time on, Leah had a new mum – if only on paper.

The happy couple were doing a good job of hiding it. Mandy was crying so much, she couldn't speak, while Leah's father looked as indifferent as if a cashier had asked if he wanted to round up for charity. They kissed the briefest of kisses, like reluctant child with a grandmother on Christmas morning, then held hands as they walked back the way they'd come.

'I didn't want to make a big deal,' Mandy said, through the sobs. 'I've made some sandwiches at home and got some sausage rolls from Tesco. The nice ones, not the value ones. There are some Mr Kiplings as well. I know it's not a wedding cake but you can't beat a French Fancy, can you?' She paused for breath. 'We'd love to have you over.'

Leah wanted to say no. She couldn't face being around her

father much more, and the inevitable talk about weather would drag on until the sun extinguished itself.

But Mandy was so nice. A better person than Leah and, without question, a better person than her father. Perhaps something about Jennifer and karma had stuck, because Leah figured Mandy was going to be in her life, regardless of whether she'd chosen it.

'OK,' Leah replied. 'I just have to make a couple of calls first.'

THIRTY-ONE

Zac was heading to Deborah's after school. He had started doing so when he was younger and Leah was at work – but now it was the routine. It meant whatever he wanted for tea, some sort of glorious dessert, and free rein to watch YouTube, or play games. There had been vague notions that he could go to the wedding, though there was no relationship between him and his grandfather. Deborah was a grandmother figure for him and Leah had no idea if, or how, Mandy would end up fitting into that.

Those were questions for another day.

In the present, Leah dutifully headed around the now notorious roadworks outside the Shell garage, across to Mandy's house. It was a classic two-bed semi-detached, five minutes' walk from the house in which Leah had grown up. One of those council houses built to withstand a tsunami, and then sold off by the government in the eighties for the price of a weekly big shop.

The inside was as Leah would have guessed. The walls were lined with trinkets and tat. There were ceramic teapots and commemorative plates; some sort of coronation spoon set and what looked like a complete collection of *Buffy the Vampire Slayer* figurines in a cabinet. There wasn't a single wall that wasn't covered with some print, or display.

Leah had met Mandy a handful of times in the run-up to the wedding. Those had been attempts to make it less awkward that a stranger was about to be her stepmother – and had always happened in cafés. Leah had never been to her house.

It only now dawned on her that this was also to be her father's home. He'd been living in the house since leaving prison, and still had conditions for his release. He was, once again, living in the same town as Leah. Five minutes' walk from where she grew up. Fifteen minutes from where she now lived. She could run into him anywhere.

A table was set up at the back of the living room, with a spread of food that screamed Britain. There was a bowl of ready salted crisps, some tidy triangle cheese sandwiches on one side, with ham and tomato on the other. The promised Mr Kiplings saw twenty French Fancies arranged in a neat square.

'I didn't know what people might like,' Mandy said, to her pair of guests – plus her new husband, who had arranged himself on the sofa. 'I have invited the neighbours but, um...'

The glance to Leah's father betrayed something she had never expressed out loud to Leah. Paul Pearce had been in prison for twenty or so years. He'd killed a person – and nobody wanted to live next door to that.

'There's no alcohol,' Mandy said. 'I know you're driving anyway but Paul's got to see his probation officer in the morning, so I've told him he can't drink the night before.' She waited a moment for him to chip in and, when he didn't, she called across: 'Isn't that right, dear?'

There was a mumble of acknowledgement, though little more.

Not for the first time, Leah wondered what Mandy saw in him. Her father was tugging at his suit again, creating enough static to power the television he probably wanted to be watching. The aggression with which Leah grew up had been replaced by whatever this was. He no longer seemed frightening, just boring – which was an improvement.

Gloria had disappeared off to the toilet and had either done a runner, or was dealing with some sort of IBS, because she hadn't been seen in ten minutes. That left Mandy and Leah in the kitchen together. Mandy was fussing around, offering drinks, and showing off a new milk frother she'd bought. 'Bit of a wedding present to myself,' she added, which left Leah wondering whether she should have bought them a gift. What could a person buy for an abusive father? It would've been something for Mandy.

As Leah was feigning interest in the frother, she realised Mandy was a step closer than she had been.

'I know about you and your dad,' Mandy said, though Leah doubted she did. Not really. Not all of it. 'I know what he did, or bits of what he did. That he wasn't a good dad. I'm not expecting you to forget any of that, nor should you. I just...' Mandy tailed off and it felt as if she'd forgotten something she'd rehearsed. 'What I'm trying to say is that I'm glad you're the bigger person.'

She reached out a hand that hovered between them and then she touched Leah gently on the upper arm.

'I know I've said this before but I don't want to replace your mum. I'm not expecting you to call me anything other than Mandy, or Mand. I just want to say that I'm around and I'm here if you need anything. You can call or text, or come round. And, with Zac, I know you're being careful with him and your dad. I understand all that – but the offer is there if you want to build bridges. Or not. Whatever is comfortable for you.'

It had all come out in typical Mandy fashion. The words blurred into one another, as if she couldn't get them out of her mouth quickly enough. It was endearing, though. Leah had no idea how to feel about the relative newcomer in her life – but kind people who bought twenty French Fancies to feed, at best, four people, should probably be welcomed.

'Thank you,' Leah said, which underplayed things, though she wasn't sure what else to say. 'We'll see how things play out.' She tried to think of something better, though nothing came, other than: 'Thanks for the invite.'

Mandy was close to tears again and grabbed a sheet of kitchen towel from the holder. She dabbed her eyes and talked about how it had been a lovely day. 'Just what we wanted,' she insisted, although there had been no evidence that Leah's father had invested in any of it. 'I did talk to him last night,' Mandy said, nodding towards the living room and lowering her voice. 'I was wondering if there might be something you and he had common ground on. Maybe a common interest? I'm not saying you should spend time together. It's just... he's been reading a lot about fishing recently, for instance. He used to be into it when he was young. I know it's probably not your thing – but maybe there's something that *is* your thing. Something you can maybe talk about together?'

'We'll see,' Leah said, which is what she used to tell her son when he was much younger, and would lose the plot when she told him 'no'.

At that, Gloria blundered back into the kitchen with the flustered air of a person who'd just spent fifteen minutes in the toilet and needed to tell someone about it. She eyed Mandy, looking past Leah, and saying 'Can you give us a minute?' without actually saying it.

Leah got the hint and sauntered back into the main room. She picked at a cheese sandwich and then took one of the cakes. If Zac had come, he'd have polished off the lot by himself.

As the sound of two women talking in hushed tones seeped from the kitchen, there was little else for it. Leah crossed to the other end of the living room and sat in the armchair, facing her father on the sofa. It was the first time they'd been one-on-one since prison the year before.

Leah had thought about that meeting a lot since it had happened. Their first contact in two decades had involved her accusing him of something he knew nothing about. Something that she knew more about than he did. He'd been uncooperative but, perhaps, in that one instance, he had reason.

Not that she'd tell him that.

'What did you think?' he asked. He was still fidgeting, tugging at his jacket and hitching up the trousers.

'I think she's way too good for you,' Leah replied.

He snorted and raised an eyebrow. 'I'm not going to argue with that.'

Her dad wriggled some more and muttered 'damn thing' under his breath.

'Is that your old court suit?' Leah asked.

'It was what I was wearing when I got sent down,' he replied. 'They give you all your stuff back when you get out, so they had it kept more or less as new. It's a bit big but I didn't want to buy a new one.'

His honest reply to what she'd meant as a partial dig made Leah feel a little silly. She didn't think he'd noticed the snark and he certainly hadn't risen to it.

Or maybe he had.

She felt him searching for eye contact that she steadfastly refused to let him have.

'I am different,' he said quietly.

'I expect anyone who's been in prison for most of the past thirty years to be different than when they went in.'

He didn't react which was probably worse than getting angry.

Leah's father was the man who had punched her mother in the face in front of her. He'd broken his wife's arm, leaving her to set it with a pillowcase. He had constantly walked out, got himself into trouble, and then returned when it suited him. He'd glassed a man in a pub, and gone to prison for assault. He'd killed someone drink driving, while already banned for a previous offence. Leah knew who he was – and she had grown into a person able to cope with his cruelty. What she couldn't face was... this.

'You being at the wedding meant a lot to Mandy,' he said.

'What about you?'

Leah was avoiding his gaze. She used to barricade her door with her bed in case he came looking for her. There was an escape route planned: out the window, onto the shed, and away. It's why she still walked into places and immediately clocked the doors and windows. She was always aware of the closest exit.

'It's too late for me,' he replied. 'Nothing I can do now changes anything from before.'

'You could say sorry.'

He thought on it for a second. 'Would that make it better?'

Leah didn't answer, because of course it wouldn't. Like attempting to clean up a North Sea oil spill with a toilet roll. They were so far past apologies – and Leah didn't want one anyway.

Father and daughter sat across from one another in silence. Two metres at most but continents.

'I messed it up,' he continued after a while. 'All of it. Sometimes I think about being a kid 'round here, me and my mates out messing about near the farms. Fishing, scrumping, getting into all sorts of boltholes. I somehow went from that to... *this*.'

It was a very different attitude compared to the man she'd met in a prison mess hall all those months ago. The one and only time she had visited him. He'd been combative then, his usual self. Either something had changed since then, or he'd taken acting classes. Leah couldn't figure out if he was after her sympathy, or if it was genuine self-reflection. She didn't know whether she cared.

It was probably the first time he'd ever talked about being young to her. He'd been a perpetual old man and, in some ways, he looked fresher now than he had during his days of terror.

'Where was all that?' Leah found herself asking.

She readied herself for a withering reply about how he'd already said but she wasn't listening properly. Or that she should already know. Instead he pointed towards the window and described the route out of town that led past Jennifer's and Charles' farms.

'I've been spending quite a bit of time there this last weekend,' Leah told him. 'It's where those three boys went missing.'

'Oh...' He thought on that for a moment, though his mind was elsewhere. 'We used to go to the woods and build rafts to get across the river. I used to know that area so well.'

Leah wasn't sure how the connection came, other than that she had sat in his living room earlier in the day. That, and he would be around the same age as Leah's father. 'Do you know Charles Garrison?' Leah asked.

'Huh...' Leah's dad mused for a moment. 'Been a long time since I heard that name.'

'But you know him?'

'I suppose I did. His dad owned one of the farms that backed onto the woods. He used to let us drive cars on his land, even when we were thirteen or fourteen.' A pause. 'Not Charles, though. Charlie. He'd come fishing with us sometimes. I wonder what happened to him.'

'He still lives there,' Leah replied.

'Does he?'

Her father appeared genuinely surprised, even though it was a town from which so few left. Leah hadn't – even though she had more reason than anyone to get away. She'd never quite been able to figure out why.

Any moment they were having was gone as Mandy entered the room, phone in hand. 'Have you seen the news?' she asked, not hiding her surprise. 'They've arrested someone. Something to do with the missing boys.'

THIRTY-TWO

Leah found relief in sitting in somebody else's kitchen. Daniel sat cradling a mug that had 'Honk For Hedgehogs' embossed on the side. He was in jogging bottoms and a top that had at least three different stains splashed across the front.

He saw the funny side, pointing to them one at a time. 'That's from where Isaac threw up on me this morning; this one's from Pam, who threw up just after I'd cleaned up her brother. This other one is from where I dropped spaghetti on myself.'

'You were eating spaghetti for breakfast?'

He yawned. 'A neighbour dropped round some meals yesterday.' A pause. 'No, the day before. They've been in the fridge because I haven't had time to cook for myself. I was going to do toast but there's no bread – and the spaghetti was right there.' That got another yawn.

Daniel's wife had died in childbirth, leaving him with the devastation of losing his wife, plus twins to take care of. Leah visited him twice a week as part of her job. She would see how he was doing and usually ended up helping out with various jobs.

'Is there anything in that mug?' Leah asked him.

Daniel seemed bemused by the question, before checking the cup. 'Oh... I must've finished it.'

Leah had assumed as much from the way he'd been holding it since she arrived. He yawned again, so she filled the kettle and flicked it on, then started washing up the plastic bowls and cups in the sink. He told her not to, that he was about to – but it looked far more like he was about to fall asleep.

'Was it a bad night?' Leah asked.

'I swear they do shifts. One of them's awake – and, when I finally get them back to sleep, the other wakes up. I don't know if it's better like that, or with two of them up at the same time.' He nodded towards the tablet on the counter. 'They're asleep now.' The screen showed a camera image of an unmoving pair of cribs.

Leah told him he could wait in the living room and she'd bring him in a tea. He made vague suggestions that he was fine, that he'd make the drinks for her, though he protested with the vigour of a starving man being offered a KitKat. By the time Leah had finished washing up, made the drink and carried it through, Daniel was curled up like an ageing cat, asleep in an armchair.

Leah tried to edge back out of the room but a creaking floorboard gave her away – and Daniel sputtered awake with a surprised 'Huh'.

He spotted the drink on the table and unfurled his limbs, before the panic filled his features.

'They're still asleep,' Leah told him. 'You were only out for a few minutes.'

'Oh, right...' He blinked half a dozen times and then noticed the clock on the wall. 'I think I've got a Tesco delivery coming today. The bank holiday pushed everything back.' He fumbled, looking for a phone that he eventually found wedged into the cushion on which he was sitting. He jabbed at the screen and then said: 'It's Wednesday, right?'

'Exactly.'

He yawned and apologised. It was the most tired Leah had seen him. 'It's not usually this bad,' he said.

Leah was standing over him. 'I was about to tell you that I'm impressed. The house is clean and the cupboards and fridge have plenty of food for the twins.'

She'd barely spoken but his bottom lip was bobbing, eye twitching. 'Right. Yeah. I thought you were gonna— Yeah, I mean I have been trying. It's just...'

It was a lot.

Leah told him she was going to recommend him for a local grant that would allow him to get a paid cleaner once a week. There was minor panic in his eyes until she told him the paperwork was already done. He simply needed to check it over and sign. She said there was another scheme similar to meals on wheels, though she wasn't certain he was eligible. She'd check the criteria and come back to him by Friday.

Daniel said his mum was coming down at the weekend but that she hadn't been able to get time off work. 'I don't like asking her, either,' he added. 'She's going to take them for a couple of days.'

'What are you going to do?'

'Sleep.'

He said it deadpan but then started laughing with such mania that he couldn't stop. He was holding his stomach from laughing so hard and it took a coughing fit for him to calm down. If anyone deserved two days off to sleep, it was him.

Another tablet was on the windowsill and he eyed the

sleeping twins and then yawned. It proved infectious, setting Leah off.

'Everyone's talking about the missing boys,' he said, his gaze flicking upwards. 'The nurse came on Monday and she was saying she's not going to let her kids walk to school anymore.' He puffed out a long breath. 'It's about the only thing I've been following. You've got to have something to keep an eye on when you're up at three in the morning. Did you hear they'd arrested someone?'

It was a testament to Daniel being understandably absorbed in his own hectic world that he thought this might be news. As it was, everyone in town was obsessed with the arrest from the night before. The person hadn't been officially named, which inevitably meant everyone online knew exactly who he was. Someone had taken photos from their bedroom window of a man being bundled out of a neighbouring house in the nearest town. The man looked like the person Dylan had described at the police station, in that he had short darkish hair. Beyond that, who knew?

From what people had been saying online, he worked as a security guard at the gym next to the retail park. It was the big one near the bowling alley and cinema, that everybody seemed to hate. It was frequently in the news whenever pregnant women, or blokes who'd lost a limb in a catastrophic work accident, unsuccessfully tried to cancel their membership. Every few months, someone seemed to end up being asked to download a form and fill it in using a pen that had ink in a specific shade of black, which could only be seen if there was a new moon. They'd have to send one copy to head office, hand deliver another to a PO Box number at a trading estate on Guernsey, do the Macarena for a manager, and then verbally give their notice, in Esperanto, to a man in a Guy Fawkes costume, who only appeared if a person really believed in him.

Either way, if the gym had a PR manager, that person's week had just got significantly worse.

With the Facebook comments section, it was difficult to know what was true and what was actionable libel. From what Leah had seen, there did appear to be a general consensus that more than one person thought he was creepy around the gym. Also plenty of claims that it was his van that had been found.

Daniel was eyeing the tablet on the windowsill, as his twins – mercifully – continued to sleep. 'Makes you think, doesn't it?' he said. 'You just... drop them off at a friend's house, and then...'

Leah never brought up what had happened to her friends around the people with whom she worked. Most were locals and knew anyway. When it came to Daniel, neither of them had ever raised it. There was a chance he wasn't aware. A part of Leah always enjoyed that uncertainty.

Regardless, considering the new father had a lot on his plate already, the concern over missing children that weren't his was something he could probably do without.

They talked in circles for a while, though Leah had the sense Daniel would probably be better off asleep. She told him she had to get back to the office, and had him sign the papers for the cleaning grant, before heading on her way.

Leah was almost off the street when she realised she was driving past rows of green wheelie bins. She stopped and looked behind to where Daniel's bin was very much at the side of his house. There was a moment in which she considered texting him, though figured there was a good chance he was already asleep. She hoped he was. Instead, Leah parked and walked back along the road, where she dragged his heavy, full, bin away from the side of the house and left it on the kerb.

By the time Leah got back to her car, she had somehow missed three calls. All were from Jennifer, who knew Leah had gone back to work. As Leah was about to message and ask if everything was all right, her phone rang again. This time she answered it.

'Are you free?' Jennifer asked, by way of a greeting.

'Um... maybe.'

'The police are on the way to the hotel,' she said. 'They've ID'd the bones.'

THIRTY-THREE

Leah was technically on work time but could always fudge things when it came to being in exact places at exact times. It wasn't the sort of job with firm clock-in and -out procedures. Plus, her manager was always nipping out early to pick up his daughter from nursery, so it all broadly worked out.

Jennifer said that the police wanted to tell her in person what they had discovered with the bones – and had called to ask where she was. They were coming from a neighbouring town, with an imminent arrival. She wanted someone to be there when she was told, for which it was hard to blame her.

It took Leah fifteen minutes to get into town, having been delayed by those roadworks near the Shell garage. She should probably have paid better attention to Mandy the previous day and taken an alternate route. Leah parked in the same spot at the hotel as the day before and headed around to the gate at the side of the main building.

The previous day, she had walked confidently past the 'residents only' sign, but, this time, a man in a suit was polishing the sign itself. As Leah went to pass, he held out an arm and asked which room she was in.

Leah realised a moment too late that she should have said something like 'twenty-one', though she'd already replied: 'I'm not.'

'In that case, I'm going to have to ask you to leave.' His lips smiled, his eyes said she could go screw herself.

'My friend's in that garden,' Leah said, pointing past him.

'If that's true, you'll have to go through reception.'

He was the sort of man who looked like he should be holding a clipboard at all times.

'If I could just—'

'I don't *want* to call security,' he replied, with a tone that made it sound an awful lot as if it would make his day to call security.

There was little point in arguing, so Leah headed back to the front of the hotel. She waited in a line for twenty minutes, only for the woman on reception to tell her to head right through, along with a set of directions and a code for the internal door.

By the time Leah reached the communal garden, Jennifer was sitting by herself on the bench in the centre. She was out of the hotel dressing gown this time, instead wearing jeans, with a T-shirt that read Rowdy Roddy Piper on the front.

'Have the police been?' Leah asked.

That got a spacy nod. 'Just left,' Jennifer said. 'They've asked me to go in and make a statement on camera but I told them I needed a few hours. Someone's going to come back to pick me up later.'

It was big. Leah could see it in the other woman's distant stare. She wondered if the bones somehow *did* belong to her friends. That was surely as big as it could get.

But, no. It was even more shocking than that.

'Why do they need a statement?' Leah asked. 'What did they find?'

'Mum,' Jennifer replied softly. 'The bones belong to Mum.'

THIRTY-FOUR

'I thought your mum walked out?'

Leah wished the words hadn't come out but it was too late for that.

Jennifer didn't respond anyway.

'They found your mum's bones?' Leah tried. It didn't feel believable, but so much of the past few days had been the same. Unlikely, barely comprehensible, revelations – one after the other.

Jennifer was nodding, though her gaze was somewhere else. 'They told me they need to do a second round of tests on the bones that's stricter than the first, so it's not a hundred per cent.'

'So it might not be her...?'

'They said it's unlikely to be anyone else. I think the second round of tests is a legal thing.'

Leah tried to remember what Jennifer had said about her mum. It was definitely that she'd walked out and was not coming back. Something about an affair.

'Are you glad it's not your friends?' Jennifer asked.

Leah realised the other woman was looking to her and, in

her moment of shock, she had forgotten to look surprised. *Knowing* the bones didn't belong to Vicky, Jazz and Harriet was one thing; *acting* like it another. There was a flicker of something in Jennifer's face, though Leah couldn't read her.

'I suppose it might have been better if it was them,' Leah replied, carefully. 'At least everyone would know what happened.'

Jennifer had been eyeing her but seemingly accepted the reply as she turned away. They sat quietly for a minute or so, listening to someone bumping a suitcase along the crumbling tarmac of the car park.

'I don't know what to think,' Jennifer said. 'Dad said Mum walked out and I suppose I didn't really question it. People are going to ask why I didn't, aren't they?'

It was a fair question, although Leah knew the answer. The majority of people grew up in calm households with parents who more or less got on. If not, there was some sort of support network, with grandparents, or friends. That hadn't been Leah's experience and it didn't sound like it was Jennifer's. Things that seemed bizarre to most could be everyday happenings to others. Leah's father had walked out on them dozens of times, which wasn't to count the occasions he had been arrested. If either of her parents had left and not come back, a young Leah would not have been surprised.

'How old were you when it happened?' Leah asked.

'A bit older than Dylan.'

That would've been around the same time that everything happened with Leah and the sleepover, give or take.

'Mum and I never really got on,' Jennifer said. 'She was always saying I needed to try harder at school, that sort of thing. She was always getting at me but I think...' She stopped and chewed on her top lip thoughtfully for a moment. 'I think she just wanted me to have a way out of the farm. She probably felt stuck and didn't want that for me.'

Leah stretched and took the other woman's hand again. She still didn't know whether she trusted her but the moment felt real. Jennifer allowed it to happen and squeezed Leah's fingers gently.

'She'd argue with Dad all the time and say, "I didn't sign up for this." She told me more than once – to my face – that I was a mistake but maybe she was *also* talking about the farm? About him. She'd ended up with a life she didn't want. There was definitely a time when she wanted to sell and move – but he didn't. Going home from school always felt like walking into a warzone.'

A chill slipped down Leah's back because she knew that. The best days were the ones in which she was ignored and could be alone in her room. The worst was when she'd get through the front door to find smashed furniture, or her mother bleeding and pretending she'd slipped.

'You should tell the police that,' Leah said. 'I'm sure they'll understand.'

That was a guess, although, when it came to someone like Leah's liaison officer, she *had* understood. It had turned into a twenty-plus-year friendship.

Jennifer was nodding.

'They're going to ask whether you tried to see your mum after you were told she left,' Leah added.

Jennifer released Leah's hand and hmmed quietly to herself. It felt like she'd considered the same. 'It's hard to remember how you feel in a moment. When I was fifteen, I was so angry at her. She'd been saying for years that she regretted having me. Then she left and, to be honest, it was better for a while. Dad did his own thing and left me to do mine. But there was no more shouting, or things being thrown. Nobody telling me I was a mistake. I assumed she'd come back at some point, or at least call. It wasn't like she left a number. I thought that if she didn't want to contact me, then why would I want to contact her? Then time passes. It had been a month and I'd not heard anything. Then two. Three. Suddenly, you've moved on.'

Leah knew that too. There was a time after she went to live with Harriet's parents that it all started to feel normal. It hadn't taken that long. Trying to explain that to someone who'd lived in a happy home growing up was hard. The idea that a parent might not be an important part of a child's life baffled them.

'Did your mum take her things when she left?' Leah asked, before immediately correcting herself. 'When your dad *said* she left?'

'I didn't really go in their room,' Jennifer replied. 'Dad said she'd packed some of her clothes but it's not like I went into their wardrobe to check. About six or seven months later, we took some bin bags of her things to the charity shop. Dad said she wasn't coming back, which seemed obvious by then.'

There was truth in that, considering the woman was buried at the end of the field.

Leah wondered if Jennifer knew what was coming. This was the sort of thing they made documentaries about. If it wasn't for the pair of boys still missing, this would be the biggest story in the area for the next month.

Jennifer pushed herself up and stretched her neck. Someone had come out of one of the other rooms that opened onto the courtyard. He started striding towards the door that was signposted as the route to the gym and sauna – but stopped when he saw the two women. He stared in the way people do when trying to figure out if they know a person. When Leah matched his gaze, he turned and continued through the door.

Jennifer had taken a few steps away from the bench and stretched a second time. 'The beds here are so uncomfortable,' she said. 'Plus why are hotel pillows always so bad? Doesn't anybody notice they're flat?'

It felt more of an explanation for stretching her neck than a conversation starter. The sort of thing Mandy would talk about for an hour straight.

'What do you actually feel about the bones being found?' Leah asked.

Jennifer blinked with surprise, as if she hadn't considered something as basic as feelings. 'Nothing,' she said, before correcting herself almost instantly. 'Not *nothing*. But it's very new. It's not like I've spent the last twenty-odd years wondering about her. I barely remember her. I assumed she'd abandoned me.'

'But she hadn't...?'

That got a slow nod of what looked like realisation. 'I suppose...'

There was a moment of quiet as Jennifer returned to the bench. She rolled her head in a circle while holding onto her neck.

'Do the police think it was your dad who killed her?' Leah asked.

'Who else?'

Leah didn't have an answer to that, although Jennifer seemed remarkably at ease. 'It's just... if your dad killed your mum, it's a big deal. It's really big. People are going to talk about this for years. You'll never escape it.'

Jennifer opened her mouth to reply but seemingly thought better of it. Nobody knew what she was talking about better than Leah.

'How did *your* mum die?' Jennifer asked after a while.

It was probably a natural reply, though it caught Leah off guard.

'She killed herself,' Leah said. 'Jumped in front of a train.'

It had been a long time and there was so little emotion in her voice. Leah couldn't remember how she'd felt at the time. Not upset, probably resigned. It felt like something that was always going to happen.

'Oh...' Jennifer replied.

It was an enormous understatement, although Leah often heard the same when people asked. If they didn't already know, nobody expected such a reply.

'I dream about it sometimes,' Leah added. 'Usually the train driver. I wonder what he saw and how he felt.'

There had been times in which Leah had considered looking him up. He'd been named at the inquest, so it wouldn't have been too difficult. Each time, Leah stopped herself because what would *he* get from such a conversation? Not everything was about her.

'Why did she do it?' Jennifer asked.

Leah thought on that. How to sum up an adult lifetime of abuse and mental health issues in a simple sentence? She'd been a terrible mother, though not all of it was her fault.

'She had problems,' Leah replied. 'Depression, mainly – but Dad used to beat her up. She'd always take him back, regardless of what he did. The quietest times were when he was in prison.'

Leah knew it was all true. She had lived it – and yet it was hard to square with the boring man who'd sat opposite her the day before.

'I looked on Facebook earlier,' Jennifer said, changing the subject.

That sounded ominous.

'People reckon that Dylan knows more than he's saying. Even Alfie's mum replied to something about it. I texted her and asked her to delete it but she ignored me.'

This was something that Dylan and a teenage Leah shared in common – though the accusations against her mercifully pre-dated social media.

'She's hurting,' Leah said. 'Her son's been missing for five days and she's lashing out at anyone she can.'

The explanation appeared to spur an idea with Jennifer, if it hadn't been there already. 'Can you talk to her?' Jennifer asked. 'I'll give you her number. You can say that Dylan's telling the truth...'

She was pleading, although, with Leah's doubt and suspicion, it was hard to know if this was a natural attempt to protect a son, or something more sinister.

'I can't do that,' Leah said. 'She doesn't know me.'

'That's why it would mean a lot coming from you!'

It felt like an insult, even though it wasn't. As if Jennifer had called on Leah specifically to deal with these sorts of things. Perhaps she had? Leah had been wondering how and why she'd allowed herself to end up how she had. Deep down, she knew. It was the guilt that had been building her entire adult life. Her fifteen-year-old self felt like a different person and, in a lot of ways, she was. It was still her, though.

'Where's Dylan?' Leah asked.

'They gave him his own room,' Jennifer said. 'It's connected to mine but also separate. They sent him schoolwork but he doesn't want to look at it, and it's not like I can force him. He's playing his games and watching his videos. I think he's been messaging his friends, but who knows what he's seen online. I have no idea when we'll be able to go home.'

At that, the gate on the other side of the garden clicked open and the man in the suit who'd been polishing the sign entered. He did a quick scan of the courtyard and made to continue towards the door for the gym but stopped when he saw Leah. As he frowned, she gave him a little wave, unable to stop herself. That got a deeper scowl, before he marched away.

'Have the police told you much about the person they arrested?' Leah asked.

'Dylan did an ID thing this morning.'

Leah was so shocked this information had been dropped into their conversation so late that she could only manage a stunned 'Oh...'

'I thought it'd be like TV, where they walk people in,'

Jennifer said. 'But it's all on an iPad. They show you pictures of people and ask you to pick out anyone you recognise.'

'Did Dylan ID anyone?'

The response was something between a shrug and a shake of the head. 'Sort of. Not really. There was one guy he thought it could be, but he wasn't sure. They don't tell you if it's the person arrested. We got back here and then, an hour later, they were calling to say they wanted to talk to me about the bones. They're coming back again later.' She laughed hollowly to herself. 'I might as well move into the police station.'

The two women settled again. Despite her suspicions, Leah found Jennifer fascinating. They had so much in common, especially around their upbringings. The fact they appeared to think in the same way about so many things was what worried Leah the most. She knew the things of which she was capable.

'Are you sure you won't talk to Alfie's mum for me?' Jennifer tried again.

'I really can't. I'm supposed to be working anyway. I have to head back.'

Jennifer failed to hide her disappointment as she huffed with annoyance. *Fine!* she didn't say.

'Do you know when you'll be back?' Jennifer asked instead. 'I know you have work, and Zac, but I suppose... it's been good to have someone to talk to.'

Leah pushed herself up. She had a sense that bloke in the suit would likely return in the coming minutes. Arguing with him was something with which she couldn't be bothered. She told Jennifer to keep in contact and headed for the gate.

It had been like so many of Leah and Jennifer's conversations – broadly friendly, yet with an almost overwhelming sense that she'd missed something. Leah never felt as if she quite knew the other woman.

Leah was almost back at the car when she realised the thing

that felt off about this particular chat. It was the 'Nothing', quickly followed by 'Not nothing' when Leah had asked Jennifer what she thought about the bones being found. Maybe not a big deal by itself – except Leah had the sense that Jennifer had known all along her mother was buried at the farm.

THIRTY-FIVE

Leah's afternoon passed in much the way it should have. She visited another person at their home and then returned to the office to get through the paperwork. She picked up Zac from Deborah's house, put up a half-hearted argument to say that the other woman shouldn't feel obliged to cook for them, but ate the shepherd's pie anyway.

She was back at her house in the early evening, Zac upstairs as he usually was. The online excitement and accusations over the previous night's arrest had been replaced by confusion. The man had been released without charge and, according to the police was 'no longer part of inquiries in relation to the missing boys'.

Many of the comments about him being a creep had been deleted, either by the people who wrote them, or an administrator realising it wasn't a good look.

The class WhatsApp group seemed to have the real story. Someone said that he'd burned out his own van and reported it stolen. He was nothing to do with Dylan's version of a kidnapper and everything to do with someone trying an insurance scam. It wasn't lost on Leah that this meant the van that had been found was nothing to do with what Dylan had described. That left the number of things provably true about his story as more or less nothing.

Communication from the police had been patchy – which left people, parents especially, worrying there was still some child-snatching man in a van out there.

It didn't help that two boys were still missing. It had been five days and, though Dylan was back, the chances of finding the others alive felt bleak.

Jennifer's 'nothing' and then 'not nothing' had been sitting in Leah's thoughts. It felt like a half-second of honesty that was quickly corrected when Jennifer realised how it sounded.

And it made up Leah's mind.

She headed upstairs and apologised – again – to Zac. She had to nip out and asked if he was going to be OK by himself. He was fifteen and shrugged it off with a bemused 'Yeah' that looked more like an 'Of course'. She clearly felt worse about it than he did. Although he was technically in his room by himself, Leah forgot that young people communicated in a different way to how she had. If she wasn't *with* her friends, she was by herself. Now, there was messaging and online gaming. If they wanted to be, kids were never *away* from their friends.

'Do you want to do something this weekend?' Leah asked. 'Make it up to you...?'

Her son seemed unbothered by this – and it was probably true that he didn't need her around to have a good weekend. Time had passed so quickly from the days when he had.

'I'll pay,' she added – and they were the magic words.

Zac had been propped on his bed but pushed himself up so that he was sitting. He lowered his phone as his eyes lit up. 'Laser Quest?' he said.

It was a curious pursuit in that it had been popular when Leah had been at school and then it felt like it had gone out of business. Now, it was back in a big way – presumably because it allowed young people to shoot things in real life, just like on their games, without actually hurting anyone.

'Maybe Josh as well...?' A hint of a grin crept onto his face. 'You do know what Laser Quest is, don't you?'

'I'm not *that* old.'

Zac laughed. 'There's no way they'd invented lasers when you were a kid. What did you do instead? Throw rocks or something? Rock Quest.'

He grinned and Leah joined in with the laughing.

'They've opened a new zone,' Zac said. 'They're calling it the bolthole and Matty reckons it's so much better than the original. You have to book online but, if you're paying, maybe you can do it...?'

'For you and Josh?'

'Maybe a couple of others...?'

He'd played her, though Leah deserved it.

'I'll book four of you in for Rock Quest, right?'

He smirked. 'Something like that.'

'All right, send me the link and whatever day and time you want. I'll see what I can do when I get back.'

Zac turned to his phone and started thumbing in some details. 'Great, so that's six of us...' He caught his mum's eye and gave his sweetest smile: the same he'd had when he was small enough to fit in her hand.

'I'll see you later,' Leah told him. By the time she'd got downstairs and picked up her car keys, her phone was buzzing with messages from Zac. Leah was buying him off and knew it.

Nothing... Not nothing.

There wasn't much more important than her son, if anything, but there were still two boys missing. Other people's sons. Leah was convinced Jennifer already knew her mother was buried in that field, which left her wondering how much else she knew about what had happened in the past few days.

Leah drove away from town, following the directions of

Google Maps. She continued past the field with the ancient oak and the wild flowers that hadn't yet bloomed, continuing on towards the coast. As Leah banked away from the country lanes, dark clouds hovered over the sea in the distance. Leah rarely visited the beach and the only time she'd been in recent years was to drop off Zac and his friends for an afternoon of sun, ice cream, arcades, and chips. She had left them to do their thing for a few hours, then picked them up as the sun began to set.

Leah followed the road along the front of the promenade, passing the arcades and pubs with their St George's flags at the front. On the handful of occasions she had visited when she was young, it seemed like every shop sold fluorescent buckets and spades, or those windbreakers that needed to be malleted into the sand. Even when it was sunny, the gales howled.

Jennifer had described a 'horrible glass thing near an old post office', when talking about where her ex had ended up. In the search for that, Google sent Leah past a giant B&M Bargains to what was now a Wetherspoon's. The pub was called 'The Mail Room', which wasn't a bad giveaway, as Leah parked across the road.

Orange was beginning to spread across the horizon, and the beer garden was rammed with pink-skinned Brits who'd been in the sun for too long. Much longer and those dark clouds would arrive to really put a dampener on things.

Leah hurried past the pub and up a small hill, hoping to get a view of anything that looked particularly 'horrible' or 'glass'.

It wasn't a big search. At the top of the slope, partly hidden behind a wall, was the upstairs of a house with a window that spanned the entirety of the top floor. And beyond, presumably, Jennifer's ex.

THIRTY-SIX

The wall was comfortably taller than Leah with no obvious way to approach the house itself. Which was likely the point. Leah continued a little along the street until she found a gate with a buzzer at the side. With little idea what else to do, Leah pressed the button and waited.

It took twenty or so seconds for a tinny woman's voice to chirp 'Who's there?' through the speaker.

'Is Steven in?' Leah asked.

'Depends who's asking.'

Despite the size of the house and any preconceptions Leah had about the type of person who lived within, the woman sounded delightfully common. The 'Who's asking?' had a distinct edge.

'My name's Leah Pearce. I think he might know the name...?'

There was a crackle and what sounded like an under-the-breath swear word. 'Hang on,' she added, before things went silent.

Leah waited as nothing happened. When she turned back

to the seafront, it felt as if the storm clouds were playing a game of What's The Time, Mr Wolf? She'd turned her back a few minutes and it had crept along the coast to sit on the edge of town. There was a freshness to the air, along with a breeze. It would likely be raining within minutes. From somewhere on the street below, there was the sound of a glass breaking and then a communal *wahey!*

There was a click to the side of the gate and, as Leah turned back, Steven had emerged from a second, smaller gate that Leah hadn't spotted. The last time Leah had seen him, a police officer had been escorting him out of Jennifer's house as she accused him of hitting her. Domestic abuse was a touchy subject for Leah and she tended to believe women unquestionably.

This was awkward.

'Leah Pearce, huh?' he said. 'Did Jen send you?'

That got a shake of the head.

'Why are you here?'

'I was hoping for a chat.'

'What about?'

'When you were saying that Jennifer probably killed all three boys, you said we should ask her why you broke up. I figured I'd be better off asking you.'

Steven had his arms folded as he weighed her up. It took a couple of seconds for him to unfold his arms and sink down from his heels.

'I shouldn't have said that,' he said, tone softer, waiting for a reply that didn't come. 'For the record, I don't *actually* think she did anything like that. I didn't then, or now. I was annoyed because I shouldn't have to find out my son's missing from a police officer, instead of his mother.' He glanced across to the approaching clouds and bristled from the wind. 'Have you got a coat?' he asked.

'I think there's one in the back of my car.'

Steven half-turned, eyeing the house and giving the sort of wince a person did when they and their partner had recently had an argument. 'Where are you parked?'

Leah pointed down the hill towards her vehicle opposite the pub.

Steven eyed the cloud again. 'I'll get a jacket from inside and meet you by your car. I think we're going to get wet.'

The coat in the back of Leah's car was a thin anorak, not particularly suited to rain or, to be honest, weather in general. In terms of the functions a coat should perform, it failed at every one – other than having pockets, which was always a bonus.

Leah waited as, across the road, the beer garden had largely cleared out in anticipation of the downpour.

Steven headed down the hill a few minutes later, wearing the sort of jacket someone on the way down a mountain might have. It was bright yellow and all toggles and zips, as if someone had invented a straitjacket for Pride week. His hands were in his pockets and he barely broke stride as Leah slotted in alongside him. They walked in the direction of town, following the road that traced the line of the beach.

'Have you seen Dylan recently?' he asked.

'Not for a couple of days.'

That got a sigh that was almost lost to the breeze. 'I spoke to him on the phone yesterday but he said they're more or less locked down in a hotel. I could visit but I don't want to risk getting into another argument with his mum. That's the last thing he needs. I'm hoping to see him on Saturday.'

There was a misty damp to the air, though no actual rain. Across the road, a line of smokers were crowded under an overhang outside a working men's club. The board outside was advertising Fleetwood Snack as the weekend's tribute act.

'If you want to know the real reason we split up, it's because Jen's impossible to live with.' Steven waited for a response that

Leah didn't give. 'I know people say there's two sides to a story, and she'll have hers, but that's the truth. I couldn't handle the mood swings. She'd go entire days without talking to me because I'd forgotten to pick up something from the supermarket. The worst thing was the house. It was always "hers", even though I was mostly paying the mortgage.' A pause. 'I'm still paying part of it.'

'I thought she'd inherited it?'

'She did but it's been remortgaged twice since then. She tells them the money's for repairs and renovations but you've seen the state of the place. The whole place is a money pit. It's so expensive to keep going. I was covering about seventy per cent of the payments, probably more, but always felt like a tenant. Because she grew up there, she had her own ideas about where everything went, how things worked, and wouldn't listen to anyone else.'

Leah could see both sides on that. It must be hard for Jennifer to welcome somebody into her childhood home and accept them moving things around, or wanting to make changes. On the other hand, partnerships were supposed to be about compromise. If it was supposed to be *their* home, no wonder Steven was annoyed at a lack of freedom.

Steven was still talking: 'Dylan was getting into trouble at school. There was an incident with him bullying someone in a younger year that got him a three-day suspension. Something else about stealing from the canteen. I wanted to take away his PlayStation and fishing rod – but Jen was like, "Boys will be boys", whatever that means. You can only discipline a kid if you're both into it. If I take stuff away and she gives it back, it doesn't work.'

It was easy for Leah to see how things had spiralled with the lack of discipline. How that girl had been groped and assaulted by Dylan because Jennifer hadn't told him off for lesser things.

Meanwhile, Steven's frustration burned, as if he'd been

wanting someone to tell for a long time. They continued walking as the rain just about held off. The street lights were on, sending speckled circles of dusky orange onto the pavement in front of them.

'I know I should've stayed around to try to work within, rather than without, but... Jen knows how to needle me. How to get me going. She always had. She'll do it on purpose, even when Dylan's there. For a while, I thought I should stay for him – but, in the end, I figured it's no way to live when you're that age. Nobody wants to hear their mum and dad going at it all the time.'

It was largely the same thing Jennifer had told Leah earlier – though she'd been talking about *her* parents, while Steven was talking about *them* as a mother and father. Jennifer had ended up in a situation replicating the one she'd hated.

That didn't mean it was her fault.

They were at the entrance to the pier, where the dings and pings of the arcade chimed across the chill. Nobody seemed particularly bothered about the weather as a line stretched along the rail for the ice-cream stall. The smell of vinegary chips clung heavily in the air, making Leah's mouth water.

Not only hers.

'Do you want some chips?' Steven asked, say what you smell and all that. He patted his belly, on which there didn't appear to be any fat. 'I probably shouldn't but...'

Leah hadn't been hungry but the smell of the vinegar was too much. She told him yes and then they crossed the road to where the doors of Chippy Chippy Bang Bang were open. Steven offered to buy, though Leah paid for her own. The bloke behind the counter told them they were almost closing so it was large chips for the price of a regular – and he'd 'wang in' a sausage for good measure. The grease instantly soaked through the white paper and, as they stepped back outside, the heat of the chips and the chill of the air was almost overwhelming.

It had been a long, long time since Leah had eaten chips at the seaside. So long that her friend Vicky had been with her.

Leah and Steven crossed the road and walked a short distance to an empty bench a little past the pier. The clouds were rolling around, though emptying themselves further along the coast. The sheer anger of the sky had a melancholic beauty as Leah sat with the chips on her lap and watched.

'Kids at school have been saying that you're not Dylan's real dad,' Leah said.

She hadn't been sure if she was going to bring it up but Steven wasn't the person she thought he was. Or, more to the point, he wasn't the person Jennifer had made him out to be.

As it was, Steven wasn't surprised. 'That's from Dylan,' he said, 'Though, really, it's from Jen. She's told him that on and off for years, usually when she's angry at me.'

He wiped his fingers on his jacket and pulled out his phone. He scrolled through a series of photographs and then held it up for Leah to see. It showed a pair of boys in different images, edited so that they were side by side.

'That's me and Dylan,' Steven said. 'Just look at us. I was ten when that was taken and he was nine. We could be twins.'

Leah didn't need to look too closely to see he had a point. Even now, with Steven as an adult, he and Dylan had the same eyes, nose and mouth.

Steven put away his phone and picked up a chip. Leah did the same, though hers were soggier from the vinegar. She'd gone over the top on the salt as well – and they were heavenly.

'This is her trying to turn him against me,' Steven said, slightly before he'd finished his mouthful. 'We'd all be in the living room and she'd go, "You know he's not your dad." It was trying to wind me up but also trying to get him to choose her over me. How much am I supposed to take before I walk out?'

'Does Dylan believe her?'

'I don't know. What's a kid supposed to think when his mum's telling him that?'

Steven grabbed his sausage and angrily bit away the end. In this case, his brimming fury felt justified. It was a different version of events compared to Jennifer's, though Leah had been questioning the other woman's honesty over more than simply this. It was why Leah had come to visit her ex.

With a sigh, Steven slunk lower onto the bench. 'She says Dylan doesn't want to see me and, to be fair, it's not like he's saying anything different. I'd love to see him every other weekend, or whatever – but it's more like every two months at the moment. I know I'm the one who left but...'

He tailed off and scoffed a trio of chips that he'd mashed together. Leah was making good progress with hers, though the abundance of salt meant she'd need a drink sometime soon.

Ahead, the clouds had largely slid along the coastline, leaving a dark blue overhead. The lights of the arcade on the pier shimmered a reflection on the black of the rippling ocean.

'Did you hit her?' Leah asked.

'No! God no!'

Steven was so animated, he dropped the rest of his sausage. He tried to catch it on the way down but only succeeded in batting it away from the pavement and over the wall onto the beach below. He leaned further forward, presumably watching it nestle in the sand as treasure for a lucky seagull.

He slumped back into the seat. 'I've not hit anyone since I was about twelve and some kids jumped me. I've never hit Jen. *Never*. I've definitely not hit Dylan, either. This is what I mean, though. She was telling people back then that I had, and she still is. I don't know what to say or do about it. It always felt like she was doing all she could to make me leave, because then she could be the victim.'

Leah passed him her untouched sausage, saying she didn't want one anyway. She wasn't sure she'd get through the full portion of chips. He took it with a mumbled thank you and then bit off the end. Steven chewed and she could sense him stewing. She wondered how many times he'd gone through this with his current girlfriend. Probably a lot.

'She used to tell me that she regretted having Dylan,' Steven said. 'I don't think she ever told him but maybe she did. I did a lot of reading about postnatal depression and it might've been that. I spoke to a doctor on her behalf, because she wouldn't go – but there wasn't a lot they could do without her. It went on for years but, if it's still going on now, is that still postnatal? Or is it just depression?'

Leah didn't know how to reply. It was only a handful of hours before that Jennifer had told Leah the same thing. Except, in her version, her mum had told her she was unwanted. Was *that* a lie? Was *this* a lie? Were both things true? She was stunned and must have seemed it.

'Are you OK?' Steven asked.

Leah put a chip in her mouth to avoid the question. How could she answer that? She couldn't figure out whether Jennifer was copying her mother's behaviour, and seemingly not realising. Or if she'd described her own thoughts to Leah and pretended they came from her mum.

Not that Steven had to know any of that.

Leah explained her reaction by saying a chip was particularly hot, which wasn't a great lie, but was accepted.

'Are you friends with her?' Steven asked, and then: 'Are you going to tell her everything I've said?' He didn't sound overly concerned. Perhaps he wanted her to know, though didn't want the argument involved in telling her himself.

Leah didn't need to think about the second question, though the first required a little more consideration.

'I don't think we're friends,' Leah replied after a while. 'But maybe we are? I'm definitely not going to tell her any of this.'

Steven had somehow finished all his food and started

balling the paper. Leah had around a third of hers left, probably the part that made it 'large'. She offered it to Steven and he took it without question. Unloading years of frustration was hungry work.

'I remember when you came back,' he said, more or less from nothing.

'Came back where?' Leah replied.

'To school. We were all in the same year and you were off for a month or two because of what happened with your friends. There was this Monday where you just appeared.' He clicked his fingers like a magician summoning a card from thin air. 'Everyone was like, "You'll never guess who's back?" – and there you were. There was that yard at the front of the main reception building and you were walking across it by yourself.'

Leah didn't specifically remember Steven on that day – but she remembered the staring. She saw the open mouths. She was supposed to report to reception in order to find out her temporary timetable and, as she walked across the playground, everyone had stopped to look at her. There was a time in which that memory burned so bright that it was almost paralysing. Then she must have blocked it out because it hadn't been in her thoughts for years – not even at the film premiere, when she was in the spotlight.

Steven must have seen something in her. He'd stopped eating and gave a soft 'Sorry'.

Leah told him it was OK, and it probably was, except the suppressed memory was suddenly right there. Someone walked behind them, heading towards the pier and Leah shivered. Those had been her loneliest days, when she was the zoo exhibit. Even the teacher's gazes would linger a moment too long.

'You probably don't remember,' Steven said, 'but I tried talking to you once. You were outside the library on that bench where kids who were in trouble got sent, before they went in to see the deputy head. I don't think you were in trouble for anything, it was—'

'It was quiet,' Leah interrupted to say. 'Nobody bothered you there.'

He snorted a fraction at that. 'Nobody except me, I guess. I remember you looked really, um... lonely...'

He left a gap for Leah to fill, which she didn't. She *had* been isolated.

'I asked how you were and you sort of shrugged me off. It's OK, I got it. You'd have had everyone trying to talk to you.'

That was true. There was a paradox in that Leah had no friends in her life at that time – and yet there were more people than ever trying to talk to her. Because she had no way of knowing their motives, she had brushed off everyone. After a while, they had stopped trying.

Leah didn't want to talk about it. In many ways, it was the worst time of her life. She needed to change the subject again.

'Did you kill the class rabbit?' she asked.

Steven reeled, probably as much from the abrupt change of direction than the accusation. 'No! It was lost and it wasn't my fault. I wasn't even home. Dad left the cage open and I don't know what happened after that.' He sighed. 'I'm never going to live this down, am I? It's been almost thirty years and people still bring it up.' He balled up the remaining chips in the paper and dumped everything in the bin at his side. 'Was that from Jen as well?' he asked.

'Yes but I remember it, too. As soon as she said your name, I thought about the rabbit.'

Steven was shaking his head. 'You lose *one* rabbit...'

Leah giggled at that, mainly because of the implication that everyone should be allowed to lose an animal, as long as they didn't lose two. She thought of Jennifer saying he'd driven over a cat and it felt either untrue, or an exaggeration of something that had been an accident.

Steven hadn't laughed, though he wasn't angry, either. The sky was dark, the stars starting to glimmer intermittently around the departing clouds. The rain hadn't arrived but the chill had. Leah pulled her jacket tighter and cupped one hand in the other. Steven was seemingly unaffected in his straitjacket.

Leah hadn't set out to discover some gotcha relating to Jennifer. Steven and Charles would have their own agendas and viewpoints but the picture they painted of Jennifer was similar. They spoke of a troubled woman who'd lie with little concern or compassion. Perhaps that was Leah's impression of her as well.

'You know she's obsessed with you,' Steven said.

'Jennifer?'

'She always has been, ever since your friends disappeared. That's why I couldn't believe it when I saw you in her kitchen. Back then, she used to talk about trying to be your friend – and, suddenly, all these years later, you're there with her.' Steven pushed himself up and arched his back. There was a crick and he groaned in pleasure. Leah stood herself and her knees ached. He gave a gentle smile. 'The perils of turning forty,' he said.

'What do you mean obsessed?' Leah asked.

They were under a street light, bathed in a glum orange. Leah couldn't see Steven's features any longer but she saw the shrug. 'She always had this scrapbook. It had loads of cuttings from papers about you and your friends. When there were anniversaries, she'd keep those articles. She'd print things from the internet, too. There was so much stuff, she had to start a second volume.'

Leah stared as a chill unrelated to the temperature whispered through her. Steven saw it but made the wrong assumption.

'There's no reason for you to know that. I don't know if she still keeps it. Maybe I shouldn't have said anything?'

Except Leah *did* know about the scrapbook – the first volume at least. She'd seen it, held it, and showed it to the police.

Jennifer had told her it belonged to her father.

THIRTY-SEVEN

Leah dozed, never quite falling into a real sleep. Her suspicion of Jennifer had been growing steadily, though there was no evidence she'd done anything wrong in relation to the missing boys. Leah could hardly go to the police with a feeling, especially because that feeling was based on her own past.

'Takes one to know one' wasn't something to take to the authorities, any more than 'He who smelt it, dealt it' could be used as evidence.

Mo and Alfie were still missing – and it had been almost a week.

As all that spun around her mind, Leah gave up any attempt to sleep and got up. She tidied the kitchen and made Zac a sandwich for his lunch. He was old enough to do it himself, though Leah hadn't quite got out of the habit. His claim that she 'made it better' felt spurious, though there was probably a compliment in there somewhere.

The morning drizzle meant Zac asked for a lift to school. Leah hurried to get her own things ready for work, while trying to make herself presentable as a person who'd slept through the night at some point in the past week.

He was in the passenger seat, fidgeting in the way he did when there was something he wanted to ask. In the corner of her eye, Leah caught him opening his mouth a couple of times before closing it. The other tell was that he wasn't staring at his phone.

'Something you want to say?' Leah asked in the end. They were stopped at a set of traffic lights.

'We were wondering if we should invite Dylan to Laser Quest.'

Considering everything going on, and the possible revelations Zac could have made, the mildness of this was something of a relief.

'I'm sure he'd appreciate it,' Leah said.

'I thought you might want to ask his mum first? We know he's in a hotel but he said his mum isn't letting him leave.'

'There were photographers outside the hotel,' Leah said, before realising she hadn't actually *seen* anyone taking pictures. Jennifer had *told* her they were there, which is why she and Dylan weren't leaving. Except Leah had driven through the gates twice in and twice out. There could've been people hiding in the bushes, but the only media Leah had seen were at the farm.

'I'll have a word with her,' Leah added, and then: 'I didn't think you and Dylan were friends...?'

'We're not, but I suppose...'

Zac let the sentence hang as Leah realised the similarity of her situation to Dylan's. She'd even talked about it the night before, when Steven remembered her returning to school as a lonely teenager. Dylan would surely be feeling the same – except he had kids like Zac wanting to include him.

'Everyone wants to try the new bolthole zone,' Zac said.

He'd talked about the same thing the evening before, though Leah's mind had been elsewhere.

Bolthole.

Huh.

It was an odd word and she'd heard it somewhere else recently.

'Why do they call it that?' she asked.

'Matty says it's designed as this bunker thing. There's a narrow tunnel that joins it to the other zones.'

He continued explaining the vagaries of the Laser Quest layout but Leah had switched off. She knew where she'd heard the word before.

Zac continued talking as Leah made enough noises to make it seem like she was listening. It wasn't long until she pulled into the school's drop-off zone. There were no protestors this time, though still a line of students waiting to be ticked off on the clipboard list.

Leah headed to work and went through the motions. She visited a couple of people and returned to the office to enter things into the system and check in with her manager. There was an anxious buzz as her colleagues whispered and wondered about the missing boys. Nobody wanted to say it but six days was too long. People rarely came back alive after being missing for that length of time. That's if they were found at all.

As lunchtime rolled around, Leah drove the couple of miles across town and knocked on the door of the semi-detached house. She didn't think she'd return of her own accord, yet here she was.

Mandy opened the door and immediately broke into an enormous smile. 'Leah! I wasn't expecting you. Not that you aren't welcome. It's lovely you're here. Are you staying? Shall I put the kettle on? There's still some Mr Kiplings left if you want those? Or we can go out if you want—'

'Is Dad in?'

It was the question Leah never thought she'd ask. She'd had a low level of dread about running into him around town – now she was actively asking for him.

Mandy's smile faded a fraction, though not by much. She was wearing an apron and wiped her hands on the front. 'He had a probation appointment this morning but said he was going to the allotment after. The officer managed to sort him a plot. Something to keep him interested and out of trouble.'

Leah wasn't sure she could handle her alcoholic, violent father turning into someone who grew marrows. Was he going to end up showing them off at county shows? He'd done too much for things to turn out this way.

'Which allotments?' Leah asked.

'The ones up past the church. Do you know it? Everyone needs a hobby, don't they? He took a radio up there.'

Mandy offered so much information for every small question that Leah figured she would be her new husband's worst nightmare if he ever did act up. The police would ask her what had happened, and she'd give them a full life story, with itemised days, times, and places.

'I know it,' Leah said, taking a step away from the door.

The hint of disappointment on Mandy's face was impossible to miss.

'Thank you,' Leah told her. 'Not just for this.'

Mandy touched her heart. 'Oh, love. You're so welcome. After all you went through, it's my pleasure.'

Leah was unsure how to respond, so she left with a nod and a smile, heading back to her car and driving up to the allotments.

She'd never been before, though it was as she could have guessed. Ramshackle sheds and greenhouses dotted the landscape, with narrow paths winding past the rectangle plots. Everything had a number and, though Leah didn't know her father's, he wasn't hard to find. While the other pieces of land had lines of neat plants and vines, her dad's was almost entirely dirt. He was sitting on an upturned bucket next to a shed, vaping while listening to the gentle babble of talk radio.

There was little, if any, evidence that the plot was being used to grow anything. Instead, her father was staring into space. As far as she knew, he didn't have a phone – though he'd clearly discovered vapes. The mobile phone revolution had happened within her lifetime, though Leah couldn't quite remember what people looked at before phones. Perhaps it was this? Perhaps it was nothing?

Leah's father stood when he spotted her, frowning with confusion. 'Is Mandy OK?'

'She's fine.'

Leah opened the gate. It was only attached via one hinge and swung crookedly inwards.

'The boy?'

Leah propped the gate back into place and continued around the dirt towards her dad. 'His name's Zac – and he's fine too.'

Her father's frown deepened. 'Did I do something?'

'Lots of things – but that's not why I'm here. I need to ask you a question.'

This confused him even further. He repeated 'A question?' as if he'd never heard of the concept. He lowered himself back onto the bucket, and pushed his vape into a pocket, as Leah stood over him.

'When we talked at Mandy's house, you told me that, when you were a kid, you went fishing in the woods nears Charles' house. There was something about getting into boltholes but I can't remember exactly what you said.'

This also seemed to bemuse her father. 'Is there a problem?'

'I'm asking you a question, Dad. There's no hidden agenda.'

As Leah said that, she realised there *was* an agenda – but it didn't relate directly to her father.

He blinked. 'I don't remember, either. I was saying that we used to play out there.'

'I get that – but what did you mean by boltholes?'

'Some of those farms had bomb shelters. This area produced lots of the food during the war, so it was a target for the planes. I don't know if they ever got used at the time but a bunch of us used to play in them. This was ages ago.'

Those shelters would have been built eighty years or more before. They were on farms that were now barely used. How many people would've played in those shelters over the years? And, of those, who'd still be around and remember?

Leah's head was racing.

'Was there a bomb shelter on Charles' farm?'

That got a shrug. 'That was the main one we played in.'

THIRTY-EIGHT

Leah's father was in the passenger seat of her car. Her *actual* car. The vehicle she drove every day. He was in it.

Thankfully, he didn't say anything as Leah drove to the outskirts of town. He spent the entire time looking through the window like a dog taking its first journey in the front. He'd mumble things like: 'Oh, that must be new', as if the world should have paused while he spent all that time in prison.

When they reached Jennifer's farm, the number of satellite vans had dwindled to two. Leah's father pushed against his seatbelt and angled to look around her, though remained quiet.

Leah parked at the end of the driveway that led down to Charles' house. Her father creaked and eked his way from the vehicle, holding his back as he moved. Leah led him towards the farm but, before they reached the house, Charles was outside. His body was braced, fists balled, apparently ready for an argument with a trespasser until he realised it was Leah.

'You're back,' he said, talking to her, before turning to her father. There was a second or two of squinted realisation. 'Paul...?'

'Hey, Charlie lad.'

The two men eyed one another with curious interest.

'I heard you were...?' Charles said, leaving off the 'in prison' bit.

'I was,' Leah's father replied. 'Been out a couple of months now. I just got married. This is my daughter.'

He nodded to Leah and she bristled at the sound of 'daughter' in his mouth. He'd never acted as if she was, quite the opposite.

'I'm sorting myself out,' he added, before: 'What are you up to?'

They were moments away from slipping into reminiscing mode, which was something Leah couldn't bring herself to listen to. After everything he'd done, she couldn't accept her father being normalised.

'Is there a bomb shelter on the farm?' she asked, which cut directly through something Charles was saying. His twitching eyebrow told her that, had it been only them, he'd have been furious. With Leah's father at her side, he controlled himself.

'I told you there was,' he said.

Leah wasn't going to argue, though she was certain he hadn't. Then she realised he had – in a roundabout way. He'd been talking about bomb shelter drills, and she'd assumed he meant at school. Then he'd moved onto something about the Home Office and a petition to get a posthumous medal for his dad. Leah had washed over things, assuming he was borderline mad. Except he'd meant he'd done bomb shelter drills *at the farm*. He'd told her and she hadn't listened.

Charles had partially turned back to her father but Leah wasn't about to let it go. 'Did you tell the police there was a shelter?'

She already knew the answer – and it came with an incredulous: 'I'm not telling them anything. I told you how they only bother when it suits them. They're useless, the lot of them.' He turned to Leah's dad: 'I've been trying to get them to come out for years because the noise, the trespassing, all that. They're not interested. Then, when they want something, they're knocking on my door, expecting me to ask "How high?" when they tell me to jump. No chance. I made them go get a warrant. See how they like it.'

If he was expecting support from Leah's dad, then all he got was a vague nod of acknowledgement that he'd been heard. He took that as agreement anyway, turning back to Leah and throwing up his hands. *See?!*

It wasn't the time for Leah to argue. 'Can I see it?' she asked.

'See what?'

'The bunker.'

His eyes narrowed. 'Why?'

Leah wasn't sure what to tell him. Because of a feeling? A guess? A coincidence that the town's laser tag centre had named their new zone the same thing her father had described at a wedding she hadn't wanted to attend? Because Dylan was a constant trespasser on this farm – and Leah didn't believe his story?

Takes one to know one.

That was the real reason – because Leah knew Jennifer. Maybe Dylan as well.

'Because I'm curious,' Leah said. 'Dad was telling me about playing in the bunker when he was a kid.'

Charles looked to her father, who shrugged to confirm this was true. Leah had fudged the truth in dragging him out to the farm, saying there was someone who'd want to meet him.

'It's not nice down there,' Charles said. 'Last time I tried it was rusted shut.'

That wasn't a shock, given the state of the rest of the farm.

'Where is it?' Leah asked.

For the first time since she'd met him, there was something of a twinkle in Charles' eye. The sort of expression she thought he'd probably have after watching a YouTube compilation of the world's greatest bicycle crashes. If he had any idea what YouTube was.

'Do you remember?' he asked, talking to Leah's dad.

That got a hint of a smile. 'Of course. There weren't as many cars here back then...'

And then they were off. The two older men walked side by side across the uneven land, although it was more of a hobble on Leah's dad's side. They made small talk about where things used to be, stopping on three separate occasions to reminisce about throwing rocks, or whatever else it was they used to do. Two big kids talking about nicking apples and making a run for it. The irony wasn't lost on Leah that it was the precise sort of low-level criminality about which Charles seemed to complain.

The farm was even more of a mess than Leah had thought from her previous visit. Some areas seemed to be in endless shade, leaving battered, rusting cars sunk in gloopy patches of mud. There were so many vehicles and parts, none of which were less than sixty per cent rust. The farmland was vast, though most areas didn't look as if anyone had been there in years. Moss and weeds had overtaken entire sections, giving an apocalyptic feel to much of the place. After the fall of mankind, Charles' farm would blend right in.

The helicopters and drones of previous days were gone, leaving the gentle murmur of the river somewhere in the distance. Leah followed the two men towards the back of the land and the woods beyond. They were almost at the edge, but still moving, as they continued towards a hedge that was wildly unkempt. The bottom half was brown, sodden, and seemingly dead; while the top was green and sprouting in all directions –

though mainly towards a rusting car. Leah almost asked where they were except, as they rounded the car, the hedge opened to reveal a dusty clearing, hidden by the foliage. Even as Leah stood facing the metal hatch in the ground, she had to turn to check her bearings. It had appeared from nowhere, only visible if a person was almost on top of it. The sort of thing that would so easily be missed.

'The bolthole,' her father said – and it was.

'You won't be able to open it,' Charles told her, though it didn't sound unkind. More a statement of fact – which is probably why his eyes went so wide when Leah stepped across to the hatch and lifted it. She'd pulled the sword from the stone.

Charles' confusion manifested itself with a baffled stare. 'No one's been down here in years,' he said.

Leah was ahead of him. Her phone was out and she was trying to find the button that made the flashlight come on. Every time there was an update, it seemed to change.

'I've got a proper light back at the house,' Charles said.

'Send dad,' Leah told him. She needed Charles to be there. It was his bunker, after all.

For whatever reason, though probably the determination in her tone, Leah's instructions weren't questioned. Charles told her dad the torch was in a cabinet near the front door and, as he set off back to the house, Leah started for the steps. She was already two down when Charles said: 'I'll go'. She could've argued but figured she'd let him – and moved to the side, allowing the older man to go first.

Leah shone the light past him as Charles grunted his way down. When he reached the bottom, he called to her, so Leah followed. The steps were stone, with a sheen of something wet. If the hatch was supposed to shield the bunker from whatever was happening above, it was either not working – or someone with wet shoes had been down in the recent past.

Or up.

Leah was two steps from the bottom when a beam of light dazzled around her. Stars swam in her vision as she blinked through the dark to Charles, who was holding a flashlight. She could barely see him, though he was directing a stream of white towards her feet.

'There was a torch down here,' he said.

'Is it yours?' she asked.

'I don't think so. I've not been down in years but I might've left one down. Surprised the batteries still work...'

He sounded unsure but, in a display of surprising submission, handed her the light.

Leah took it, put her phone away, and flicked the brighter light towards an empty corner.

Relief.

There was nothing there.

Two steps more and the smell hit her. Charles was at her side and stopped too. It wasn't overpowering but it was there. Leah had once gone away for ten days and forgotten to empty the food waste bin under her sink. When she got home and opened the cupboard, the stench of rot and decay had made her gag. This was similar, catching at the back of her throat. As much a taste as a smell.

Leah swung the torch carefully, slowly, from one corner, following the line of the wall. The space was bigger than she thought and the light was swallowed by the dark. She walked forward slowly, into the deeper depths of the bunker. As she moved the light, Leah stopped as it reached a pile of blankets and bin bags in the furthest corner.

Charles' 'What on earth's that?' was muttered from a pace away. He sounded like one half of a bickering couple who'd been arguing for years about where the car keys should be left. Annoyance, not shock.

And then it *was* shock. He gasped as he moved towards the pile, arm outstretched.

'Stop,' Leah told him.

And he did.

Because they both knew why the bunker smelled – and what was under the blankets.

THIRTY-NINE

Charles turned to look at Leah through the murk. He'd frozen and she couldn't see his face, though the horror was there in the laboured way he was breathing.

Leah swung the light around to the steps.

'Go and call the police,' she told him. He didn't move, so she hissed, 'Go!'

There were no arguments this time about the usefulness of the authorities. No outrage at being told what to do on his own property. He simply went.

Leah held the light, directing it up the steps as Charles rushed from the bunker. He'd almost certainly intercept her father, heading the other way with the light.

There was silence, except for a drip somewhere out of sight.

Leah was alone.

Despite everything in Leah's past: despite those lies and betrayals, she had never seen a dead body. It wasn't that morbid curiosity that drove her to the pile of blankets, it was needing to know.

As Leah swung the light back towards the dread of that corner, she realised neither she nor Charles should have touched the torch. There would probably have been finger-prints, which would have been obliterated by their own.

Bit late now.

The smell grew as Leah crept towards the corner. No longer mouldy vegetables, something so much worse. She'd never experienced anything like it before – and didn't want to again.

They weren't blankets. As Leah neared the corner, she realised they were curtains. The material was heavy and brown or navy blue, each bundled on top of each other. Leah stood over them and the smell was almost overpowering. She took a shallow breath and held it as she tugged the curtain on top. As it shifted, it brought a second with it.

Leah gagged. The stench was everywhere and all encom-passing. Rotting eggs but worse. Child vomit but worse. Every-thing awful she'd ever smelled, blended together – and still worse.

Leah hurried across the room towards the hatch, where the halo of light at the top of the stairs offered some respite. Not much. The fresh air wasn't particularly fresh.

She took the deepest gasp she could and pinched her nose with one hand, holding torch with the other.

And then back to the corner, where they were lying almost peacefully next to one another.

Though their skin had started to turn a waxy greeny-grey, Mo and Alfie looked just like their photos. They were wearing some sort of pyjama bottoms: Mo was in a football shirt, Alfie in a top with the name of a band Leah had never heard of.

There was no obvious blood or wounds, though Leah wasn't about to uncover them any further to check. She considered dragging the curtain back over the top of the bodies, though couldn't quite bring herself to do it.

Those poor boys.

Leah saw them and pictured Zac with his lumbering gait and that smile. The way he'd said Rock Quest and made her laugh. He'd come from her and was the best thing she'd done with her life. She told herself that the young man he was becoming would make up for everything else she'd done.

One step backwards became two. Three.

Leah couldn't take her eyes from Mo and Alfie. Their clothes seemed tight, their bodies bloated against the material.

Three steps became five. Ten.

Then Leah was sitting on the bottom step, breathing the almost fresh air. She wouldn't leave this space until the police arrived. Somebody needed to keep watch and it was going to be her. It *had* to be her.

There was a scuffling of something near her feet and Leah looked down, half expecting a mouse or something similar.

Nothing.

There wasn't a thing there, not even an ant or a beetle.

Except Leah had learned to trust fate and trust herself. She arced the light down to her feet and slid it around the floor in a semicircle to a slim gap where the hard steps had cracked.

And there, sitting in the space – impossibly, *incredibly* – was a fingernail decorated with purply-blue zigzags.

FORTY

TWO DAYS LATER

Leah was sitting in a bright corridor by herself. Footsteps echoed in the distance, as they had the entire five or so minutes Leah had been there. It was as if somebody's job was to stride up and down at an even pace to provide the metronomic sound-track. *Clip-clop-clip-clop.*

It'll just be a minute, she'd been told – though some people had strange ideas about the length of sixty seconds.

Suddenly, a man appeared in a suit. He bounded along the corridor towards her at something close to a spring. It was Chief Supersomethingoranother from the TV appeal. He had a voice better suited to narrating a nature film, though Leah could understand why he was a police officer. If he crooned too long, suspects would end up admitting to anything.

He stood over Leah, tall and imposing, though she didn't think he meant that to happen.

'I'd like to go over what you've been told,' he said, after introducing himself properly.

His last name wasn't Supersomethingoranother, though Leah instantly forgot what it actually was.

'This is very important,' he said.

'I know.'

'And you're confident you can remember the questions?'

His nature documentary voice had become impatient supply teacher.

'I'm not an idiot,' Leah told him.

He backed away a pace. 'I'm not saying you are – but there are lots of legal, er, implications for what's about to happen.'

Leah pressed back in the chair, wanting to put space between them.

'I cannot overstate this enough,' he added.

'I get it,' Leah said.

'Good. Right. That's what I've been told.'

He moved to the side, revealing Call Me Ashley – Detective Inspector Bryan – who'd emerged silently from a side room.

Leah *did* know the questions, considering she'd spent almost an hour and a half going over them with DI Ashley Bryan that morning. Ashley had told her that everyone at the station was nervous, largely because they'd searched Charles' property and failed to find the bomb shelter. They had focused their numbers on digging up Jennifer's field, and only sent a couple of officers to the other farm. Charles had obviously not tipped them off and, because there wasn't a similar shelter on Jennifer's farm, nobody had thought to look. It had been hidden away at the back, only noticeable to people who had *really* searched. Which obviously meant someone on the force had messed up big time.

'Why would they?' Leah had said supportively, although that hadn't got an answer. It felt like someone, somewhere, was in for a massive telling off – with Chief Supersomethingoran-other trying to make sure the blame was laid as far down the chain as possible.

Leah had asked what was going to happen to Charles and, although Ashley had said there were whispers of an obstruction charge, it was unlikely. If it came, it would only draw more attention to Charles' legitimate complaints about the police, coupled with them failing to find a bomb shelter. Best to keep quiet about that part and let it all go away.

After that, Ashley had run her through the upcoming questions in the canteen, while plying her with coffee.

Three bodies had been discovered in as many days: Mo, Alfie, and Jennifer's mum. For a force more used to dealing with petty thefts and Saturday-night fighting, it was a lot to be cracking on with.

Leah had spent a lot of time talking to police in the preceding days. When the officers had arrived at the bunker, she'd pointed them to the fingernail and said Jennifer had been picking off identical ones the previous weekend.

She knew her own thoughts about what had happened, though hadn't aired them. The police had retrieved the fingernail and, while others dealt with the horror underneath the curtains, a couple of officers had been dispatched to talk to Jennifer.

When they mentioned the fingernail to her, where it was found, and what else was in the bunker, they had expected denials and resistance. Leah had assumed the same – but, later, when an officer visited her at home, it was to say that Jennifer had listened, shrugged, and told them she'd killed both boys.

Simple as that.

Leah had needed the officers to tell her the same thing three times before it went in. Her suspicions around Jennifer had been strong but little more than misgivings.

Except Jennifer had caved at the first sign of evidence and that was that.

Almost.

'Are you ready?' Ashley asked.

The chief officer had moved out of the way and Leah stood.

Over the course of their talk in the canteen, Leah had come to the conclusion that Ashley was a decent bloke. The sort who'd be first in the stocks at a summer fete where everyone paid a quid to lob wet sponges at him.

He led her through a door into a whitewashed room.

When it came to real life looking like the television, this was how Leah pictured interrogation rooms. There was a double tape deck, a pair of cameras in the corners, a mirror on one wall, and a table bolted in the middle, surrounded by four chairs.

Jennifer was already there, wearing grey joggers. Her purply-blue hair had faded, although it could've been the light. She smiled as she saw Leah, like old friends meeting in a pub after a year or two of not seeing each other.

Ashley sat and Leah did the same – although she was at Jennifer's side.

The detective inspector went through the rigmarole of starting the tapes and pointing out the video cameras. He listed the day and time, before introducing himself.

'To confirm, you have been offered legal advice but declined?' he said firmly, talking to Jennifer.

'Right.'

'And you've requested the presence of Ms Pearce in place of a legal representative?'

Jennifer turned sideways to look at Leah and smiled again. 'Yes.'

'To be clear, and for the avoidance of doubt, Ms Pearce is here because you want her to be. Nobody suggested this to you and it is entirely your idea?'

That got a nod.

'I need you to say the words,' Ashley told her.

'That's all correct,' Jennifer said. 'I want her to hear this.' She looked up to one of the cameras, staring down the barrel. 'I said I would tell you all everything – but only if Leah was here. This was my idea.'

Leah was suddenly nervous. When an officer had said that Jennifer was refusing to speak unless Leah was present, she had first said she didn't want to be there. The smell in that basement had felt like an end, something she would never forget. Besides, she didn't particularly want to see Jennifer.

But without her, the parents of Mo and Alfie weren't going to get their answers, so Leah had gone with it. Ashley had thanked her and told her what was going to be asked. He had run through various scenarios and said it might take a while, because they didn't know if Jennifer would talk again past this.

Leah felt Jennifer watching her but couldn't match it. She was sitting next to a killer.

The first question was the big one – and Ashley didn't hang around.

'Did you kill Alfie Carpenter?' he asked.

There was a half-second of silence and it felt as if everyone was breathing in.

'Yes,' Jennifer replied. She was still looking at Leah, her tone unwaveringly calm.

'Did you kill Mohammad Hakim?'

'Yes.'

Neither Jennifer nor Ashley reacted to this, though Leah could sense the chief super guy in the other room letting out a big breath. It was one thing to admit to something in a hotel room when nobody was recording, another entirely to do so on camera in an interview room.

They had what they wanted.

'How did you kill them?' Ashley asked.

And they were off.

Leah stared at a spot on the wall, as Jennifer bored a hole through her. The story was told almost entirely *to* Leah, who refused to acknowledge the person telling it.

Jennifer said she had smothered the boys while they slept in their separate tents, calmly moving from one to the next until they were both dead. She spoke with the same emotion as someone telling a colleague that a server needed resetting.

She woke up Dylan in the early hours and told him that, if he didn't do what she told him, she would go to jail and they'd lose the house. He would be homeless and, because his dad didn't want him, he'd have nobody.

He helped her move the pair of bodies around the back of Charles' land, through the hedge, and into the bunker. She then made him memorise the cover story about the man with the van, before leaving his fishing rod by the riverbank.

Leah turned fully away as Jennifer said that she had made her son wait it out in the bunker for the time he was apparently missing. As his friends began to rot, he hid with the few scraps of food Jennifer left him. On the day he'd been found, Jennifer had headed across in the early hours, knocked on the hatch, and told him where to go. Then he'd been picked up – and Leah more or less knew the rest.

The discovery of the burned-out van and the failed insurance scam was something Jennifer had never expected.

Ashley had been calm throughout, as with the time he'd interviewed Dylan. There was no emotion, or judgement – only the questions he wanted to ask with little elaboration. After all that, there was still another big question. Perhaps even bigger than the first.

'Why?' he asked.

'Why do you think?'

It was the first time Ashley seemed stumped by anything said on either of the occasions Leah had met him. He pressed forward in his chair. 'What do you mean?'

Jennifer shifted in her seat as much as she could, so she was facing the woman at her side. Leah had an idea of what might be coming.

'Look at her,' Jennifer said.

Leah wilted under the stare.

'You're going to have to spell it out,' Ashley said.

'She's famous,' Jennifer said.

'I'm not,' Leah replied.

'They just made a movie about you.'

Leah wanted to point out that the movie wasn't *about* her, though there seemed little point. In the town, if nowhere else, she had been the face of the documentary. A documentary that wasn't guaranteed to be seen anywhere. It had just had a screening in a community centre to try to drum up publicity.

Except, Leah would always be the girl who was left.

'Everybody knows you,' Jennifer added, her voice just about holding. 'They've been talking about you for twenty-five years. They're *still* talking about you.'

It had been a week ago that Leah had sat with Jennifer in the kitchen in the early hours and she'd felt a bond to the other woman. To a horrifying degree, she still felt it.

Jennifer had been getting louder and was almost in tears – except they were tears of rage. 'You don't even want it,' she shouted. 'All the times we talked and that's what I can't believe. How can you not want it?'

Ashley had gone quiet and Jennifer's question echoed around the small interview room.

Leah half expected someone to intervene, anyone, though no one came. Nobody spoke. She realised everyone watching this needed to hear it. Mo's and Alfie's parents certainly would.

'My friends disappeared,' Leah said – which wasn't a lie.

'And you're famous because of it.'

'I'm not. Nobody knows me outside town. Hardly anyone is going to watch this film outside of here.'

Jennifer thought on it – and, for a moment, Leah thought she saw a flicker of reality. It didn't last long: 'You are! I asked for you and the police knew who you were. At the hotel, after we'd been talking in the garden, this guy came up to me and asked if you were Leah from the movie.'

'Those are still people from around here. I didn't ask for any of that.'

'But you got it.' Jennifer took a breath and lowered herself back fully onto the chair. Not quite relaxed but as close as she was likely to be. This is why she'd wanted Leah there. 'I thought Dylan would end up like you,' Jennifer said, first quietly – and then louder. She turned from Leah to the camera. 'I did it for him. I've spent all my life watching Leah get famous because of her friends, then all year with this film getting made. And I thought, "Why not us?"'

Leah had chills. She was now watching Jennifer, who was ignoring her and talking to the camera. It was hard not to remember the times they'd touched hands in solidarity. The memories they'd shared about the way they had been raised – and the parents who'd shaped them.

That was the thing with parents. Whenever someone won a big film award, they'd go on stage and thank their mum, dad, or both. They would tell everyone how their parents shaped their upbringings.

But that worked both ways. Good parents raised good kids and, sometimes, not always – but sometimes – a bad parent would raise a bad kid.

'We had nothing,' Jennifer said. 'We almost lost the farm at least three times. It costs so much to look after. The money just disappears. Some girl made up a story about Dylan at school and he was suspended. Everyone thinks we're scum – and I spent all that time watching you and... I wanted what you have.'

She turned to look at Leah, emphasising the final part – and it was impossible for Leah not to feel guilt.

None of this had been on the list of questions, of course. Ashley hadn't said that he'd go silent. Nobody had predicted this could happen – and, suddenly, it felt as if it was only Leah and Jennifer in the room. Another chat around the kitchen table.

'Did you kill your mum?' Leah asked – and the moment the words came out, she felt Ashley tense in the seat at her side.

That hadn't been on the list of questions, either – and Leah was fairly sure she shouldn't be asking. But what were they going to do? Stop the interview? The police needed her and Leah knew it.

The two women were staring at one another now – and Leah saw the fire burning in Jennifer's eyes. When she'd asked for Leah a week before, it wasn't because she wanted support or a friend, it was because she wanted to be seen with her.

'Why would you ask that?' Jennifer replied.

'Because *somebody* killed her.'

They continued eyeing one another for a second or two longer, until Jennifer turned to Ashley. 'I'm not answering that,' she said.

Except Leah wouldn't let it go. 'You told me about your dad and the potential bodies when you found out the police were getting a warrant for Charles' place. It was the same conversation. You knew he wouldn't help them but couldn't risk them finding the bunker before Dylan reappeared. Or, worse, finding Dylan in the bunker with his friends. So the police put all those people on *your* farm, instead of the one next door.'

Jennifer was shaking her head, staring ahead. 'I'm not answering that,' she repeated, even though no question had been asked.

'If you didn't kill her,' Leah added, 'then you must have known where she was the whole time. You made up the stuff about your dad and other girls, trying to get them to dig in the right place.'

Jennifer turned a fraction and looked to Leah, eyes narrow. Leah expected a denial, or perhaps some sort of abuse. What she didn't expect was the hissed '*Careful...*' that came.

It sounded like a threat and, as Leah stopped herself from saying anything more, she figured it probably was.

In an interview room, in a police station, on camera, Leah

was not going to push. She sat back, arms folded, being as careful as she'd been told to be.

'Do you ever feel guilty?' Jennifer asked. It was more in her usual tone, the way most of the conversations she'd had with Leah had gone.

'For what?' Leah replied.

'That you're the one who's left.' She clicked her fingers. 'All your friends gone like that and you're still here. And you get to be a mum, and live your life – and none of them did.'

They were staring at one another again – but Leah flinched first. She slipped her chair back and stood. 'We're done,' she told Ashley – and then she headed for the door.

FORTY-ONE

Leah was sitting outside the coffee shop, enjoying the breeze. Fresh air had never tasted so good as in the past few days.

Across the plaza, the boys had headed into the Laser Quest half an hour before and were presumably busy shooting one another, or possibly throwing rocks. They'd be in the bolthole, which was a word Leah would never forget. Zac had told her it was the name of a multiplayer zone in one of his shooting games, which is where Laser Quest got it from. 'Everyone knows what it means,' he said, by which he meant his friends, who played the same games.

Leah knew now.

Dylan wasn't with them, of course. He was staying with his dad, on the coast, in that 'horrible glass thing'. Leah could see better than almost anyone what lay in his future.

The coffee was bad, though Leah was aware she shouldn't be drinking caffeine this late in the afternoon.

A chair scraped to her side and Deborah slotted herself in. She was carrying a tray and delicately placed a cappuccino on the table for herself, a second flat white for Leah, plus two almond croissants.

'Have both if you want,' she said.

Leah laughed at that. A long time ago, shortly after Leah had gone to live with them, Deborah had taken Leah to a bakery and told her she could have whatever she wanted. The idea of choosing something and not being concerned by the price had been bewildering. Through habit alone, Leah had picked a jam doughnut as it was the cheapest thing. After she'd finished, Deborah had asked if she wanted anything else, which had got a default 'no'. Except Deborah had bought a second jam doughnut anyway and put it in front of her. 'In case you change your mind,' she'd said. No minds had been changed because Leah's rake-thin frame had ached for a second cake anyway – and she'd devoured it as she had the first.

After that, if they were ever in a similar place, Deborah always bought two.

'It's been a long week,' Leah said.

'A long year,' Deborah replied.

And it had. From the moment Owen had turned up to start filming his documentary, Leah's life hadn't quite been the same.

Leah bit the croissant and then finished her first coffee.

'Thank you for coming,' she said.

'It's my pleasure. I'm always here if you need me. Same for Zac.'

It was true and it had been for a quarter of a century. If bad parents did sometimes make bad kids, then Leah had been saved because Deborah was the opposite.

'I've not been able to talk to you the last few days,' Leah said, holding up a hand to stop Deborah interrupting. She needed to get it out. 'I wanted to tell you that, even with Dad's wedding, even though I technically have a step-mum, that I really appreciate everything you've done for me. And Zac. You're the mum I wish I had.'

Leah broke and Deborah knew her well enough not to say anything. She rested a hand on Leah's shoulder and waited.

There weren't enough napkins on the table so, when the time came, she shuffled off in search of more. When she got back, she'd somehow half-inched an entire dispenser with about three-hundred inside.

'You don't have to say thanks,' she said softly.

Leah dabbed her eyes, caught her breath. She knew she wouldn't get through it but there was so much she couldn't put into words. How she could never say thank you enough – because some of what Jennifer had said had stuck. Vicky, Jazz and Harriet never did get to grow up. Deborah never saw her real daughter become a woman, go to university, graduate, get married, have kids – all that stuff, or none of it. Nobody would ever know the person Harriet would have been.

'It's not your fault, love,' Deborah said. 'I don't mean it quite like this is going to sound. But there's a new scandal now, isn't there? People will move on.'

Deborah paused. Perhaps she had a point, even if it was morbid and awful.

'That's what you want, isn't it?' Deborah added. 'For people to move on?'

Leah thought – because Jennifer was right on that too. Leah's friends had disappeared and she was left. Her entire life had been defined by that, and there was a degree of local fame to it, even though Leah had never craved it. Never asked for it.

But people moving on *was* what she wanted... wasn't it?

EPILOGUE

FIVE MONTHS LATER

Leah had been in a prison visiting room once before. It had been around a year and a half before, when she'd seen her father. It had been only them in a large room with vending machines on either side. He'd been belligerent then, before his apparent reinvention. Leah still assumed he'd turn back to the demon she knew he was – but, for now, the mask was being maintained. She had been keeping a relationship with Mandy, meeting every ten days or so.

What Leah didn't tell her was that, every time they saw each other, it was because Leah was looking for hints of bruises or scrapes. The moment Mandy started having frequent run-ins with doors or stairs would be confirmation her father was back to his old self. And then... Leah wasn't sure what she'd do. She had a few ideas.

It was impossible not to think of her dad as Leah sat in a similar spot, this time surrounded by other people visiting prisoners. It was a wide-open room, with long rows of plastic tables and chairs, all bolted to the ground. There were a lot of husbands and boyfriends, sitting waiting for their partners to be brought through from the cells. A couple of wives or girlfriends, as well – plus a smattering of teenagers waiting for their mums.

Leah was none of those things. On the form she had to sign to get in, she had identified herself as a friend – though she wasn't that, either.

There was a gentle hum of shuffling feet and bodies among the visitors. Nobody had their phones to look at and, in the absence of that, didn't know what to do to pass the time.

Then there was a clunk of a door, a momentary silence, and the clatter of footsteps on a hard floor. The female prisoners were led into the visiting area in a row, before being directed off to various tables to see their loved ones. The din rose as everyone spoke over the top of one another. Guards were standing in the corners and walking the aisles.

Jennifer was wearing similar joggers to the last time Leah had seen her, though her hair was cleaner and greyer. She'd lost weight, not only on her body but her face. Her cheeks were sallow, eyes deeper set. Leah was sitting and Jennifer stood on the other side of the table, waiting for the guard to release her from the cuffs so she could sit.

'I wasn't sure you'd add me to your list of visitors,' Leah said. She'd thought a lot about the first thing to say, half expecting hostility – which didn't come.

'You're always welcome to visit,' Jennifer replied – and they were back in her farmhouse kitchen once more, with the dots of police officers in the distance. That anger from the interview room five months before had gone. The more Leah had thought about it since, the more she figured the fury hadn't been specifically for her. It was the unfairness of how things had panned out. They were the same age, from the same town, with similar upbringings. Except, as far as Jennifer was concerned, Leah's life had worked out – while Jennifer had been left with a farm she couldn't run and could barely keep. 'There's going to be a lot of time for you to come and say hello,'

Jennifer added. 'I think I'd quite like that. I'm going to be here a long while.'

That was true enough.

'You pleaded guilty,' Leah said, even though it was something that had happened months before. Jennifer's sentencing was due, and the delays were more to do with reports that would determine how long she remained in prison. There would be no trial and Leah wouldn't have to give evidence.

'Why wouldn't I?' Jennifer asked.

As well as considering her opening line, Leah had thought a lot about the next part. It was the reason she was there, after all.

'I don't think you did it,' she said.

'Did what?'

'Any of it.'

In all Leah's thoughts about how this might go, she'd had visions of Jennifer storming out, maybe shouting. She'd thought there could be a resigned shrug, a 'Whatever'. What she hadn't expected was... nothing.

Jennifer hadn't reacted and Leah might as well have asked her favourite colour.

'I don't believe you knew there was a bunker there,' Leah added. 'I know what you told the police. I've read the news articles – but it was Dylan who was always trespassing on Charles' farm to get to the river. That bunker is hidden right by the hedge he would've been cutting through.'

It had been playing on Leah ever since she sat on the bottom step of that bunker and found Jennifer's nail. They had spent a week becoming something close to friends. They had shared things and, to an extent, lived in one another's heads. Some of that could be faked but not all of it.

'Who cares what you think?' Jennifer said, although there was no particular harshness. It was more of a fact because Leah's opinion was that and nothing more.

'I can't picture you holding a pillow, or a bag, something like that, over the faces of two teenage boys. Honestly, I doubt the police do either.'

'Have you been talking to people there?'

Leah stayed quiet at that because of course she had. Although Leah didn't need to give evidence, the run-up to sentencing had meant every part of her witness reports had been checked. She'd seen the doubt in the eyes of people like Ashley.

'The police botched things so badly with the search that they'll take any win,' Leah replied. 'This is a victory for them – because you confessed – and they're obviously going to take it.'

'So what's the problem?'

Jennifer was remarkably cool to the point that Leah wondered if she, too, had been having imaginary conversations to run through these scenarios. She'd known for a few days that Leah was coming.

Takes one to know one.

'Dylan was the person who took a gun to school. He—'

'*Air* gun,' Jennifer corrected.

'That's what he says now. He's the one suspended for touching girls.'

Jennifer's features hardened: 'The girl who said that is a liar. He turned her down and she went to her teacher, making up all sorts.'

It felt as if Jennifer believed her son on that part – and perhaps he was telling the truth. But it was still his gun and still he who would trespass and explore his neighbour's farm.

Leah had seen how protective Jennifer was when she stormed Mrs Hawkins' house that Sunday morning. There was a fury that Leah had rarely seen before – and if it hadn't have been for Nick and Deborah, things could have ended very badly. Mother and son shared a lot – but he kept *that* part of his life secret.

'Dylan killed his friends, didn't he?' Leah said. 'He suffocated them one at a time, then came and calmly told you what he'd done. He even knew a place to hide them. A place you didn't know existed.'

No response.

'Who came up with the story of the man in the van? You or him?'

'Do you really think a fifteen-year-old could come up with all this?'

There was something in Jennifer's stare: perhaps a challenge. Because Leah knew without any question that a fifteen-year-old was more than capable of such things.

Takes one to know one.

'You talked about karma at the hotel,' Leah said. 'You mentioned your dad but you were thinking of Dylan. Wondering if it would come back on him. Or you...?'

That got a shake of the head.

'Did he set you up?' Leah added. 'I do wonder about that, because it seems such a silly thing to leave a fingernail in that bunker, plus you must have known you'd lost one or two. You'd have gone looking, surely? Unless it didn't happen when the boys were left down there – and Dylan placed it just in case someone found them. That fingernail meant the police would look at you, instead of him.'

Jennifer glanced sideways, making sure none of the guards were too close. She leaned forward, not too far to catch their attention, but enough that she could speak quietly enough for only Leah to hear. 'You don't know what you're talking about.'

The words were hissed, which made Leah think she *did* know what she was talking about. Nothing else had got a reaction.

Was it possible that Dylan could have left that nail as an insurance policy? He hadn't necessarily set up his mum, because he wouldn't have known the bodies were going to be found. But, if they were...

Jennifer leaned back, arms folded. She glanced to the side again because one of the guards was on the prowl. He walked along the back of her, wordlessly checking from side to side. Leah waited until he had moved a few tables along. There was chatter all around, though visitors and inmates were only interested in their own lives and conversations.

This was Leah and Jennifer, nobody else.

'Did you know your mum's bones were in the field?' Leah asked.

Jennifer's eye twitched, though she said nothing. The police were yet to charge anyone for that and the assumption was that Jennifer's father was responsible. In truth, it was unlikely the facts would come out. Everyone was dead, except Jennifer, who wasn't speaking about that.

Still no answer.

'I think you did tell the truth about one thing,' Leah said. 'You wanted to be famous. Or, maybe, you *used* to want fame but realised it was unlikely now. But it's not only you. You said Dylan was obsessed with YouTubers and TikTokers and the money they made. He wanted to do that making fishing videos – but he never had the audience. When he started talking about having three-hundred subscribers in the police interview, you cut him off – because you knew what he could say.' Leah paused. 'It's much more than three-hundred followers now, isn't it?'

Jennifer's eye twitched again and it felt as if she didn't know. There had obviously been visits between Dylan and her, though – because of his age – Dylan's father would have been present, else there would have been other supervision.

'I've seen Dylan's videos where he talks about losing his friends and his mum,' Leah added. 'I've seen the GoFundMes, with people donating for his future – and he's got almost half a million followers now. He hid for a few days and allowed himself to be found. Nobody knew the bodies would be found but, even with that, he's the boy who was left. He's me – but with modern tech.'

Jennifer opened her mouth and started to say something, stopped, and then tried again: 'He's got *half a million* followers?'

'Zac explained how exponential growth works on there. He says there's a point when you get past about ten thousand, and it keeps going. Because more people are seeing your posts, you end up in more algorithms, which gets you more followers. Then more people see your posts, and so on. That half a million will be a million soon, then two. Who knows where it'll end?' Another pause. 'He's famous.'

Jennifer was open-mouthed, a fish gasping for air. 'Half a million...?'

'You said it when we first met. *Dylan* wanted to go to the premiere of the film. He told me the same thing. *He* applied for tickets and didn't get them. That's why you let him have the sleepover in the first place. Isn't that odd for a fifteen-year-old? Zac wasn't interested and neither were his friends. I was there and it was all people our age and older. Then, when Dylan and I were alone in the interview room, and you were in the corridor, he said something like, "Everyone's been talking about you all year".'

'That's true.'

'I know – but why would he care? When people want to talk to me about the sleepover, it's never teenagers. I'm Zac's mum to them. I'm a free taxi. Everything with Vicky happened in the dark ages for them. They think DVDs are ancient – and they definitely think we are.'

Jennifer was still, though that eye was twitching again. 'Why are you saying all this?' she asked.

Leah pressed back in her seat. It felt as if she'd been on edge since the moment Jennifer had sat. So much that had been running through her mind had come out. Esther was her outlet for one big thing in her life, though there had been nobody to run all this past. Finally, after months, she'd said it out loud.

'When we were alone in the interview room, Dylan asked if I'd ever seen a dead body. He did it really quietly, so nobody else would hear. It felt like it wasn't such an innocent question.'

Jennifer was nodding slowly but then her jaw hardened. She didn't bother to lean in when she replied. 'Let's say that's all true.' She shrugged. '*All* of it. You never believed your friends were killed by the man with the van that Dylan talked about. I was watching and there wasn't a single second you thought that's what happened to them. Nor when I told you my dad was obsessed with the case and that the girls could be in our field. I looked into your eyes and knew you didn't believe me.'

In all the times Leah had run through the way things could pan out, it hadn't occurred to her that things could be turned around.

'Then there was the tarot reading. The seven of swords: the queen of lies and deception.'

'Nobody believes that stuff.'

'Maybe – but you were shocked. I saw that, too. You were shocked because it was true and that card was you.'

Leah was mute. She had been stunned when told what that card meant. She had expected it to be a load of old nonsense and, though she still thought it was, her reading had been unerringly based in reality. In the months since, she had wondered why Jennifer had taken her to the psychic healer for the Tarot reading. If she knew where Dylan was, what was the point? Unless it wasn't about her at all. She was the one who had pushed Leah to go first.

Leah thought she had spent those days analysing Jennifer – but perhaps the opposite had been true.

Jennifer was still going. Clearly, she'd also had a long time to think about their week of friendship. 'When I told you they found my mum in the field, I asked if you were glad it wasn't your friends – and there was nothing in your face. You always knew they weren't on the farm. But the only way you could have been so certain they weren't there is if you know what happened to them...'

'I don't know what you're talking about,' Leah said, though her insides were twisting. She wasn't sure what she'd wanted from the visit – but it wasn't this.

'Who'd suspect a fifteen-year-old?' Jennifer continued. 'Maybe someone who already knows what a fifteen-year-old is capable of.'

'No,' Leah replied – but Jennifer wasn't done.

'That's why you were suspicious when Dylan asked about seeing a dead body. Because you have and you know what it's like.'

'The only bodies I've seen are Mo and Alfie.'

That part was true at least, not that Jennifer could be dissuaded from her belief.

The two women stared at one another, each knowing they weren't going to get the answers they wanted. They were both confident of their own truths.

Jennifer leaned in and whispered, even as a guard approached to tell her to stop. 'Look out for my son for me,' she said. 'I think the pair of you have a lot in common.'

PUBLISHING TEAM

Turning a manuscript into a book requires the efforts of many people. The publishing team at Bookouture would like to acknowledge everyone who contributed to this publication.

Audio
Alba Proko
Sinead O'Connor
Melissa Tran

Commercial
Lauren Morrissette
Jil Thielen
Imogen Allport

Data and analysis
Mark Alder
Mohamed Bussuri

Design
Emma Graves

Editorial
Ellen Gleeson
Nadia Michael

Printed in Great Britain
by Amazon

37151362R00169